BLIND SPOT

Center Point
Large Print

Also by Dani Pettrey and available from Center Point Large Print:

Sabotaged
Still Life

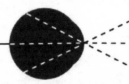

Chesapeake Valor
Book Three

BLIND SPOT

Dani Pettrey

CENTER POINT LARGE PRINT
THORNDIKE, MAINE

This Center Point Large Print edition
is published in the year 2017 by arrangement with
Bethany House Publishers,
a division of Baker Publishing Group.

The text of this Large Print edition is unabridged.
In other aspects, this book may vary
from the original edition.
Printed in the United States of America
on permanent paper.
Set in 16-point Times New Roman type.

ISBN: 978-1-68324-579-7

Library of Congress Cataloging-in-Publication Data

Names: Pettrey, Dani, author.
Title: Blind spot / Dani Pettrey.
Description: Center Point large print edition. | Thorndike, Maine :
    Center Point Large Print, 2017. | Series: Chesapeake valor ; Book 3
Identifiers: LCCN 2017039215 | ISBN 9781683245797
    (hardcover : alk. paper)
Subjects: LCSH: Large type books. | GSAFD: Suspense fiction.
Classification: LCC PS3616.E89 B58 2017 | DDC 813/.6—dc23
LC record available at https://lccn.loc.gov/2017039215

To Janet Grant:
For being a fearless warrior,
friend, and advocate.
I'm blessed to partner with you
on this crazy writing journey.

BLIND SPOT

Prologue

Luke crouched behind an orange shipping container, dreading to think what it held.

Captain Jose Augero puffed on a cigar on the dock beside the *Bainbridge*. The stale breeze coming off the water was scant relief from Kuala Lumpur's sticky night air.

Flicking a mosquito from his neck, Luke turned from his study of the captain to watch headlights sweep over the shipping yard. Creaking echoed above him as the crane arm swung overhead, settling on a metal container three over from his position. Clamping ahold, the crane lifted the massive container high in the dark, starless sky and settled it onto the ship.

Luke held his breath as a black sedan stopped less than ten feet from the captain, spotlighting the man in a glare of headlights. Seconds later Harris Sayid stepped out of the car with a lift of his chin. "Jose."

This is it. Luke exhaled as adrenaline coursed through his veins. Inching closer, he prayed the shadows concealed him from the men, and that the container he was using for cover wasn't the next to be transferred to the ship.

"Sir." Jose gave a curt nod, his dark eyes

illuminated by the headlights. "I told you I have this under control. No need for you to oversee."

Sayid stepped forward. "Need I remind you what happened to your predecessor?"

"There's the difference. I'm not foolish enough to let a federal agent aboard my vessel."

Sayid waved off the cigar Jose offered him.

Jose shook his head. "You and all those rules . . ."

Sayid ignored the comment, disgust for Jose evident in his narrowing eyes. "I'm here to inform you we have a change in plans."

"Oh?" Jose flicked ashes on the pavement. "Hopefully not a cargo switch. The weapons and parts have just finished loading."

"No. Not the cargo—the destination. And it would do you well not to utter such words about what you carry."

"It's only my men here, and unlike Jackson's, my men fear and obey me."

Every fiber of Luke's being burned with the urge to stop this shipment in its tracks, to take the men out *now,* before the weapons and whatever parts they were referring to reached his homeland, but he'd been ordered to stand fast. *Listen and report.* While he understood the reasoning behind it, it felt innately wrong not to act. But if he did, it wouldn't stop the threat. It would only fuel it. A war was headed for U.S. soil, and tonight there wasn't a thing he could do to stop it.

"Why the change?" Jose asked at Sayid's silence.

"Baltimore is too hot right now. There's a fed there who has latched on to the paltry information he thinks he uncovered on the *Hiram*."

Jose chuckled. "You can't stop *one* federal agent?"

"He's been relentless—not to mention extremely lucky—but his days are numbered."

Luke swallowed, knowing exactly whom they were referring to. His contact in Baltimore had informed him that has childhood friend Declan Grey had uncovered the arrival of Anajay Darmadi on the *Hiram* and was doggedly pursuing what he believed, correctly, was a pattern of terrorist activity. Luke's finger itched on the trigger, every instinct whispering to squeeze it—to protect Declan, to protect them all.

"In the meantime, take the shipment into Galveston. Our man from Houston will transport the cargo back east."

"You're the boss, but isn't Houston and the Galveston port how the other fed got onto us in the first place?"

"That needn't concern you. *That* fed is dead. Soon the Baltimore one will be as well."

"Fine, but it's going to cost a hefty sum to

11

get the manifest changed at this late date—to cut through the red tape."

"I understand. Just take care of it."

Jose nodded, exhaling a gray puff of smoke.

Sayid's jaw tightened in the lights bouncing off his profile.

"And the doctor?" Jose asked.

"He'll be liberated when the time is right." Sayid swatted a bug off his damp white shirt, clinging to his back in the thick humidity. He studied Jose. "Why does the doctor matter so much to you?"

"I told you," Jose said. "The doc and I made nice on his journey over. I don't like him rotting in some prison cell."

"He won't be there much longer." Sayid's smile turned to one of malice. "And then their empire will crumble into dust."

1

Declan Grey started his day as he did every other. He showered, shaved, dressed, drank a strong cup of black coffee, ate two slices of cinnamon-and-sugar toast, and then headed out the door to work, calling his friend Griffin for a quick chat as he drove.

The office was humming when he arrived, and he was pleased he'd made it nearly half an hour early, despite 695's horrific morning commute.

Today was the meeting he'd been pushing for with his boss for nigh on a month. An attack was headed for U.S. soil, and no one was doing a thing to acknowledge it—let alone stop it.

He entered the meeting room, planning to have time to run back through his argument before Alan King showed, but his boss was already there, deep in conversation with a woman. Both had their backs to him.

The woman was five foot seven, athletically lean and toned, her brown hair almost identical in shade to Tanner's. His gut sunk. *Tanner.*

It *was* Tanner. He knew her—knew the way she angled her head so her hair fell slightly over her right shoulder when she was deep in thought, knew the graceful curve of her neck, knew . . . *too much*. He cleared his throat, and they both turned.

The black dress she wore fit well, falling mid-knee, a few inches of fabric caressing the subtle line across her shoulders, leaving him wanting to . . . He shook off the thought, frustrated.

Something captivatingly drew him to her . . . and yet strangled him at the same time— as if he were underwater in her presence. All sound evaporated, he couldn't breathe, his vision grew limited, until all he saw was her. It was surprisingly peaceful, albeit alarmingly disorienting.

It had begun the day she'd entered his life, nearly a year earlier, showing up in his hospital room, dressed like a nurse, bent on obtaining answers about her friend's murder.

The surprising sensation he experienced in her presence had steadily grown in intensity until it now engulfed all else. He wasn't sure if he liked the effect or if he was drowning in it. His heart said the first, his head the latter.

One plus was his certainty that he no longer felt anything but friendship for Kate Maxwell— hadn't for months now—and considering how deeply in love she was with Luke Gallagher, the man who'd been his best friend for years, before his disappearance over seven years ago . . . it was a very good change. His crush on Kate was over, and in hindsight that's all it had been—a crush, along with genuine friendship, of course. But now . . . *now* he was drowning in the middle of an unanticipated ocean and a part of him reveled in being surrounded by the unknown.

He had the decision before him: fight the undertow or give in to his feelings and see where the current pulled him.

"Agent Grey," Alan said, stealing back his attention, "I'd like you to meet the Bureau's newest crisis counselor."

Declan blinked. Had Alan seriously just said—?

"We're well acquainted," Tanner said, before he could finish his thought.

She settled into one of the conference room chairs, and he sat down beside her, his shoulders stiff. "Not sure I'd say *well* . . ."

There was so much about her he didn't know, so much he longed to. What she liked and didn't like. How she spent her downtime. What scared her, if anything. What thrilled her, though he already knew rushes of adrenaline did. At least she spent most of the year finding it through healthy means via rock climbing, white-water rafting, kayaking, snowboarding, and the list went on. She was an all-weather and all-season athlete much like him.

She sighed. "Of course you'd say that."

He tucked his chin in. "Meaning?" He'd meant it as a compliment, an indication that he wanted to know more, but it didn't appear she was taking it as such.

She flipped open her folder, shaking her head. "Never mind."

"All right then." *Moving on . . .* He opened his case folder, convinced he'd never understand women—Tanner Shaw least of all.

Griffin entered the offices of Grant & Brentwood Investments.

"Mr. McCray," the receptionist greeted him. "Mr. Grant said to head on back."

"Thanks, Jen." He walked the long, narrow, glass-walled hall.

Haywood Grant occupied the corner office at the end. He'd started the firm more than twenty years earlier, running it solo for the first dozen years before bringing on his partner, Lowell Brentwood, and, much more recently, Emmitt Powell, who had yet to earn his name as part of the firm's.

"Griff." Haywood smiled and stood as Griffin entered the office. "How are you, son?" He clapped Griffin on the back.

Haywood had coached his, Declan, Luke, and Parker's Little League team, the Chesapeake Pirates, for three seasons before moving from their hometown of Chesapeake Harbor. But after three key developmental years, the *son* stuck. As well as the bond of a boy and his first coach.

Their paths had crossed now and again over the years when Haywood visited his brother who'd still lived in Chesapeake Harbor, and then more recently when a mutual acquaintance recommended Haywood's accounting and investment firm. Griff had been visiting Haywood annually ever since, today being an exception to the otherwise yearly schedule.

"Come on in," Haywood said. "Let me shut the door."

Griff wondered what level of privacy the glass-walled office really provided.

Haywood returned to his seat as Griffin took his.

"So what brings you here today?"

Griffin exhaled, joy bursting inside. "I need to withdraw some funds from one of my accounts."

"Oh?" Haywood sat back, interlocking his fingers. "Another rehab project?"

Griff flipped houses—or, as he preferred to say, *restored* them—before putting them on the market. "Not this time. I put down a deposit on a plot of land in Sweet Air. I'm going to build Finley's and my home on it, and I want to pay for the land before I start construction." The farmhouse he'd been flipping when he'd met Finley was way up in Thurmont. He'd sold it to a very happy couple, and he and Finley were now renting a place in the Sweet Air area, which they'd fallen in love with.

Haywood leaned forward with a wide smile. "Well, that's great. Congratulations." He shook Griffin's hand, and Griff noticed the lack of wedding band on Haywood's. He prayed Haywood's ring was being fixed, sized, or forgotten on his nightstand, but a glance around the office revealed the pictures of Carol were gone.

"I hope to see that beautiful wife of yours at the retreat kick-off tonight." Haywood continued to smile.

"She'll be there." He wanted to say "And Carol?" but wasn't sure the best way to proceed. "Will your kids be there again?" he asked.

"I'm afraid not this year. Maggie and her husband moved to Denver six months back, and Jack can't get away from the hustle and bustle of New York."

"That's too bad."

"And since you always inquire about Carol, I'll save you some trouble. We called it quits a few months back."

"I'm sorry to hear that."

"Well, after Jack moved out and we shifted to an empty nest, we realized we had nothing else in common. It just wasn't working."

So you make it work. At least that was his commitment to Finley and their marriage. It was for life. They exchanged vows, and he'd honor them until the day God took him home. Finley deserved him to be the man he'd promised to be. She deserved the world.

"Well, let's get down to the nitty gritty and get you that land," Haywood said, rolling his chair to his computer.

A knock rapped on the door, and Haywood's jaw tightened along with his broad shoulders.

Griffin looked over his right shoulder at the doorway.

Lowell Brentwood stepped into the room. "Sorry to interrupt . . ."

"Yes?" Haywood responded to Lowell, his tone tight.

"When you're finished here, we're going to congregate in the meeting room to finalize the retreat presentation."

Haywood nodded, but didn't look at his partner. "I'll be there."

He said it pleasantly, but the tension in the room was palpable—thicker than a Chesapeake Harbor fog rolling in across the dark water on a cold October night.

Lowell excused himself, shutting the door

19

behind him but continuing to stare through the glass wall until he moved out of their line of sight. *Weird.*

Griffin had interacted with Lowell numerous times over the years, and always saw him at the firm's annual client retreat, but he had never noticed such a strain between the two. It would be interesting to see how the men interacted at the retreat.

He and Finley were looking forward to the time away to soak in the gorgeous Hunt Valley setting. There were plenty of places to hike between Oregon Ridge and Loch Raven, to watch the sunset over the fall foliage, and to ride horses less than half an hour from where he planned to build their home.

Typically, the retreat was for the firm's wealthiest clients, but because of Haywood's fondness for his Pirates, he always invited them and, graciously enough, their significant others. Now that he thought about it, Lowell never seemed a fan of their presence, so maybe that was the source of the partners' tension.

Haywood cleared his throat. "Where were we? Ah, money for your land. How much do you need?"

Griffin's gaze narrowed. Was that perspiration on Haywood's brow?

"Is everything all right?" he asked.

Haywood swiped his forehead and rubbed his fingers. "Fine."

The man sitting before Griffin was hardly fine, but he let it go and they proceeded. It wasn't until they were nearly finished with their business and Haywood appeared no more at ease that Griffin took a chance and asked again.

Again Haywood said he was fine, but this time, he scrawled something on a neon yellow sticky pad, pulled off the top slip, and handed it to Griffin.

Meet me at Le Scala restaurant at noon.

Griffin nodded once and slipped the note into his pocket, his mind racing through the endless possibilities.

"Always good to see you, son."

Apparently, he'd be seeing him again in three hours. About what, he had no idea, but from Haywood's appearance, it was far from good.

"As I've been saying since our discoveries on the *Hiram* two months ago, I believe there is credible evidence of an imminent terrorist threat against our country," Declan said, getting straight to the point. Alan indicated Tanner had insight to add to the meeting, but had not elaborated.

Curiosity nipped at Declan. What insight? Would she make his third plea to his boss that they continue strongly pursuing this investigation easier or more difficult? With Tanner, it usually fell somewhere in between—challenging yet helpful. He prayed that was the case in this situation because he needed all the help he could get.

Alan shifted, his hands balling into pale fists on the conference table's black top. "Agent Grey, what evidence are you basing this belief on?"

"Mr. Darmadi's dying words: 'The wrath is here.'"

Alan flicked his hand, dismissing Declan's greatest argument as if it were an annoying fly. "That is not evidence—you know that. Over the last two months, in all the hours and manpower you've dedicated to this pursuit, have you found a shred of *evidence* to substantiate Mr. Darmadi's declaration?"

"There's been . . . chatter." Declan exhaled, knowing his boss would dismiss this as casually as he had Darmadi's dying words.

Alan pushed back in his swivel chair, his long, slender fingers twitching on the armrests. He was losing his patience. "Chatter?"

Declan cleared his throat, stretched his shoulders until his muscles contracted in the center of his back, and took a deep breath before responding. Everything rode on this. "Yes, sir." He pulled out his notebook. "I've been listening for code words." He flipped through the transcript pages until he found the one he wanted, highlighted and tabbed.

Tanner glanced over, curiosity dancing in her beautiful brown eyes, but she didn't say a word.

She was usually the first to speak and the one to protest or argue most vehemently, and she was good at it. It made for some of the best verbal sparring and deep discussions he'd ever had. He found her savvy wit and intelligence both impressive and sexy. Yes, much to his chagrin, he thought Tanner Shaw all those things and more. He admired the woman, and she'd come to mean a great deal to him.

When it had happened—when his feelings had shifted and become far, far deeper—he wasn't quite certain, but it had definitely happened.

"And?" Alan tapped his fingers.

Declan swallowed. He needed to focus, to speed this up. *Get your head in the game, Grey.* "I've heard chatter about the *family* expanding."

Alan cocked his head. "What family?"

Declan moved to the whiteboard, where he placed his surveillance photos. "A man from Malaysia immigrated four years ago and has been steadily bringing over an intriguing number of 'nephews.'"

Alan frowned. "Nephews?"

"Yes, sir. Supposed relatives. Young Southeast Asian men in their early twenties—all Muslim."

He paused briefly but wanted, *needed,* to keep pounding the importance of this case into his boss's shortsighted mind. "Several are on student visas, pursuing degrees in biochemistry, chemical engineering, or biology. The first young man he brought over now specializes in virology."

"Smart nephews."

"All fourteen of them?"

"Have you checked if they really are his nephews? Some families are large."

"Documentation in that area is easily bought, but we're digging deeper, and we have the CIA regional department overseas digging as well. Mack's been a great help."

Michael "Mack" Jacobs was his main contact at the CIA, the agent who served as a liaison between Declan and whatever region he needed help from. Over the years, he'd become a friend, the two meeting occasionally for dinner or a cup of joe in Georgetown, where Mack resided, or he'd come up Declan's way for a pickup game of rugby with the guys.

Parker was leery of anybody in the CIA, but he too liked Mack as a person. He just didn't trust the *agency* as an entity, said he didn't like the *read* he got off most agents—said they were called "spooks" for a reason. But even he agreed they were a necessary agency, just not one he wanted any part of.

Alan exhaled, steepling his fingers. "This had better be worth it."

"It is. I'm telling you, I can feel it in my gut."

"Well, luckily for you, Miss Shaw believes she has something too, and I hope it is more concrete than her gut and some chatter." Alan indicated for her to proceed.

"Thank you." Tanner nodded, and Declan found himself literally sitting on the edge of the swivel chair, scooting out from the conference table before his knees knocked the underside of it again.

"Over the last few months, I've been in regular contact with Mira," she said.

"The woman taken from the house where Anajay Darmadi was staying?" Declan asked.

"Yes. After your raid on the house, my former organization, the Intercultural Resource Center," she said, no doubt more for Alan's information than his, "safely placed her in a new location and have been working with her to make a new life for her here in America."

"That's wonderful," Alan said, "but its pertinence to the case . . . ?"

That was rude. What Tanner did was beyond admirable, but that was Alan—always direct and focused on the case at hand.

"That's great," he said, truly admiring her work and compassion for those in need.

She tucked her hair behind her ear. "Thank

25

you," she responded, clearly surprised. He hated that his respect and admiration for her work surprised her. He wanted her to know how genuinely he believed in what she did, in how she relentlessly fought for the rights of the marginalized and oppressed. It was just *how* she sometimes went about it—without any concern for her safety—that terrified him.

"Miss Shaw?" Alan grunted.

"Right," she said. "Mira confided in me that before the house was raided, men were coming through at a regular pace. From there they were moved to strategic locations to wait until they were called upon."

"Called upon by whom?" Alan asked, straightening.

She had him. *Finally*. He was reeled in, or at least interested.

"She didn't know. No names were used."

"What do you know of this woman? Can she be trusted?"

"I know she was brought over against her will on a ship from Malaysia. Her father sold her to a man who in turn handed her over to a different man after the ship docked in Baltimore's port."

"Did she say who bought her from her father?" Alan pressed. He wanted the facts and wanted them quickly.

You've got this, Tanner. Fighting his impulse

to let Alan have it for being so bullish, Declan said a silent prayer for God to guide and strengthen her. He knew she could handle the situation, and her occasional hostility toward his attempts to protect her was a clear sign that she was no fan of his treatment. He didn't blame her. It was just that when it came to Tanner, a highly protective mode kicked in—so strong, he felt helpless to control it at times.

"She can describe the man, but she doesn't know his name. She thought he was the captain of the ship that transported her to the U.S. She said he's American."

Declan's muscles coiled. The captain of the *Hiram*, the merchant ship sailing under a Malaysian flag, who snuck Anajay Darmadi into the country was American. A former soldier who was currently serving time for smuggling and treason.

Could it be the same man? Randal Jackson had smuggled in not only Darmadi but dozens of refugees whom he and his crew treated like slaves. If it hadn't been for Tanner's intervention, those refugees would now be the property of "business man" and loan shark Max Stallings, who too was now serving time for human trafficking.

Both men had also been linked to FBI agent Steven Burke, who'd been undercover on the *Hiram*. Whether he was under FBI sanction or not was still up for debate, but he'd been killed on the ship. Most likely by Darmadi when, Declan was guessing, Burke's true identity came to light. Burke was yet another facet of this case Declan had barely scratched the surface of.

"If I showed Mira a picture of the man I believe she's describing, would she be willing to look?" Declan asked.

Tanner's eyes narrowed. "You're thinking Randal Jackson, aren't you?"

He nodded. "Will Mira look at his picture?"

"I can ask," Tanner said cautiously.

Alan stood, collected his files, and smoothed his jacket. "Here's what we're going to do. You two are going to work this together."

"Excuse me?" Declan swallowed. He already had a partner. Not that he wouldn't mind the time spent with Tanner.

"What?" Tanner's face brightened.

Of course it would. Any chance of danger.

"Agent Kadyrov is on bereavement leave for her father's death out west. So in the meantime, you two"—he pointed between them—"see what you can get out of Mira, dig a little deeper on this 'family' and the nephews, find out what the CIA learns on their end through Mack, and pay Captain Randal Jackson another visit in the pen *if* Mira identifies him as the man who brought her over from Malaysia." He

28

stood and headed for the door. Once in the hallway, he turned with a frown on his face. "*If* by the time Lexi returns to work you two don't have anything concrete, we're letting this go. It's already been two months, and I fear we're chasing nothing but ghosts."

2

Griffin took a seat at a two-person table in the upper brick-walled loft of La Scala. A rectangular window overlooked Little Italy, where Declan lived, and a balcony overlooked the bocce ball court on the lower level.

He'd asked Lucio, the maître d', to send a man fitting Haywood's description up when he arrived. Before long he led Haywood to their table.

Haywood surveyed the secluded area, and relief swept across his face. He hung his jacket across his chair and took a seat opposite Griffin, his back to the bocce ball court, and Griffin's to the wall. *Always to the wall.* It was ingrained in him as a homicide detective.

Griffin waited until the server introduced himself, brought them water, and left, before leaning forward and whispering, "What's going on?" Haywood's cryptic message had been weighing on his mind for the past three hours. Time to get at it.

Haywood exhaled, his crooked fingers clasping together, shuffling. Crooked from his years of baseball, playing catcher all the way through college and breaking fingers more times than he could remember.

Haywood leaned in, whispering in his gravelly voice, "I think my partner is embezzling from my clients and setting me up to take the fall."

Griffin choked on his water. "What?"

The waiter returned for their order, and they quickly made a decision so they could get back to their discussion—Griffin ordering the spinach fettuccini and Haywood the seafood fra diavolo. The waiter departed as quickly as he'd come, providing them the privacy they needed.

Griffin looked to his friend. Was he *serious?*

Haywood's twitchy hands, flushed face, and rapidly bouncing knee all indicated a man in the grip of fear.

Haywood cleared his throat before continuing, his voice still low. "Clients of mine, John and Elizabeth Markum, came to me concerned with some discrepancies in their accounts." He shook out the white cloth napkin and dabbed his forehead with it.

"What did you do?" Griffin asked, floored.

"I assured them I'd look into it."

"And?"

Haywood glanced around, even though no one sat at the only other table on the loft. "Money is missing, transferred to an offshore account."

"Transferred by whom?"

Haywood swallowed, his pronounced Adam's apple dipping. "It shows I did it, but I swear, son, I didn't."

"Why do you think Lowell is the one who is behind it and not Emmitt?"

"Because only Lowell knows my log-in information."

Griffin frowned. "Why does he know your log-in information?"

"In case of an emergency. To protect our clients. If something happens to one of us, we can take care of each other's clients."

"Speaking of clients, has he embezzled from any of his own?"

"Not that I can tell. It'll take me time to comb through all the accounts, but it looks like he's only siphoning from my clients—I'm guessing in an attempt to make me look like the guilty party."

"So the Markums aren't the only ones he's stealing from?"

"No, but they are the only ones who have come to me about it." Haywood shook his head with a sigh. "So far I've found four accounts."

"And you didn't notice until now?" That rocked his confidence in Haywood's account management abilities.

"Lowell was careful. Covered his tracks. If the Markums hadn't come to me, it would have taken me a while to notice it."

"Okay, then we'll go to the station. I can introduce you to—"

"No." Haywood shook his head vehemently. "I don't have any proof it was Lowell. I'm not going to the cops. *Officially*," he added, looking at Griff. "Not until I have proof."

"What proof?"

"I don't know, but I'll keep searching until I find it."

"I may have another option."

"Oh?"

He handed Haywood Kate Maxwell's card.

Griffin led Haywood into Charm City Investigations, the Fell's Point private investigation firm Kate Maxwell ran. Kate had become a member of "the Pirates" when she started dating Luke during their freshman year at the University of Maryland, College Park. That is, until Luke went missing right before their college graduation, but they'd all remained close with Kate. She was family.

Griffin found her at a makeshift desk in the front room. She liked to be where the action was and where she could keep an eye on things. Her *actual* office sat empty at the end of the hall, next to Parker's lab.

She glanced up at their entry.

"Kate, this is Haywood Grant. Haywood, this is Kate Maxwell."

Kate stood, and Haywood stepped forward, extending his hand. "A pleasure to meet you."

Kate shook his hand and then slipped her thumbs in her back jean pockets. Griffin had seen her do it so many times, it must be habit, borderline muscle memory by now. "So, how can I help you, Mr. Grant?"

He dipped his head slightly. "Haywood, please."

"Okay." Kate smiled. "Why don't we take a seat"—she gestured to the circle of leather chairs and arched sofa where the group shared meals multiple times a week—"and you can catch me up to speed."

Haywood filled her in, Griffin noting a few subtle differences in his wording, but Haywood was flustered. No story ever came out exactly the same way twice.

"I'll get started right away," Kate said.

Haywood straightened. "You should come to the retreat."

"Retreat?"

"The one Parker, Declan, and I go to in Hunt Valley every fall," Griffin said. "It kicks off tonight. Avery and Finley are going too."

Her gaze tracked to Luke's file on her desk and she hesitated. "Sure," she said after a moment. "Sounds like a good plan. It'll let me meet the Markums and Lowell in a casual setting."

He wasn't surprised at her hestitation and he knew full well she'd bring Luke's file with her. Ever since she'd found proof of life—or what she believed was proof of life—she'd been unstoppable. How Griffin longed to see her move on with her life. Her devotion was admirable, even inspiring, but he feared after so many years it was wrongly placed.

"Wonderful." Haywood smiled. "Then I'll see you all there."

"Unfortunately Declan won't be able to attend this year," Griffin said.

Haywood arched his brows. "My assistant didn't mention that."

"He's got his hands full with a case."

"That's too bad," Haywood said, "but I'll look forward to seeing the rest of you." He smiled in Kate's direction. "I think you'll find our retreat a PI's dream with all the gossip that goes on."

"Gossip's not really my thing," she said.

"Oh?"

"Nope. I'm a sucker for the truth."

And anything that tied to Luke.

3

"No," Tanner said, frustration searing through her. How could a man she found so intriguing vex her so thoroughly?

"You heard Alan," Declan said. "We need to interview Mira."

"I understand the importance of the situation, but this is Mira's life."

"We're not going to harm her."

"Perhaps not intentionally, but she's hidden away, and she's scared of the men we rescued her from. There's a chance they're watching you, and if they see you go to her . . ."

"Let me stop you right there. I'd know if I was being tailed."

"You really don't think Dr. Ebeid is keeping tabs on you?"

"Tabs, probably. Tailing me, no. He doesn't have someone watching my every move. Trust me."

"You're that confident of yourself?"

"Of my ability to sense a tail? Yes."

"And if you're wrong, it could get Mira killed. I'm not willing to take that risk."

"We have orders."

Of course Mr. By-the-Book would go there.

Orders. Duty. She respected him for it, but where did compassion and instinct—doing the right thing despite orders—come in?

"Fine," she finally said after what felt like a five-minute staring contest. "*I'll* go talk to Mira." She visited Mira at least weekly, and no harm had come to her friend. She was a safe person, and Mira trusted her. Even if Declan was the one responsible for her freedom after discovering the house she'd been held hostage in, Mira was understandably terrified of men, and there was no doubt she was still in danger.

Unfortunately, none of the men arrested in the raid had talked, and nothing had been found on-site to prove a connection to Dr. Ebeid, the president of the Islamic Cultural Institute of the Mid-Atlantic and the man they strongly believed was behind the encroaching terrorist threat.

"I need to be there," Declan said.

How did she know he'd automatically disagree? "Why?"

"Because I have questions to ask her."

"Tell me what questions, and I'll ask her."

He strode around to sit on the corner of his desk, his hands—twice the width of hers, folded in his lap. "I'm afraid it's not that simple. I need to be able to respond appropriately to her answers, which will in turn dictate my next questions. It's a flowing dialogue, not a set list of questions."

From her training she knew he was right, so how did she argue that one?

Frustration surged through Tanner's limbs as they climbed the stairs to Mira's apartment. Alan had insisted that either Declan accompany her or they'd track down Mira's location and go in with a team of Alan's choosing.

Knowing that this was the better of the two options, Tanner led Declan up the nine flights of stairs, as the elevator was still on the fritz.

As they reached the top, Declan reached around her to open the stairwell door.

"Thanks." He certainly was a gentleman. Not something she'd experienced with most men over the years, and despite herself, she found it quite appealing. Swallowing, she redirected her thoughts. Now was not the time.

"Mira's the last door on the end. The corner unit." She pointed to the navy door with a gold *9K* just below the peephole.

She halted a few feet from it and looked up at Declan with the thought that she still might be able to get him to back off. His expression told her that wasn't going to happen . . . but, man, was he breathtaking. Rugged, tall, exuding strength, and yet as she'd just reflected, a gentleman. He was intelligent, loyal, hardworking—but what she loved most about him was his strong relationship with Jesus.

Yes, he had a knack for getting under her skin—now being one of those times—but the only real negative was his penchant for being overprotective with her. She appreciated his concern—and to be fair he didn't know just how much she could take care of herself—but it was a festering point of contention that kept her heightening feelings for him even more heated and at the surface.

He dipped his head. "Are you okay?" he asked at her beyond-embarrassing gaping stare.

"Sorry." She blinked. "Zoned out."

His lips twitched into a smile.

Greeeatt. He saw right through her, which only vexed her more.

Once again directing her focus off Declan Grey and on to Mira, she said, "Mira's going to be startled to see you . . . a man, accompanying me, especially one so . . ." *Virile. Manly. No.* She couldn't say those adjectives out loud.

He arched a dark brow. "One so . . . ?"

"Intimidating," she blurted without thinking, though it was accurate. With his sturdy physique and commanding presence he could easily intimidate Mira.

He frowned. "You find me intimidating?"

"I can see . . . where other people would."

He linked his arms across his broad chest, a slight smirk on his lips. No doubt at her flustered responses. Why couldn't she just act normal around the man?

"But not you?" he said, taking a step closer.

Sandalwood and a hint of spice filled her nostrils, reminding her of cozy nights in front of the fire at her friend's log cabin. Of course he'd smell enticing. What had he said? Oh, right. "I mean you're clearly good at what you do and well trained, and with your build . . ."

His lips twitched again in pleasure. "My build?"

"You know what I mean. You're six-three. One of your hands is bigger than both of mine combined."

He took another step closer. *Cardamom*. That was the spicy, aromatic accent. "But *you* don't find my build intimidating?"

She found it . . .

She immediately cut off that thought, pulling her eyes from his adorable chin dimple. They'd gotten so far off track her head was spinning, and she needed to be on her game, needed to keep Mira safe and feeling secure. She didn't know what a good man Declan was. It was Tanner's job to convince her. "We should go in," she said.

She turned and knocked on Mira's door before Declan could say anything else that could further dizzy her thoughts or emotions. "Mira," she called in a low voice, "it's Tanner."

After a moment the door cracked open and Mira smiled up at her, but fear quickly replaced the happiness in her friend's almond-shaped eyes at the sight of Declan standing beside her.

"Don't worry," Tanner said in her most soothing tone. "He's a friend." Theirs was most definitely an unexpected friendship, and certainly a different type of friendship than she'd ever experienced before, but she'd truly come to value his opinion, depend on his presence, and long for time with him, despite the heated frustration he often raised inside her.

As her mom would say he "tickled her ire." But while she'd never admit it aloud, the frustration resulting from their verbal sparring was strangely addictive. He kept her on her toes and incited a cascading rush of adrenaline coursing through her. He brought her to life. Clearly what was wrong with her was no little thing. She never chose the easy path.

After a few moments' hesitation and another reassurance from Tanner that Declan was in fact a friend, Mira let the chain drop, the metal clanging against the door as she pulled it open and stepped back.

Declan followed Tanner inside Mira's place. The apartment was small but tidy with touches

41

of her homeland here and there. A Malaysian cloth with traditional batik design lay across the back of what appeared to be her reading chair, and a *labu sayong*, a glossy black clay jar, sat on the small window box beneath bird-print curtains.

He only knew what the items were because he'd been with Tanner at the Ten Thousand Villages store when she'd picked them up for Mira, to make her friend feel more at home. Tanner was thoughtful that way—in ways he wasn't—and the more time they spent together, the more he longed to be kind like her, or at least closer on the spectrum.

"I will get some tea," Mira said, still not making eye contact with Declan. Tanner was right. Unfortunately, Mira was intimidated by him. Understandably so. He couldn't fathom the horrors she'd endured. But that made the purpose of their visit all the more vital. A monster like Ebeid needed to be stopped, and Mira might just be the key.

Until they knew what exactly they were facing, what type of attack the men Mira had been held hostage with had planned, it was nigh on impossible to combat.

Waiting to start the questioning when he wanted to plow headlong into it was hard, but pressing Mira would get them nowhere, so he would follow Tanner's lead. While the women stood at the counter waiting for the water to boil, he took a seat at the round white kitchen table—the chairs ice-cream-parlor style with white-and-blue-checked seat covers. They reminded him of his gram's, though hers had been a yellow-and-white crisscross pattern.

As Tanner and Mira talked quietly in Mira's native tongue, Declan's mind drifted back to childhood afternoons at Gram's house, sitting at her table, his legs dangling in the air as she prepared an ice cream sundae for him after school. His mam was home, but he always stopped by Gram's on the way home from school. Sometimes all the guys—Griffin, Parker, and Luke—joined him, the four seated around the table with ice cream on their chins and Gram humming Irish lilts as she worked about the kitchen. Good memories.

Pulling himself from the past, he glanced about at the furniture in Mira's apartment. It was in nice condition, and he was betting Tanner had found it.

Tanner really was amazing. It was not surprising she'd worked with the Global Justice Mission helping rescued sex-trafficking victims in Cambodia before returning to the States last year. He bet she had been equally amazing in her work with the Intercultural Resource Center before she joined the Bureau.

Mira carried the tea over on a tray with three

white cups, a short white teapot with blue flowers, a creamer, and a sugar bowl. She set the tray in the center of the table and, as she and Tanner sat, Mira observed Declan, though still careful not to make direct eye contact. She was more than wary—she was scared of him.

Causing her any fear or trepidation was not his intention. He didn't mind when criminals feared him, but not Mira. He smiled as she poured his tea, then lifted the cup and said, "Thank you."

She nodded, the smidge of a smile gracing her face. She had beautiful cocoa skin, dark eyes, and long dark hair. She was a beautiful woman, and he feared what horrific things may have been done to her.

He sat back, determined to let Tanner take the lead.

"Mira, may we show you a picture?" Tanner asked.

"Of who?"

"The man we believe was the American ship captain who brought you over from Malaysia."

Horror flickered in Mira's eyes. She pulled her arms in close to her body and crossed her legs. Basically balling up as much as possible while in a seated position. "Why?" she asked.

"Because if you can identify him, we can add another count of human trafficking against

44

him," Tanner said, but there was so much more riding on it. So many possible follow-up questions.

Mira stiffened. "I can't."

Tanner reached for her hand. "I know you are worried about your sisters back home, and I understand why you fear for them, but making sure men like that captain stay behind bars is the best way to protect them."

Mira pondered that a moment and then nodded. "A-All . . . right." She swallowed.

Declan had Captain Randal Jackson's mug shot on his phone, so he handed it to Mira. "Is this the man who bought you?" he asked quietly. The words were so cruel, the action brutal.

Tears welled in Mira's eyes, and she nodded.

Tanner clamped Mira's trembling hand in hers, and Declan offered her his handkerchief.

His muscles coiled and tensed. Jackson was a monster. What had he done to this poor woman for so much fear to live in her sorrow-filled eyes?

He hated to keep questioning her. It felt like the most insensitive thing, but they were here to stop a terrorist threat. He couldn't lose sight of the mission. He had to ask. It was his job. "I'm sorry to prod, but it would be really helpful if you could tell us what happened once you landed in America."

Mira looked to Tanner, who nodded.

Mira sniffed, holding back burgeoning tears welling in her eyes and began, her voice uneven and shaky. "We came to Baltimore. I did not know where I was. I later heard Baltimore."

"And then?"

"I . . ." Tears slipped from her eyes.

"It's okay," Tanner said, resting her other hand on top of their clutched ones. "You can trust him. He's trying to help."

Thank you, he mouthed, and Tanner nodded.

He took a deep breath, praying Mira continued.

"A man came to *collect* us from the ship," she said with disdain.

"Us?" Declan said.

"Me and the others."

"How many?"

"Twenty-one, I think."

Fury pounded through Declan at the horrific injustice of it all. "And the man who came to collect you?" he asked.

Mira said something in Malaysian, her gentle features pinched fierce.

Declan arched a brow at Tanner.

"Evil man," she translated.

Evil man sounded about right. Tanner's jaw tightened in sync with his. They both loathed injustice. One thing they had deeply in common. Hardwired into them by their Creator.

"They put us into groups," Mira said, her

46

voice cold, devoid of emotion—she'd distanced herself from the painful memory. He'd witnessed it in other victims of abuse. He believed it was a God-given mechanism to battle against the evil confronting them. "I was placed with three men. Two Malaysian and one Indonesian."

"When was this?"

"Three years ago this summer."

Horror tracked through Declan. *Three years?* That meant Mira had only been seventeen at the time. He'd be paying Captain Jackson another visit in the pen, and Jackson had better pray the Lord provided Declan the willpower not to lay waste to him.

"Another man came for the others, and they were put in a white van, just as we were. We pulled out of the lot, and I never saw the others again. Me and the three men were taken to the house where you found me."

"So you have no idea what happened to the other people?"

"No. Only that they went with the lanky white man in that van."

Lanky? White? "Any chance you recall his hair color?"

"Blond."

"Anything else noticeable about him?"

"He had a . . . scar along the right side of his neck and was missing his right . . ." she traced

47

the side of her head and said something in Malaysian to Tanner.

"Earlobe," Tanner supplied, turning toward Declan. "He was missing his right earlobe."

Lennie Wilcox.

Declan exhaled, his blood pressure rising. He would have to hit the hiking trail later today to work off some of the righteous anger churning inside.

Mira's eyes widened at Declan's response. "Do you know this man?"

"I've tried to arrest him many times, but I've never found a witness to ID him."

Mira looked to Tanner in panic, and a flood of words rushed out in Malaysian.

Tanner spoke back, her tone soft, even, and reassuring. She looked to Declan. "I told her she didn't have to identify him."

And that's how Lennie Wilcox was going to get away with it *again.*

"She still has two sisters back in Malaysia," Tanner said beneath her breath. "She's terrified to go to the authorities because she fears what retaliation might come. She's only speaking with you because you are with me."

He nodded, but he wasn't there to hurt Mira or get her family harmed, only to obtain vital information that could protect thousands of lives, and then they'd leave her in peace. He had no intention of bothering her again, but

48

this was necessary for the safety of his home and the country that he loved. "I understand," he said.

"Who is the man with the scar?" Tanner asked him.

"Lennie Wilcox."

Understanding registered in Tanner's eyes. Lennie Wilcox was Max Stallings' right-hand man, and the one running Max's business while Max was in prison. Max ran a horrific scam, promising people a fresh start in a bountiful country and then basically enslaving them by giving them low-paying jobs and charging them exorbitant amounts for their necessities, all the while keeping them living in his buildings; no other word but *slums* could do them justice.

In addition, he'd been in the smuggling business for at least three years according to what Mira had just shared. Much longer than he'd realized. That would definitely require further investigation.

"And the evil man who came for you? Was he American?" He noticed she hadn't described him—probably in an effort to disengage her thoughts of him as much as possible.

Mira shook her head. "Arabic. Egyptian, I believe."

"You don't think . . . ?" Tanner said, casting a furtive glance at Declan.

"Jari Youssef." He nodded, his mind going to the same man. "That was my first guess. It makes sense."

Jari Youssef had worked for the Islamic Cultural Institute of the Mid-Atlantic and was also the man who'd picked up terrorist Anajay Darmadi when he'd been smuggled into the country. Jari had been shot in the backseat of Declan's Suburban as he was taking him in for questioning and had died on the scene. No doubt killed by the members of the cultural institute in an attempt to be certain he didn't talk.

Declan called fellow agent Tim Barrows and asked him to text the photo they had at the office of Jari Youssef. When it arrived he showed it to Mira. "Is this the man who picked you up?"

Mira nodded as the door blew in, a brief second of terror flashing in her eyes before a gun retorted.

4

Declan swung around, moving to grab Tanner and yank her behind the kitchen table, which he was about to kick over, but the man who'd busted his way in had already grabbed her. He stood with one arm wrapped around Tanner's waist, her back flush against his chest, the muzzle of his Beretta wedged to her temple.

"Drop the gun or I shoot," the man said as a second man entered, his gun aimed at Declan's head.

As he turned back to Tanner, her expression was different than he'd expected. Instead of fear, he saw cold calculation.

He didn't have the shot, not the right angle. If she moved just a little to her left, perhaps . . .

Before he could finish his thought, Tanner stomped down with her heel on the man's instep. He flinched, and that was all it took for her to elbow him in the solar plexus, reverse head-butt him, and swing around, relieving him of his gun as his free hand flew to his dazed head.

The second man turned to fire on Declan, but not before Tanner got her shot off—straight to center mass. The man stumbled back, lifting his gun. She fired again, this time right between his eyes.

She kneed the first man with impressive force in an area he wouldn't soon recover from and stood over him with his own gun pressed to his head as he crumpled to his knees. "Who sent you?" she demanded.

Declan stood, gun aimed to back her, but it was pretty apparent she required no backup.

Where on earth had that come from? He'd always suspected there was something about Tanner he couldn't put his finger on, but he'd never have guessed . . . Those were no simple self-defense moves, especially not the two perfect shots she'd gotten off under such heated circumstances. Her actions—or rather, reactions—bespoke of military or agency training. His interest in Tanner, along with his curiosity about the source of her skills, skyrocketed.

Declan stood over the man kneeling on the floor. "The lady asked you a question."

Sound echoed in the hall and both he and Tanner stilled. *Boot steps coming up the stairs.*

"There are more coming," he said. He thumped the man on the back of the head with the butt of his gun to knock him out and glanced into the hall. Men were rushing up the long zig-zagging stairwell. "We need to move." He surveyed the space. "The fire escape!"

"But . . . Mira." She knelt at her friend's side, tears tumbling down her face. "We can't just leave her."

He stepped to her, crouching beside her while covering the door with his gun. "Honey, she's gone. If we stay, we will be too." He reached for her hand and after a reluctant breath, she took it.

They moved to the living room window and he thrust it open, indicating for her to go first.

Kicking off her heels, she stepped onto the fire-escape platform. He followed, a bullet shattering the glass mere inches above his head, shards plunging down on him, embedding in his skin, slicing across his shoulder blades and the back of his arms. Ignoring the stinging pain, he followed Tanner down the first flight of stairs and onto the next platform.

Bullets ricocheted off the metal platform above.

Tanner moved quickly, the muscles in her slender arms toner than he'd realized. She was strong, hanging from the rails until she jumped three feet across an opening that led straight down to the pavement nine stories below.

A bullet pinged off the bar above Declan's hand, and with a gigantic leap he followed Tanner across the divide. She covered him with fire as he landed on the shifting platform. He found purchase and grabbed Tanner by her arm. "Let's go."

Only two men were on the fire escape, which meant others were likely racing to meet them once they reached the ground. They needed to speed up their descent. Once within a safe distance from the ground, Declan tugged Tanner toward him, cradling her waist and holding her tight.

"What are you doing?"

"Leaping," he said, his heart feeling as if it was jumping off far more than just the fire escape.

They landed on the pavement, the soles of Declan's shoes making contact first, his knees slightly bent to cushion the jar of the jump. Not wanting to let go of Tanner, he forced himself to set her down. Her eyes met his and she blinked quickly.

"Your six!" she hollered.

Declan spun around in time to see two men rounding the backside of the building.

He scanned the alleyway. An SV650 Suzuki motorcycle sat parked fifty feet away.

He nodded in its direction, and they raced for it.

"You know how to drive one of these?" Tanner asked, having never seen straight-laced Declan on a motorcycle.

He hot-wired it while she covered them with fire, and within a matter of seconds they were speeding out of the north end of the alley and onto Pratt Street, horns blaring as Declan maneuvered his way into oncoming traffic.

It was all wrong. She'd gotten her friend killed and then just left her. Logically, it was what had to happen. Loath as she was to admit it, she knew Declan was right. If they'd stayed, they'd most likely be dead, but that was exactly why she'd left her past life—so she didn't have to make choices like this.

She knew in her gut she never should have let Declan come along, regardless of what her new boss ordered. She should have walked away instead of compromising Mira's safety. Declan had promised he wasn't followed, promised Mira would be safe, and he was wrong. But ultimately, the guilt was hers to bear. *She'd* gotten her friend killed.

A black SUV came barreling behind them down the three-lane one-way road, and Declan rolled on the throttle, swerving masterfully between the cars stacked up at the red light. Tanner braced herself for the sudden stop, certain he wasn't going to run it. And yet he did. Veering through cross traffic, again to the blaring of horns and several hollers, he weaved his way to the other side, the SUV swerving to the right and jumping onto the sidewalk to avoid oncoming traffic stopped at the light.

When they reached the next light, Declan yelled, "Hold on, this one's gonna be tight!"

This one? She tightened her hold around his waist, careful not to put any pressure on his bleeding, glass-covered back.

He opened the throttle and nearly soared through the intersection, the engine roaring as he continued to weave his way through oncoming traffic.

With a screeching of tires, the SUV slammed to a stop. Tanner looked back to see the bald driver hollering something as he hit the steering wheel. There was no sidewalk for him to swerve onto this time. He blasted the horn, but nobody moved. She had no doubt, however, that as soon as the light changed and traffic loosened up, the SUV would be coming after them.

A couple of blocks later Declan's knee hovered a mere inch above the ground as he banked hard left into an alley, making a superior turn. He straightened, gliding around obstacles blocking their path as if he'd designed the course, but moments later the SUV turned into the alleyway, tires squealing, ramming and knocking over the boxes and crates Declan had so masterfully weaved around.

"They're still behind us!"

He banked hard left onto Fleet Street, his

bike again nearly horizontal to the ground at a forty-degree angle to the pavement, his Docker-covered knee nearly breezing the asphalt.

The SUV followed, its wheel rims sparking off the brick of the building as it tore out of the nearly too narrow space.

"Time to lose them for good." Declan revved the engine, shifted direction, and headed for the waterfront industrial area, making a right onto Boston Street and then another right a half a mile up onto the railroad path. He ran along the rocks beside the track as a train blistered past. Tanner's hair whipped about her face as the train wheels clanged, reverberating in her ears and chest just barely over the motorcycle's roar.

The rock path was too narrow for the SUV to fit. It had to wait for the train to pass, and thankfully it was a long one.

Two men climbed out and took off on foot behind them as the SUV reversed, no doubt searching for a parallel route.

Declan swerved right into an opening she feared even they wouldn't make it through and came out into a marina industrial park.

He yelled at the guy stationed at the gate. "Hey, Bill, open the gate! We've got company coming."

Bill opened the gate, and Declan sped through with a wave of thanks.

The gate slid shut behind them with a clang.

Declan pulled into a boat warehouse on their left and cut the engine. "We should be safe here. I'll update backup and call local police to put an APB out on the SUV. Any chance you caught the license plate?"

"MCV-989."

The beauty of Maryland. Front plates were required.

"Great job," he said.

Great job? "Are you insane? We just got Mira killed!"

5

Declan followed Will Russel into his office, Tanner right behind him.

Will was the owner of the marina industrial park that sold, stored, and serviced boats. Will and Declan's dad went way back—friends from a fishing gig when they were both young men starting out in the maritime business. Will had moved away from fishing and into selling boats, but after Dec's dad retired last year, both men could still be found on the water each morning before dawn, ready to start their day with some fishing. Being on the water was their form of breathing. Just as his job had been his, until recently. Somehow thoughts of Tanner had crept into his mind, growing in intensity until he spent his days thinking of her—or the *her* he'd believed her to be.

"There's a first-aid kit in the closet," Will said. "Use the space as long as you need it." He stepped out the door.

"Thanks, Will."

Tanner stood with her back to Declan. He shut the door and stepped in front of her.

Tears streaked down her cheeks, her eyes puffy and red.

59

Without thinking, he pulled her into his embrace. She pushed against his hold, but he didn't release. She looked up defiantly, with pained anger clouding her beautiful eyes. "You got Mira killed, and I let it happen."

"I'm sorry, Tanner, but we had no way of knowing—"

"I told you." She pounded his chest. "I told you, and now she's dead." She stopped fighting his hold after a moment, sobs taking over, wracking her slender body.

He let her take her sorrow out on him. He deserved it. However it happened, Mira was dead because she'd talked to them. But . . . "No one followed us there. I'm sure of it."

So how did they know?

She shook her head against his chest, finally leaning into him, letting him shoulder the weight of her grief. "So you're saying it was just a coincidence?"

"Not necessarily."

"Then what?" She swiped at her eyes in an attempt to stem her tears. Never had a woman's tears cut so deep inside him. His heart was breaking for her, despite his disappointment over her hiding her past from him. There was no doubt Kate had run a background check when Tanner had shown up in their lives, so why hadn't she told the gang?

He swallowed, shaking off the thought.

Now was not the time. *Focus on Tanner—on what she needs.* "They weren't following us, so . . . they must have been watching Mira." It was the only thing that made sense.

She looked up at him, and his heart melted. All he wanted to do was fix her pain. "No one knew where she lived except me and a few volunteers from my old job who helped move in furniture."

"Maybe one of the volunteers worked for Ebeid."

Her eyes widened. "What if you're right? What if I led them there?"

He gently brushed a strand of hair from her cheeks. "You can't blame yourself."

Her shoulders drooped. "How can I not?"

"Because we both know Ebeid sent those men. They pulled the trigger. They killed her."

"Because she talked to us."

"And for that I'm so sorry." He truly was. "But we were doing our job."

"Believe me"—she swiped at her eyes again—"I know all about that."

He arched a brow. "Your training?" He couldn't wait to hear the truth about her past.

"I know I need to tell you, but I need a minute." Her bottom lip quivered. "I just lost a good friend."

He swallowed. "I'm sorry, Tanner. What can I do?"

"Just hold me," she whispered, nuzzling back into his embrace.

He smoothed her hair as she rested her head on his chest. "There's nothing I'd rather do," he whispered in a moment of brutal honesty.

She gaped up at him, surprise flooding her face, but it couldn't hold a candle to the shock that engulfed him as he cupped her cheek in the palm of his hand and lowered his mouth to hers.

Warmth radiated through him as she, defying all logic, kissed him back.

The exchange was soft . . . slow . . . tender, and all breath left his lungs until she jerked back, blinking up at him.

She shook her head as if shaking herself out of a fog. "What's wrong with me?"

Definitely not the response he was hoping for, but given the circumstances . . .

"I just got my friend killed and I'm giving in to my feelings."

He staggered back. "*Your* feelings?" *She* had feelings for him?

She took a deliberate step back, putting distance between them. "I shouldn't . . . I can't . . . Not now."

He reined in his instinct to move closer and instead remained rooted in place, adrenaline burning his limbs.

She swiped a hand through her hair, shifting

restlessly. "We need to get that glass out of your back and get back to Mira. We shouldn't have left her alone."

He nodded, still in shock. Tanner held feelings for *him*? He wasn't the only one?

He cleared his throat, the taste of her strawberry lip gloss still on his lips. "I'll make the necessary calls." God would have to give him the focus to think straight. "We can take care of me later."

"You have glass in your back."

"I'll be fine."

She retrieved the first-aid kit from the closet. "Make your calls, and then I'm getting it out. I'll work fast."

"Fine, but on one condition," he said.

She arched her brows.

"While you're at it, you tell me who you really are."

Tanner had known this day would come. She couldn't hide from her past forever, couldn't hide it from her friends any longer. Today was her day of reckoning. She prayed they didn't feel differently about her afterward, but how could they not?

Declan started by calling the office and sending Tim Barrows and his team to Mira's apartment. Then he called local police—who'd already sent a squad to the building after several neighbors reported gunfire—and lastly he called Parker to process the crime scene. By the time the two of them returned to Mira's, everyone else would likely already be on-site.

When Declan finished his calls, Tanner sat behind him on a cold metal stool, took a deep breath, and focused her thoughts before clamping the first piece of glass with the tweezers. Her hand was finally steady after that kiss and the rush of emotions riddling through her. "This is going to sting."

"I'll be fine."

She pulled the shard out, and he didn't flinch. He wasn't going to let her stall much longer, and in some way, it'd be a relief to get her secrets off her chest and see where things landed. She prayed they landed well. Declan and the entire gang had become her family over the last year. She couldn't imagine losing them. Declan's opinion in particular held far more weight than she'd expected.

"I'm from Israel," she blurted out, seeing no way to be subtle at this point. Subtle had been lost the moment her ingrained defense response kicked in. The admission of her country of origin felt strange. She hadn't spoken of it for so long, other than to the human resources division at the federal office where she now worked.

Declan, to her surprise, remained quiet and still, silently encouraging her to continue.

Taking another deep breath, she did. "My family—well, my parents and grandparents—still live there."

"And you lived there until . . . ?" His tone was even, calm, despite the news she'd just dropped on him and the shards of glass she was pulling from his back. He was so steady. So strong.

"Until I was twenty and finished my mandatory service in the Israeli army."

"So the skill set . . . ?"

"Mainly came from my time in the army."

"Mainly?" he asked as she tweezed another sliver of glass from his right shoulder blade, trying to ignore the strength of the broad shoulder span she'd just been leaning on moments ago.

She exhaled, focusing on his question. "My father," she said as she dropped the shard into the metal bowl she'd located, and it clanged on top the others.

She could almost sense his brows furrowing.

"Your father?" he asked, curiosity coloring his tone.

"He's Mossad." Basically Israeli CIA. Her father was an elite field agent. One of the top in the agency. "I'm his only child." And unfortunately, a woman, as he liked to constantly remind her. "He began teaching me self-defense, combat, and shooting skills at a young age." As far back as she could remember. *"You must know how to defend yourself."*

"It was very important to him that I be self-sufficient, self-reliant." And while she appreciated that, a little love and affection, a little nurturing would have been nice too, but her father appeared incapable of it, and her mother followed his lead.

"And you left because . . . ?"

She swallowed. "I wanted to come to school in the States." She'd wanted a new life. "I had aunts and uncles and cousins living in Maryland, so I came to Towson University." Carrying one suitcase on the plane, leaving her life and her domineering father behind. "I obtained my psychology degree and then went to work for the Global Justice Mission, then the Intercultural Resource Center, and now the Bureau."

"To work for the Bureau you have to be an American citizen," he said as she removed the last piece of glass from his back.

"I became an American citizen upon graduation from Towson. I knew even if I'd be traveling with my work with GJM, this was my home." Now even more so since she'd met Declan and his friends.

"But your parents are still in Israel?" There was a deeper question there, since she'd already stated as much.

"Yes."

He clearly wanted to ask more, and she knew precisely what he was getting at. Why had she left her homeland and her parents? What was the state of their relationship now? But he was kind enough, or just polite enough, to refrain from asking outright.

"Kate doesn't miss this sort of thing in her background checks, and she's not usually one to keep things quiet," he said. Given the high-profile jobs they all had and the security surrounding them, background checks were routine.

"I asked her to keep it quiet."

"She must have trusted you enough to do so."

"She understood why I'd left that life behind."

"Why did you, if you don't mind my asking?"

He wanted to know the truth, the full truth, and after their kiss, she felt it only fair to tell him. If things were moving beyond friendship— or even if they weren't—he deserved to know. In fact, it would be a great relief to finally stop carrying the secret.

"I left because I wanted to serve people in a different way, in a way that didn't involve killing, but after today, I fear I am doomed to having death follow me."

"Killing?" Surprise drenched his throaty voice.

"Because of my shooting skills, the army assigned me to sniper school."

He turned, his eyes wide. "*You* were a sniper?"

"I know. Not me at all," she said matter-of-factly. "Now take off your shirt."

6

Declan's brows shot up. "Excuse me?"

"I need to clean your wounds out, and most likely stitch a couple of the deeper ones. I can do it easier if your shirt is off."

"Oh. Right. Of course." He fumbled with his buttons but managed to get his shirt off and tossed it on the table.

She swallowed, trying not to gape. His torso was made for a gym poster. His rippling, sculpted muscles didn't really come as a surprise, but the charcoal and cobalt howling wolf tattoo on his chest certainly did, along with a myriad of scars—a combination of bullet wounds and knife cuts and burns—all healed-over memories of injuries he'd endured on the job.

He retook the chair he'd been sitting in, his back to her, and she retook her seat, praying for focus.

Twenty minutes later they were back on the bike, Tanner's arms wrapped around his waist as they made their way to Mira's apartment.

Tanner, a sniper?

He struggled to picture the compassionate,

loving woman he had come to admire serving as a sniper. It was a necessary job. Griffin had served as a sniper for the Baltimore Police Department SWAT team before transitioning into being a detective. Now Tanner's occasional comments or hints of comradery with Griffin made sense. But it was no wonder she'd left that and eventually gone into helping combat sex trafficking with the Global Justice Mission. It gave her a chance to love on others and, on a soul level, that's who she really was—the embodiment of compassion.

The knowledge of her past didn't alter his impression in the least, though he now understood why she resisted his overprotectiveness. She wasn't being reckless. She possessed the skills to take care of herself in those situations. Now he really felt foolish.

He turned down Mira's street, blue and red lights whirling in the distance, his mind rattling with so many thoughts and unasked questions. Had Tanner's dad wanted her to remain in the army, or had he wanted her to follow in his footsteps by joining Mossad? And what about Tanner's faith? She was most certainly a Christian. A strong one. What about her parents? When had she come to accept Christ as her Savior, and had that caused a fracture in her relationship with them? His gut said yes, but that was her business. Hers to share if and when she wanted to. He prayed one day she'd feel comfortable enough and trust him deeply enough to share all of that with him, but for now he'd wait.

They pulled to a stop outside of Mira's building, and he offered his hand as Tanner climbed off the bike, her cold fingers intertwined momentarily with his before Agent Barrows called his name.

He and Tanner exchanged a look—one that spoke so much more than words could express. They, for better or worse, were in this together.

"Ready?" he asked.

She nodded, not looking the least bit confident, but taking a deep breath, she moved in stride with him toward Tim.

He gave her hand a squeeze before letting go as they reached Agent Barrows.

As anticipated, local units were on-site, and according to Tim, the SUV had been stopped just north of the Baltimore Harbor Tunnel, the men thankfully in custody. However, a battle between local authorities and the Bureau was brewing. Given the nature of the case and participants, it was the Bureau's jurisdiction, but local cops had been very helpful in nabbing the SUV, so Declan believed it was best to tread carefully.

Relief filled him as he spotted Parker's Land Rover. The more people Tanner had on her side, the better. She had a lot to answer for with the unknown suspect's death, but it had been a warranted kill, and he could attest to that. He just needed to keep his head in the game, but after that kiss . . .

A tremor of delight shot through him at the memory.

"Can you run us through what happened here?" Tim asked as they stood by the cordoned-off front door of Mira's building.

"Why don't we step inside?" Declan suggested.

"Of course." Tim nodded.

They climbed up to Mira's apartment, Tim huffing a little at the end. While not exactly out of shape, Tim had let his physical performance slide a little over the last year. After his wife left him, he'd turned to food for solace. Declan was all for self-control, but losing a wife in any manner had to be gut-wrenching. He was placing no judgment, had only sympathy for the pain Tim must be going through. Not that they ever spoke of it.

Fellow agent Matt Greer greeted them, as well as Parker, Avery, and the rest of the Bureau team that Tim had brought with him. Two local police officers remained, the two teams needing to work together until the case was fully shifted over to the Bureau.

Tanner's eyes welled with tears as her gaze shifted to Mira, her body illuminated by Avery's camera flash. Avery's gentle gaze conveyed her depth of sorrow for what Tanner was going through. Though conveying emotion wasn't his strong suit, Declan hoped he could provide some solace as well.

"Let's step into the bedrooms," Tim said, "so Matt and I can get your statements."

"I'll take Declan in this room," Matt said, pointing to the second bedroom. Declan had expected their separation, but he didn't like it. He watched Tanner disappear with Tim into the first bedroom, his mind racing through all she'd have to explain, and wondering how Tim would react.

His time with Matt went quickly. He got straight to the point, hoping to be back out with Tanner as quickly as possible, but the other bedroom door remained shut.

Parker stepped to his side. "What on earth happened here? Looks like professional hits," he murmured in his low Irish lilt.

Mira's definitely was. Her attacker's, in a manner of speaking, was as well. But the truth about Tanner wasn't his to share.

"I'll let Tanner explain back at Kate's." Meaning Charm City Investigations, where the gang was planning to share an early dinner. While this was Bureau business, he still wanted to employ the talents and expertise of his friends, even if only in a consulting manner.

"Dude, what happened to your back? It looks shredded." Parker gaped at his blood-covered, glass-sheared shirt.

"One of the suspects shot the window while I was climbing out."

"You should have that looked at."

His gaze fixed on Tanner as she exited the bedroom followed by Tim, a bewildered expression on his brow. "I already did."

Parker followed his gaze, and a slight smile crossed his friend's lips. "She okay?"

"I hope so."

When Tanner stepped back into the living room, Declan's gaze fastened on hers. He, to her utter shock and amazement, had been her rock in this storm. Biting her bottom lip, she glanced back to Mira. She'd promised to keep her safe, and now she was dead. How was she going to live with the guilt and sorrow?

She swallowed and stepped to meet Avery as she moved in to hug her.

"You okay?" Avery asked.

No. She nodded.

"Declan said she was your friend." Avery glanced back at Mira as Parker covered her body now that his exam and Avery's photographs of the crime scene were complete.

Tanner nodded again, afraid if she spoke, the tears would flow.

Avery rested her hand on Tanner's arm, her touch warm against Tanner's cool skin. "I'm so sorry."

"Thanks."

"Any luck with prints?" Declan asked Parker.

"All unknowns. Sorry. Other than Mira's, Tanner's, and yours, of course."

Parker looked at Tanner. He'd run her prints, so now he knew too. Soon they'd all know she used to be a killer. She glanced at the sheeted body of the man—now she was again.

"Did you find anything useful?" Declan asked.

"Two things," Parker said. "First." He held up a listening device.

"Her place was bugged?"

Parker nodded. "In three rooms."

"That's how they knew she was talking to us," Tanner said. Talking to them *had* gotten Mira killed, but not in the way she'd imagined.

"Any idea on the tech?" Declan asked.

"I'll have to examine it better back at the lab, but it's not American issued. My guess would be Russian," Parker said.

"Russian?" Declan's brow furrowed.

"Russia's black market supplies a lot of terrorist factions with arms and surveillance materials," Parker explained.

"Well, that adds another layer to this case."

"And so does this." Parker handed him an evidence-bagged slip of paper with an address

75

scrawled across it. "John Doe had this in his pocket. And according to Tim, the men in the SUV had a duffel bag with clothing and toiletries in it. It appears that John Doe, or at least one of the men, was about to take a trip."

Declan examined the address. "Houston?" he said.

Steven Burke, the FBI agent killed on the *Hiram* two months ago, had lived in Houston. "Any chance . . . ?"

"Already ahead of you," Parker said. "It's Steven Burke's address. Looks like you'll be taking a trip yourself."

"So we're going to Houston?" Tanner said. She prayed Declan didn't fight her on this one. Alan had said they were a team until Lexi returned.

Parker's brows arched, his lips twitching with a smile. *"We?"*

Declan cleared his throat. "Tanner is now a crisis counselor with the Bureau."

Parker's lips twitched again. "Is that right?"

Declan nodded.

"Well, congratulations." Parker patted her on the back.

"Thanks." But it was her first day on the job and she'd already gotten two people killed— one by her own hand. It didn't bode well.

7

On the way over to Charm City Investigations, Declan had made a call to the Houston Bureau office to talk with Chuck Franco, Burke's former partner. Declan hadn't shared much, but hearing his side of the conversation had given her the distinct impression he hadn't gotten a lot of cooperation from the man.

The evening air was cool as Declan walked beside her to CCI's entrance, and then held the front glass door open. She stepped inside to the scent of tomato sauce and cheese wafting down the hall.

Entering the main room, her heart wobbled at the sight of everyone seated on the sofa and chairs. It was time to share her past with them. In hindsight, it hadn't been fair to ask Kate to keep her secret, and now that Declan, Parker, and Avery knew, or at least suspected, it seemed pointless to keep it from the rest of them.

Before she could utter a word, Griffin's wife, Finley, raced over and engulfed her in a hug. "I'm so sorry about Mira." Concern blanketed her face. "I know how close you two were."

"Thanks."

Everyone expressed their sympathies, and

right when she was on the verge of tears, Declan stepped to her side. "You must be famished," he said. They'd both been so distracted, and she heartbroken, that they'd neglected to eat.

"We've got pizza," Parker said, gesturing to the kitchen.

"And salad," Finley added.

Avery smiled. "And cheese sticks."

Tanner's favorite, but she still had zero appetite—whether more from the events of the day or her anticipation of the discussion to come, she wasn't certain.

She blinked as the terror in Mira's eyes right before she was shot sped through her mind. She doubted the sight would ever leave her entirely. Sweet Mira was dead.

"Are you cold?" Declan asked.

"Huh?" She glanced up at him.

"You just shivered."

"Oh." She rubbed her arms, trying to hide the gooseflesh rippling up them. "I'm fine." She was far from it, and all she wanted to do was nestle back into the security of his strong arms, but instead she strode toward the kitchen. "Let's eat," she said, despite her lack of appetite.

He followed her into the small galley kitchen where she grabbed a slice of pepperoni pizza and a can of Coke before returning to the front room and taking a seat on the sofa.

Declan sat next her, exuding a sense of comfort

but also one of concern. He was worried about her. She could read it in his eyes. But to be fair, she was worried too. The entire day, the vast spectrum of emotions—sadness, comfort, terror, along with the engagement of skills she hadn't practiced in years—all bordered on dizzying.

"Should I take you home so you can get some rest?" Declan asked, clearly sensing her unease. He was good at that—reading her. Though she'd previously pictured him as stiff and always logical, he had a strong intuitive and compassionate side. She'd been seeing more and more of it lately, and she liked what she saw.

Surprise hit her as she realized what he was really offering. He was offering to take her home, rather than expecting her to explain her past and today's events to the whole group.

The softness of his expression made that clear.

While she greatly appreciated the lack of pressure, it was time. "Thanks," she murmured, "but I need to do this." She should have a long time ago.

Taking a deep breath, she scooted forward. "I have something I need to share with you all."

Before she lost her nerve, she jumped straight in—explaining how she'd grown up in Israel with her father serving with Mossad, how she'd done her mandatory service and excelled at shooting skills, and how she'd had twelve kills during her tenure—thirteen, counting today's. She finished by explaining why she'd wanted to keep that part of her past in the past, and how Kate had been kind enough to let her, but that she was glad they all knew. Then she waited anxiously for their response.

"Thank you for trusting us enough to tell us," Finley said.

"We all have a past," Avery said. "I totally get wanting to leave it in the past. That's where mine is now."

All the guys agreed, and a bit of relief Tanner hadn't anticipated swelled in her chest. How could they be so understanding, so forgiving, so nonjudgmental? Yes, she'd been doing her duty while serving in the army, and today she'd saved Declan's life, but she still remembered each kill—all thirteen of them, today's included.

Despite everyone's kind reaction, her chest felt compressed, like a lead weight was squashing it, stealing the breath from her lungs.

Please, Father, help me to release this burden to you. It's too heavy for me to bear anymore.

It was crushing her. She could see that now—the toll it was taking on her. The weight of guilt and emotions she'd shouldered rather than turning them over to her Savior. She'd felt it wasn't fair to give Him her burden—*she* deserved to carry it. But she also knew He'd already borne it on the cross for her. Why was it so hard to let go of pain sometimes? Especially when she had such a loving Savior waiting to bear the agony for her?

Thank you, Jesus.

She swallowed back the tears salting in her eyes and covered them with a cough and a quick swipe of her eyes. She prayed Declan hadn't seen, but there was little he missed. "Parker said you're heading to Houston," Griffin said, casually shifting the topic of conversation and, along with it, thankfully her thoughts.

"Yes," Declan said. "John Doe had Steven Burke's home address on his person and a duffel in the SUV. Seems Steven might still hold a key to the *Hiram* case, and possibly the terror threat that seems to be building in Baltimore."

"When do you leave?" Finley asked.

"First thing tomorrow morning." He looked to Tanner. "I took the liberty of booking our flight."

She nodded, and Declan proceeded to explain Tanner's new role with the Bureau—for which she got full congratulations, though given her first day on the job, she was second-guessing whether it was where God wanted her, despite the peace she'd had going in. Much more prayer was required.

"We're all leaving in"—Griffin looked at his watch—"a half hour."

Declan looked around the room and frowned. "Where to?"

"Haywood's retreat. Kicks off with the usual dessert and cocktail party."

"Oh, that's right. Since I couldn't attend, I totally forgot it started tonight. Tell him I'm bummed I can't make it."

"Will do, but it seems we'll be doing more than just attending."

Declan's brow arched. "Oh?"

Griffin exhaled. "I had a weird meeting with him today. He believes his partner Lowell is skimming money from his clients' accounts and setting him up to take the fall."

"What?" Declan leaned forward. "You're kidding."

Griffin shook his head. "I wish I were." He went on to relay the entirety of his and Haywood's conversation.

Declan exhaled as shock sifted through him. He'd never have seen that coming. "Keep me posted."

"Will do," Griff said. "And Katie's coming along."

Declan glanced at Kate. "He hired you to investigate?"

"Yep." She nodded.

Declan frowned. "I know you'll all do an

excellent job, but why doesn't he just report it—have someone in the police fraud department look into it? Or the Bureau fraud department, for that matter?"

Griffin shook his head. "He came to me as a friend, said if he went to law enforcement now, everything points to him. He wants us to find the proof of his innocence and the truth about what his partner is doing before he *officially* goes to the authorities."

"Sounds like we've all got an interesting weekend before us," Parker said.

"Why don't we take a minute and pray for safety and guidance?" Finley said.

Griffin clasped his wife's hand, and Tanner remembered the feel of Declan's hand in hers as they'd stood outside of Mira's apartment.

"Great idea, babe," Griffin said. "Why don't you start?"

Finley closed her eyes and bowed her head. "Dear Father, you are sending us out among wolves. Please keep us safe. Please guide us to the truth, and help us to see justice done."

A few others added their prayers, and then "Amen" rounded the room.

"Ready to go?" Declan asked Tanner.

She nodded, having ridden with him from the Bureau. "We'll need to pick up my car."

"I'll just take you home and pick you up bright and early in the morning for our flight. It leaves at six. Your car will be safe at the office while we're away."

"Six?" She was a night owl, not an early bird.

"It'll give us more time on the ground."

"Gotcha." *But . . . ouch.*

Declan held the door for her as they exited CCI, and her heart fluttered. She still couldn't believe they'd kissed. Now, as things had settled down and they were alone, it really hit home. He held his SUV door open for her, and she climbed in, her heart racing as she watched him walk to the driver's side, taking in his athletic physique in the brick building's floodlights. He was gorgeous. She'd always recognized it, but something had shifted today. Seeing him drive that motorcycle, feeling his lips on hers . . . She felt as if she were on the top of a stopped Ferris wheel, her feet dangling in the air high above the ground below, anticipation soaring for what would happen next.

"How you holding up?" he asked. "I know you're blaming yourself, but it wasn't your fault."

She frowned. His sentiment was kind, but totally false. "How was it *not* my fault?" She shifted to face him better, readjusting her seat belt to hit lower across her chest. "If I'd paid attention to who was helping move furniture, if I hadn't been questioning her . . ."

84

"If *we* hadn't been questioning her they may not have shown up today, but the fact that her place was bugged meant she'd been in danger the entire time. You can beat yourself up or you can focus on identifying her killer and the man who ordered the hit."

It's not what she wanted to hear, but her training told her he was right. She owed it to Mira to find her killer, and to do that she had to detach and focus on the facts, but her heart ached so.

He glanced over at her at the stoplight, red bouncing off his features, concern filling his eyes. "I'm not trying to be cold. I'm so sorry about Mira. I *truly* am, but I hate to see you beat yourself up. You were trying to help. There's a much larger case here, and if we don't solve it, who knows how many casualties we might be facing."

She swallowed. When he put it that way . . .

Driving the rest of the way in silence, she contemplated the truth of Declan's words. She'd been trained to focus on the larger picture. He was right, but the need to pray, to connect with her Savior overwhelmed her. She closed her eyes, praying God would heal the deep ache in her soul at the loss of her friend and that He would equip her and Declan for the case before them.

Twenty minutes later, Declan pulled to a

stop in the marina lot. She climbed out of his vehicle and walked slowly beside him down the creaking dock to Kate's houseboat, where she was staying until she found her own place. She turned to unlock the sliding glass door when his hand stilled her arm. Turning back, her breath caught at the deep emotion welling in his dark brown eyes.

He reached for her cheek, cupping it in his palm, his hand warm despite the chill in the air. He stepped closer still. "All I want to do is kiss you again," he said, his voice hoarse, his breath clouding in the crisp night air.

She leaned in to him, but a shift of movement in the pier light grabbed her attention—an armed man in black.

"Get down," she shouted, yanking Declan with her to the deck as shots fired, bullets riddling the boat around them.

Declan fired back, but shots seemed to come from all directions.

He grabbed her hand. "Into the water!"

Before she could even take a breath, they were submerged in the cold, dark harbor.

8

Declan felt Tanner in front of him as they dove deeper into the murky harbor and away from the boat, bullets propelling past them fractions of an inch away.

They'd been sitting ducks on the boat. At least in the water they had a fighting chance. He prayed Tanner was a strong swimmer because they had a ways to go before they were out of firing range.

The cold seeped straight to his bones. He could only imagine how chilled Tanner must be, slender as she was.

He tugged her leg, indicating for them to move for the surface. She followed his lead, and slowly, carefully they breached the barrier between water and sky. Frigid air crinkled through Declan's burning lungs as he breathed deeply, keeping as low in the water as possible.

Glancing to his right, he saw the men fanned out across the docks, flashlights in hand, scouring the water.

"Keep searching. They have to come up for air sooner or later," one of the men hollered. "I *want* them found!"

Declan looked to Tanner, her brown hair soaked and clinging to her face. Her lips were blue in the light of the nearly full moon, teeth chattering. He wrapped his arm around her shoulders, rubbing her back to warm her, for the brief moment he could.

He scanned the harbor, the towering brick office building across the inlet his target. It was dark except for the light over the door and far enough away it should be safe to head ashore.

Lights shifted in their direction.

They were coming

"Head for that building. Deep breath!" he said before diving back under. Lights bounced off the surface overhead as they swam.

Bullets continued spiraling through the water, one skimming Declan's left arm. He dove deeper, praying Tanner understood they needed to increase their pace, to make it farther from the docks and out of range.

Her strokes grew faster, stronger, the water streaming in the wake of her breaststroke and intermittent dolphin kick. She was doing a remarkable job.

Through the murky water he saw her moving toward the surface. He followed, hoping they were far enough out as they slowly rose above the waterline.

Lights continued to bounce off the water,

but they were finally out of reach. The men suddenly shifting into a run for the parking lot indicated they realized that.

"They're moving for their vehicles," Tanner said, her voice trembling.

If only he could warm her.

"They're going to start searching the perimeter. We have to reach that building." He pointed at its tall shadow looming a hundred yards away.

She nodded and they swam, Declan using the building's one light as a beacon.

Finally reaching shore, they remained low in the water as he surveyed the scene.

It looked clear.

"Okay," he said. "Move quickly. Straight for the south side of the building and hold."

She nodded, her head lolling slightly.

He kept her behind his right shoulder, his service weapon drawn as they raced for what he prayed was the safety of the building's shadows. Tanner stumbled along the way, but he held her upright.

Their backs finally flush with the rough brick wall, he glanced down at her. She was shivering, puddles of water pooling at her feet. He needed to get her someplace safe, someplace warm. *The office.*

He slipped his jacket off, feeling the weight of it drenched with water, but at least it gave more protection from the wind than the light-weight jacket she had on. He draped it across her shoulders, and she slipped her arms in.

"Thanks."

Headlights whizzed by the rear parking lot, but just as he was about to sigh with relief, the vehicle reversed and pulled into the lot. There was no way he was taking Tanner back into the frigid water. She was showing clear signs of hypothermia—shivering, lack of coordination, drowsiness. He felt her pulse—weak, just as he suspected. They needed to find another way of escape, and fast. *Help us, Lord.*

He held her against the building as the vehicle screeched to a stop, doors slammed, and two sets of footsteps headed toward them.

"What are you doing?" the one man asked.

"I thought I saw something," a second man responded.

"You've been saying that a lot tonight."

"I'm telling you, I saw them in the water."

"And now? You're telling me they swam all the way over here?"

"It ain't that far if your life is on the line. Now, shut up and help me look."

"This is a waste of time."

"Xavier said to search the surrounding shore-line. You go left, I'll go right."

"Fine, but I still say it's a waste of time."

Tanner looked up at Declan, steadfast determination in her eyes, despite the fatigue rimming them.

He held his finger to his lips and stepped in front of her.

The man grew closer.

Declan waited. His timing had to be precise.

Two more steps . . .

One.

Two.

Declan rushed the man, knocking him to his knees and silencing him with a quick, powerful jab to the throat.

Tanner bent and retrieved the man's sidearm, and they rushed for the vehicle the men had left running in the parking lot.

They jumped in and Declan swerved out of the lot as the other man raced after them, a bullet pinging off the roof.

"I'd head for my house," he said, accelerating, "but I don't want to risk leading them there. That is, if they don't already have people watching it. Instead, we're going to the office."

She nodded as he cranked up the heat, praying it would kick in quickly.

He handed her his cell. "Give the office a heads-up—tell them to have local units search for the men who are after us if local police haven't already been called by someone within earshot."

She swiped the water dripping from the

phone's case. "You seriously think this phone is going to work after being submerged?"

"Lifeproof case. Trust me, it'll work."

She dialed, and it connected. "Impressive."

He glanced in his rearview mirror as he sped down Boston Street toward the freeway. So far no tail. He wanted to take Tanner home and get her warm and dry, but the car they'd taken needed to be processed, and the Bureau office was definitely the safer location.

He turned down Ponca Street, and then Eastern Avenue as she finished the call. He was taking the back route to the office, hoping to lose anyone who might still be chasing them. Praying he'd get Tanner to warmth and safety. Praying he could protect her. Praying God would protect them both.

9

Griffin and Finley strolled toward the Gilmore Inn's reception area. Tomorrow morning they'd be able to see the bounty of orange, yellow, and red leaves surrounding the resort. Hunt Valley was at "the height of the foliage's vibrancy," according to the perky meteorologist they'd been listening to on the radio during the ride up, but for tonight, there was a clear, star-filled sky. The temperatures were cool and expected to dip below freezing before the night was out, but tomorrow was going to reach highs in the mid-fifties. It was Griffin's favorite time of year, and the perfect time for the client retreat—clear days for hiking and crisp nights for sitting around the resort's fire pit, roasting marshmallows for s'mores.

He couldn't wait to kiss the gooey marshmallow from his wife's lips.

He loved being married, loved waking up next to Finley each morning. Loved spending quiet moments together and all the laughter—even sorrow was bearable, as long as she was at his side. The two had truly become one, and now he fully understood what God intended for marriage. The Lord had blessed him beyond measure by bringing Finley into his life.

He marveled that it was less than one year ago. It was a lesson in how quickly life could change for the good—he glanced at Finley and smiled. Or for the bad, he thought as he glanced at Haywood and then stepped toward him, hand extended. "Haywood, great to see you. Thanks again for the invite."

Haywood clasped his hand. "Thanks for making it again this year. We so look forward to this time with our clients." He shifted his gaze to Finley. "Mrs. McCray, you're looking as lovely as ever."

Finley smiled. "Always a charmer, Haywood."

"How can I not be when you're around?" He chuckled, looking a wee bit more relaxed than he had been during his conversation with Griffin earlier in the day.

Haywood glanced around at the couples gathering in the Gilmore Inn's dining hall. French doors lined the back wall, leading out to a vast brick patio where silver pyramid-shaped heaters sparked with flames dancing in the night sky.

People mingled in small groups, mostly couples, several moving back and forth between the open bar on the patio and the round dessert tables set throughout the dining room.

Haywood swiped his nose, leaning into

Griffin. "The couple next to the far dessert table are the Markums."

"Got them," Griffin said, catching movement out of the corner of his eye.

Blonde. Tall. Athletic. Kate had arrived.

"Perfect timing," he said, turning to greet her, smiling at the fact she was actually in a dress. Basic black, knee-length, capped sleeves, but it suited her—especially the red heels.

"Haywood, you remember our friend, Kate Maxwell," he said. Having met with her that afternoon, Haywood obviously didn't need the introduction. It was more for the benefit of anyone who might overhear their conversation.

"Of course. So glad you could join us."

"Thank you for inviting me." She slipped her red clutch under her arm as Finley complimented her dangly earrings.

Lowell Brentwood caught sight of new blood from across the room and made a beeline for them. "Haywood, who do we have here?" he asked, swooping up beside Kate.

"Kate Maxwell," she said before Haywood could introduce her.

"Ms. Maxwell, it's a pleasure," Lowell said with a slight dip of his head.

"Ms. Maxwell is thinking of signing on with the firm," Haywood explained. "So I suggested she join us. No better way to find out what we're all about than during our seminar tomor-row evening."

"Agreed." Lowell lifted his glass. "Thrilled you could join us." He nodded at Griffin and then Finley and smiled. "Griffin, Mrs. McCray, lovely to see you again. Where are the rest of your friends? I hope they're all coming. The retreat wouldn't be the same without the . . . What was the name of your team, Haywood?"

Haywood hitched his pants up. "The Pirates."

"That's right," Lowell said with a cloying smile before taking a sip of his champagne. "The Pirates."

"You have a good memory," Griffin said.

"Haywood has pictures of the teams he's coached in his office. Yours is in the center. Apparently he loved coaching you all the most. I mean, it's been years and he's still got that picture."

"We won the championship all three years I coached them. And let me tell you, they were a special group of kids," Haywood said, looking to Griffin. "Plus, that picture was of my last year coaching in Chesapeake Harbor. Good memories. Good times." His gaze shifted over Griffin's shoulder. "Speaking of Pirates . . ."

Griffin turned to see Parker entering the room with Avery at his side.

"Parker." Haywood stepped forward and shook his hand. "And you must be Avery."

He cupped her hand. "A pleasure to meet you, my dear. I've heard wonderful things about you."

"Thank you so much for having me," she said.

"Another new guest," Lowell said, moving to greet Avery as Frank Sinatra's version of "The Way You Look Tonight" played softly over the speakers.

Whether requested by someone or of the DJ's own choosing, crooners were Griff's favorite and perfect for dancing with his wife. Luckily the resort provided a nice dance floor in the center of the room.

"Lowell, this is my girlfriend, Avery Tate," Parker said.

"It's a pleasure. I hope you got settled in your room okay."

"We did. Avery is bunking with Kate."

"Ah, so you all know each other. I should have assumed. You know one Pirate, you know them all," Lowell said.

Parker arched a brow in Griffin's direction. Was Lowell already loaded or just being a smug suck-up? Probably a combination of the two, but the former boded well for the purposes of Kate's investigation. The more Lowell drank, the more he tended to ramble.

"Ms. Maxwell"—Lowell offered his arm—"may I have the pleasure of showing you around the inn?"

Kate put on her working smile. "I'd love that.

Thank you." She waggled her fingers, signaling good-bye, and taking Lowell's arm, headed off with him toward the library.

"Well, that went well," Haywood said.

"And while Kate's with Lowell, I think Finley and I will go make friends with the Markums," Griffin said.

Haywood nodded. "Excellent."

"Have you had any interaction with them since they've arrived?" he asked.

"Thankfully, no. But I have spoken with the Coveys." One of the other client families of Haywood's who was missing money.

"Any sign they are on to what's happening?"

Haywood shook his head. "Not that I could tell."

"Could you point them out?" Griffin asked.

Haywood looked around. "There," he said. "The couple in the center of the dance floor."

"Why don't Avery and I join the Coveys on the dance floor?" Parker said.

"Sounds like a plan." Though he'd much rather be on the dance floor with his wife, Griffin nodded, taking Finley's hand in his. "Meet up between the party ending and s'more time?" he said over his shoulder.

Parker nodded.

"Excellent," Haywood said, suddenly shifting back to the nervous man he'd been earlier in the day.

Was there a chance he worried what they might learn from the Markums or Coveys? Was there a chance Haywood—a man he'd known practically his entire life—was lying to him?

He swallowed, praying he was not as they approached the Markums who, according to Finley, were expensively dressed.

Elizabeth wore a cocktail dress from some designer he didn't recognize when Finley whispered the name, and she had a plum cashmere wrap draped along her pale arms. John was dressed in what looked to be a J. Crew suit, based on fit and style, along with a plum-and-white pinstripe shirt and matching plum tie. The J. Crew look he recognized from Finley dog-earring the Crew catalogs with items she liked for him.

"What a fabulous location," she said loudly enough for the Markums to hear as they approached from the side. "I can't wait to meet everyone and see more of the place. Oh, hello," she said, stopping before them.

Elizabeth Markum turned toward them, her blond hair cut just above her shoulders and wisped to the side. Her large blue eyes held wariness, as did her tight jaw.

"Hi, I'm Finley McCray." She extended a hand.

Elizabeth exchanged an "Oh, great" look with her husband before shaking Finley's hand. "Elizabeth. And this is my husband, John."

"A pleasure to meet you. This is my husband, Griffin." She did a backward tap on his chest with her hand, then flipped her hand over, to place it firmly on his chest as she moved into his hold, positioning them to stay a while. Whether the Markums registered their intent, Griffin wasn't certain, but either way they didn't look the least thrilled at the prospect of company.

Was that their norm? Or did their understandable concern over stolen funds have them on their guard toward anyone and everyone? Griffin was betting a mixture of the two.

"What a lovely inn for the retreat," Finley said.

"Yes." Elizabeth used her swizzle stick to stir her drink, the color and scent both consistent with lime.

"That looks good," Finley said. "Do you mind my asking what it is?"

"A virgin lime and blackberry mojito," Elizabeth said dryly.

"That sounds delicious."

"Let me get you one," Griffin said. "I'll be right back, folks." He turned and left, heading for the patio bar before the Markums could excuse themselves. Finley could work them for a while. She was doing a masterful job.

He made his way through the milling crowd, catching bits and pieces of conversation. When he reached the bar he smiled. "Eddie."

"Mr. McCray," the bartender said.

Griffin liked Eddie. He'd been working the retreats and for the resort the past three years, putting himself through school at Stevenson University, which was just down the road. "Griffin, please."

"Okay, Griffin. What can I get you and that lovely wife of yours?"

"Two blackberry lime virgin mojitos."

"You got it." His gaze drifted to Finley as she talked with the Markums. "How you talked her into marrying you, I'll never understand," Eddie said, the two always joshing each other.

"You and me both," Griffin said, dropping a twenty in the tip jar and grabbing the drinks.

"You're too generous," Eddie said, "as always."

Griffin didn't completely know Eddie's circumstances, but God had placed him on Griffin's heart, and that was more than reason enough to be generous. "I'll catch you later."

"I'll be here the rest of the night," Eddie said. "The patio bar is open until midnight, in case anyone would like a nightcap with their s'mores." Griff was glad to see heaters at either end of the bar, but Eddie would certainly earn his wages and tips tonight.

Griffin walked back through the crowd, scanning it, wondering what Jenn and Jeremy Barrit looked like and if they had already arrived. They were the next couple on the list Haywood had given him of clients with missing funds.

"Here you go, my love," he said, handing Finley her glass.

"Thank you, dear." She angled toward Griffin. "John was just telling me the highlights of the resort."

"We've been coming for ten years now," John said.

Good job, Fin. She'd got them talking.

"This is just my third year," Griffin said.

"I'm surprised we haven't met before."

"This is my first year with Finley."

"We were recently married," she added.

"Ah, newlyweds." John smiled. "Congratulations."

Finley snuggled into Griffin. "Thanks."

"I spent most of the other retreats hiking during the day and reading at night," Griffin explained.

"So a solitary man before marriage," John said. "I get it."

Elizabeth rolled her eyes. Apparently she wasn't enjoying the conversation nearly as much as her husband, who'd relaxed a great deal.

"How long have you two been married?" Finley asked. "If you don't mind my asking. You look very happy together."

John and Elizabeth exchanged a glance, and Elizabeth's scowl softened.

"Twenty-three years," she said.

"Wow. That's wonderful."

Elizabeth's tight jaw relaxed into a smile.

Amazing, Fin.

"So what do you do, John?" Finley asked.

"I run a marina in Annapolis."

"Impressive. That sounds like a big job."

John's smile gleamed. "Oh, I don't know about that. Having grown up around boats, I love it though."

"I grew up in Chesapeake Harbor," Griffin said.

"Oh sure, I know the place," John said.

"Really?" Not a lot of people were familiar with the small harbor town southwest of Baltimore along the Chesapeake Bay.

"We sail all over the place," Elizabeth said.

"And we visited Chesapeake Harbor on one of our many Bay cruises," John added.

"How lovely," Finley said.

"Haywood's a big boater as well," Griffin said, trying to steer the conversation back to the case in a natural and what he hoped was casual way.

Apparently not casual enough. Elizabeth's jaw tightened again.

"He has a power boat," John said with a bite to his tone. "We're sailors."

"Oh, a true boatman," Griffin said, trying to regain John's favor.

"You like to sail?" he asked.

"Grew up sailing," Griffin said. "And so did Finley."

"Maybe we can enjoy a sail together sometime," John offered.

"We'd like that very much," Griffin said.

"Well, I think we're going to get settled in our room." John gave his wife a "Let's go" glance.

"Yes. I could use some settling-in time," she said, as if on cue.

"Well, it was a pleasure meeting you folks," Finley said as the couple scurried away.

"You too," John's voice drifted away.

"So they like boats, but there's clearly no love for Haywood," Finley said.

Griffin sighed heavily. "Would you have any warm feelings toward the person you believed was stealing from you?"

10

Relief flooded Declan as he and Tanner pulled into the Bureau's parking garage. He wrapped his arm around her shoulders, guiding her through the concrete structure as they made their way into the warm interior of the building's lobby.

Agent Matt Greer stepped off the elevator as they were about to step on.

"Hey," he said. "I heard what just happened. You two all right?"

"Nothing some warm clothes won't fix," Declan said, rubbing Tanner's arm. "Car's in the lot, so the processing can start."

"Yeah, about that . . . I know you like to work with Parker Mitchell, but . . ."

"He's off this weekend," Declan said. "I know."

"Yeah. Weird, right?" Matt frowned.

Parker was nearly *always* on call, or at least had been until he and Avery became serious. Now he had found a much better work-life balance. Same as Griff did since meeting Finley. He, on the other hand . . .

He swallowed and responded to Matt's quizzical expression rather than finishing that thought. "Parker has a standing invitation around this time every year."

Parker was taking Avery to the retreat for the first time, and Griffin was bringing his wife, Finley. Declan glanced at Tanner, wondering what it would be like to bring her as his significant other. The idea warmed him more than dry clothes would.

Matt arched his brows in curiosity but pushed no further on Parker's whereabouts. "I'll let Cross and his team know to head down and get started on the vehicle." He punched a couple buttons on his phone and placed it to his ear.

"Thanks. Glad to hear Cross is on." Next to Parker . . . well, no one came close to Park, but Brayden Cross always did a precise, thorough job.

"We need to get into some dry clothes," he said, hitting the Up button on the elevator.

Matt nodded, waved, and continued his phone conversation as he moved away from the elevator.

"I don't have . . . clothes . . . here," Tanner said, her words borderline jumbled.

Definitely hypothermia.

He jabbed the button again, fighting the urge to pick her up and wrap her in his arms. "No, but I do," he said. He always kept extra work-out clothes at the office.

She nodded, her eyes growing heavy, her head lolling to the right.

"That's it." He swooped her up in his arms, and she was obviously feeling *bad* because she didn't protest or even question his move.

Reaching his office, he set her on his sofa, removed his jacket and then hers. He cranked up the space heater he kept in his drafty office and moved to the secretary hutch in the corner, pulling out his FBI-issued sweatpants and sweatshirt. "Here." He handed them to her. "I'll leave so you can change. I'll be back in two."

She nodded, and he headed for the kitchen. Finding an oversized pot in the back of the lower cupboard, he filled it with hot water. Returning to his office, he elbow-knocked on the door and asked, "Okay to come in?"

"Yep," she said, her voice sounding a bit stronger.

He entered to find her drowning in his sweats, her hair still damp. He grabbed a gym towel from his cabinet. "Here," he said, chastising himself for not thinking of it sooner.

"Thanks." She lifted her hair, draped the towel across her shoulders, and let her hair fall back over it.

He retrieved the pan of water he'd set on the corner of his desk and moved to place it on the floor at her feet. "Stick your feet in. It'll sting at first, but it'll warm you up much quicker."

She dipped one foot in tentatively, winced, and then went for it, submerging both feet.

"That's my girl," he said without thinking.

A soft smile crept onto her still blue-tinged lips.

"I'm going to make you something warm to drink. Coffee, tea?" He moved for his Keurig. A gift from his mom last Christmas.

"Coffee, please."

"On it." The Keurig spit out the warm brew in no time.

"You need to change and get warm too," she said.

The sight of her in his sweats, three sizes too big, cupping her mug on his couch, warmed him quite a bit, but she was right. It was time for him to get out of the wet clothes too. "Agreed," he said, grabbing his gym bag and heading for the bathroom down the hall.

Within two shakes he was back at her side, praying the men shooting at them had been caught. But, unfortunately, there was no news, which meant they were still out there.

A rap sounded on Griffin and Finley's door shortly before ten. "It's Parker," he said, getting up to answer it.

"Hey, man," he said, opening the door to find Parker and Avery waiting in the hall. "Come on in."

"Kate said she'd be right up." Parker took a seat in the sitting area of their room. "Nice fireplace."

"Exquisite bed," Avery said of the four-poster mahogany bed dating from the 1800s.

"According to Ann, the owner, it's original to the inn," Finley said.

"Wow." Avery studied the smooth curves of the posts and the detailed carvings on the headboard.

To Griffin it was just a place to lie next to his wife. He'd take a sleeping bag in a tent if it meant falling asleep with her in his arms—where or on what didn't matter. Only Finley in his arms did.

"So what'd you guys learn?" Parker asked as Kate tapped on the door.

Griffin opened it. "Hey, Katie."

"Hey, yourselves." She carried a movie-theatre-style tub of popcorn—caramel, if his nose was working right—cradled in her right arm.

"Where'd you get that?" Parker jumped up from the wingback chair and moved for Kate and her popcorn.

Kate held up her left hand. "Back off. I'll share, but only a handful each."

Parker grudgingly obeyed, taking just one handful and downing it in seconds. "Where'd you get it?"

"Miss Ann. We've been chatting for the past hour, and she mentioned she has a DVD library and offers guests a bucket of homemade caramel popcorn on the weekends."

"No way." Parker headed for the door.

"Park," Griffin said before he could dart from the room. "Focus. Case now. Popcorn later."

Parker exhaled and held up his hands in surrender. "Fine, but have you tasted this stuff? It's as good as Fisher's."

Now *he* had to taste it. Griffin grabbed a handful and popped several pieces into his mouth, where it proceeded to melt in ooey-gooey goodness. "Wow, you weren't kidding."

"Okay, now you *both* have to focus," Kate snapped.

"Your fault," Parker said, threatening to snatch another handful. "You brought it in. You should have anticipated the consequences."

"Fair enough." She took a seat in one of the wingback chairs, tucking her right leg beneath her and dangling her left leg over her right bent knee. "So I've got some juicy details. How about you guys?"

Griffin sat on the loveseat with Finley as Avery took the armrest of Parker's chair. "Finley and I learned a few things about the Markums, but with a lead-in like that, I think we're all curious to hear what *you* learned."

"So," Kate began, "Lowell said he wants to start his own firm. He claims he's being held back and doesn't feel he can do his clients justice in his partnership with Haywood. He's just waiting until after the retreat to drop the news."

"He told you that, even knowing your 'Pirate connection'?"

"Yeah, I guess I just dazzled him with my charm." Kate smiled. "That and the liquor."

"Did he give any indication of *how* he believes his partnership with Haywood is holding him back? Did he mention anything about skimming from clients, anything like that?"

"No. But he definitely plans on leaving and taking his clients with him."

"So he's bailing on Haywood before he gets exposed for stealing from company clients."

"If Lowell is setting up Haywood, as Haywood claims, distancing himself is a brilliant move," Parker said.

"How about you?" Kate asked Griffin. "What have you learned?"

"The Markums clearly resent Haywood. I'd be very surprised if they don't confront him this weekend."

"What about the Coveys?" Griffin asked Parker.

"They seem oblivious to the fact their accounts are being skimmed," he responded.

"They went on and on about how happy they were with the investment growth they saw in their last portfolio report from Haywood."

"Which can totally be doctored," Kate said.

"Any progress on the financials?" Parker asked Kate, who had planned to take a look at them before heading to the retreat.

"It's a lot to go through, but so far it does look like Haywood is the guilty one."

No one commented or wanted to go there. They were taking Haywood at his word, but ignoring the obvious wasn't always easy.

"I know a great forensic accountant, if you want to go that route," Parker offered.

"That might not be a bad idea," Kate said. "Then I can focus on what I need to learn here."

Griffin liked that idea. While Kate was excellent at hacking and following the numbers, Thatcher Grimes was specifically trained to detect fraud or embezzlement of funds. He had a great reputation with the Baltimore PD.

"Okay, I'll give him a call," Parker said. "Thatcher Grimes is the best."

"I can send him the documents from my computer and scanner," Kate said.

"I'll ask him to get you his contact information," Parker said.

"Great. That takes that off my plate. Now I can concentrate on the people here."

"How soon do you think Thatcher will be

able to give us some answers?" Griffin asked, always impatient when it came to obtaining evidence.

"He usually gets back within forty-eight to seventy-two hours depending on his availability and how much paperwork he needs to go through."

"There is a lot in the sense that the Markums have been clients for more than a decade," Kate said, "but it looks like the skimming has only been happening over the past year, so that lessens the scope."

"But it begs the question," Griffin said, "if he's been working with the Markums for that long and with some of his clients since he started the firm twenty years ago, why start stealing now?"

"You're considering that Haywood might actually be the thief?" Kate asked.

"Yeah. I guess my mind went there." He'd been trying hard not to let it. "But the same question holds true if he's telling the truth and Lowell is the one behind it all. Why, after being with the firm for eight years, would Lowell start stealing now?"

"While we're waiting on Thatcher, I'll do some digging into both of their financials," Kate said. "See if either is dealing with personal money troubles, or if the firm is. I'll also start looking into their personal lives."

"Might as well check into Emmitt Powell while you're at it," Griffin said.

"Agreed." Kate popped a piece of caramel corn in her mouth. "I'll start digging on all of them."

"You said that with a little too much pleasure," Parker jested.

She smirked. "So I like digging up dirt."

"As do we all," Parker said. "We can all pitch in and help while we're here."

"Great," Griffin said, "but you and Avery keep the Coveys as your main focus, and Finley and I will focus on the Markums. Kate, keep working Lowell, and we'll have to double cover the Barrits and the Douglasses, when they finally show up."

"Ann mentioned everyone has arrived," Kate said. "So they must be here somewhere."

"Great. Let's head down for s'mores and hope they all have the same idea. We need to solve this before Haywood's reputation is ruined."

"If he is, in fact, innocent," Kate said, her train of thought similar to Griffin's.

He'd never envision Haywood capable of theft, but the evidence against him was strong thus far. They needed to keep digging.

11

Just as Declan and Tanner were finally warming up, a knock sounded on the door and Matt Greer entered.

Declan frowned. "I thought you were on your way out when we ran into you at the elevators."

"Nope. I'm covering Ford's shift tonight and was heading out to check into a lead when you guys came in. But I stopped on my way back and grabbed some takeout. Thought you could use some sustenance after all you've been through." He set a white plastic bag that smelled of orange chicken and General Tso's on the table. "Hope you like Chinese."

"Thanks, Matt." Declan stood and shook his hand. "How much do I owe you?"

"Please, my treat. After the day you two have had . . ."

Declan nodded. "I owe you one."

"That"—Matt smiled—"I'll take you up on."

"Any news about the men who attacked us at the marina?"

"I asked for an update on my way in, and . . ." Matt swiped the back of his neck. "I'm afraid it's not good news. The vehicles you described disappeared before the cops arrived, but Cross and his team are still working the vehicle you managed to bring in. I'm sure they'll find something useful."

Declan prayed they did, because until those men were behind bars, he and Tanner remained targets. It was a good thing they were heading to Houston in the morning—an early morning that was quickly approaching.

After finalizing their plans for covering all the bases in their embezzlement investigation, Griffin, Finley, Parker, Avery, and Kate headed down to the sunroom to grab s'more kits and head out to the fire pit. The blaze was already dancing in the night, sparks sizzling, and they were about to close the sunroom door when heated voices echoed down the corridor on the right.

"I'll check it out," Griffin said, stepping back inside.

"Okay." Finley gave him a quick kiss on the cheek as the rest of them headed for the fire pit.

He moved as quietly as possible down the corridor, his s'more kit still in hand.

"How could you do this to us?" Elizabeth Markum's voice was frenzied.

"You could ruin us. You've given us no choice," John said. "After the retreat we're going to have to go to the authorities."

116

"But I didn't do it, and soon I'll be able to prove it," Haywood countered, his tone pleading and borderline desperate.

"We've heard enough of your lies." Elizabeth turned to walk away, and Griffin quickly ducked into the hall alcove, praying she hadn't seen him. He remained stock-still as she and her husband passed by. After waiting a moment, he popped his head out, expecting to see Haywood in the hall, but he was nowhere in sight.

He spent a few moments searching, walking up and down the corridor, but after having no luck decided to head outside. He hoped he'd find Haywood on the patio, but again no luck. Instead, he located the gang seated around the fire pit and discreetly caught them up to speed on what little he'd overheard.

Avery was chatting with the Coveys—a couple in their mid-to-late thirties—and if the laughter and smiles were any indication, Avery was turning on the charm. The Barrits and Douglasses were also gathered around the fire, the former in their early forties and talkative, the latter in their sixties and looking like apparent introverts overwhelmed by the crowd. Unfortunately, they left the fire before Griffin could reach them. He'd have to catch them at breakfast.

He scanned the patio again, but there was still no sign of Haywood or the Markums.

"You all right?" Parker nudged his arm.

"Yeah. Just wish Haywood or the Markums would show. I didn't like the sound of Haywood's voice. He sounded desperate, and the Markums seemed furious."

"You think they'll go to the authorities?" Finley asked.

"I don't understand why they haven't already," Avery said, leaning in to grab another marshmallow.

"Maybe they have something in their own financials they want to hide," Parker suggested.

Now there was an interesting angle to explore.

Tanner curled up on Declan's office couch, happy to not be alone tonight, with Kate at the retreat and the shooting at the boat. She wasn't shaken per se, but Declan's presence was soothing . . . calming. She knew she didn't have to be on guard while he was near and that she could sleep in peace without a worry. It was a nice assurance.

Shifting the toss pillow under her head, she rolled on her side. Declan lay on the floor, covered with a throw blanket pulled up to his chest, his hands linked behind his head on the other square toss pillow. "Are you sure you're going to be okay down there?" There were other offices with couches, but he'd insisted on staying close, and while she felt bad he was on the floor, she loved that he wanted to be near.

He rolled on his side, propping his head on his hand, his weight resting on his elbow. "I'm good. I can sleep anywhere." Something told her he wouldn't sleep at all, rather he'd spend the night keeping guard. It brought back memories of knowing she was safe with her dad near, but Declan was a far different man from her father. They had similarities— excelling at their jobs, wanting to protect those they loved—but Declan understood the value of friendship and laughter, and of the saving grace of Jesus.

"You okay?" he asked with a lift of his chin.

"Yeah. Just processing."

He arched a brow. "Dare I ask?"

"Just thinking how much I'm enjoying this time with you."

His lips twitched into a grin. "You are unique, Tanner Shaw."

She frowned. "Why do you say that?"

"Not many—if any—women would make a statement like that after the day we had."

But it was with you.

"But I love hearing you say it."

She bit her bottom lip, waiting for him to say something more, to do something more.

"We better get some sleep. We've got an early flight."

Not at all what she was hoping he'd say.

She nodded.

"Sleep tight," he said, before closing his eyes.

God had given him supernatural restraint. That was the only explanation for what had just occurred—or rather *not* occurred. All he wanted to do was kneel by Tanner's side and kiss her good-night, but they couldn't keep kissing without a commitment. He wasn't that type of man. Though he had no idea if Tanner was interested in pursuing a relationship with him. They needed to talk, but he didn't want to push her, and there was a part of him that was nervous she'd say no. He was no coward, but being overly cautious could easily be considered a fault of his.

He exhaled. How had they gotten here? How had Tanner stolen his heart without him seeing it coming, and what did he do about it amidst a case that was threatening their lives?

12

Tanner loved the rush of a plane taking off. Adrenaline coursed through her as the aircraft surged into the still-dark sky. Being up before the sun was just plain wrong. And she'd been up for hours. First, stopping by the boat to shower and grab a duffel with a couple changes of clothes, Declan standing watch, armed and alert the entire time, and then dropping by Declan's to grab his bag, and finally on to the airport. But at least she could crash on the flight if she needed to.

The plane continued soaring up in its ascent, and she reveled in the sensation of flying. It was addictive, really. She loved traveling, especially the excitement of new adventures and the sense of freedom it brought, but in the last year she'd come to love and appreciate the value of home much more. Not to mention, having friends as close as family who loved her. It was such a blessing.

She glanced over at Declan, wondering what it would be like if he loved her, romantically. They'd kissed, but she didn't know how he really felt. And, to be honest, she wasn't sure what she truly felt in her heart for him, hadn't really allowed herself to explore the bevy of emotions bubbling inside of her because she'd believed nothing would ever happen there.

Today she allowed herself the liberty to explore and feel them all—the joy of a growing and deepening friendship, heated frustration when they argued, massive attraction, a strong sense of loyalty, confusion, elation . . . all heightened and fizzing at the surface. *Whatever* she felt for him, whether or not it could be defined or encapsulated in one word, was coursing through her like the plummet of the falls crashing and frothing the surface at Niagara.

She studied him in the middle seat beside her. He'd insisted she take the window. It was a lovely gesture, but at six-three and easily two hundred muscular and toned pounds, the poor guy looked like a crumpled suit wedged between suitcase folds.

"Are you sure I can't switch with you?" she offered again. Her being five-seven and one-thirty-five, the center seat just made more sense.

He smiled. "Enjoy the window. I'm going to have my head in files the whole time."

"If you're sure?"

He nodded, and her gaze tracked to the stack of papers piled high on his tray table, his knees pushing against the underside of the plastic tray.

He was taking the flight to reacquaint himself

with the information he'd gathered on Steven Burke since the FBI agent's murder on the *Hiram* two months back. That information included every case file Burke had worked in the last two years. Declan, if nothing else, was thorough.

Thorough and, as her thoughts wandered again, an exemplary kisser, her lips still tingling from his touch. Not that she had a ton of kissing experience to compare him against. She'd only kissed three men in her life, Declan being one of the three, but *he* most certainly left the most distinct and wonderful impression. The fact she'd kissed Declan Grey still staggered her, and yet somehow made so much sense. He was the first man who made her feel fully alive.

They had yet to broach the subject of their kiss beyond his expressed desire to do so again, but a big part of her was hesitant to be the one to bring it up. It was a new day, and something told her that today he'd approach the subject logically, say their kissing and pursuing a romantic relationship wasn't wise, especially now that they were working together.

He was too rational to leave emotion in the equation, and yet a whole new layer of emotion engulfed her now. He was different from her previous impressions. She felt as if she was seeing the true him for the first time. She'd spent the night in prayer over her growing feelings and felt God leading her straight to him, but it was complicated. Though incredibly straightforward, *he* was complicated. Now would be a really great time for him to be the former.

His elbow bumped hers as he shifted in his seat, and he smiled at her. She was dying to know what was going on in that handsome head of his.

The next morning, Griffin and Finley found a table in the sunroom. Miss Ann went out of her way for breakfast. She and her two friends, Susan and Patty, whipped up airy waffles, cinnamon-swirl French toast, made-to-order omelets, and all the sides a person could want— all fresh and ready to dive into within minutes of ordering. On the way in, they had passed Avery and Kate enjoying their coffee out on the back porch, and learned Parker was showering after a sunrise stroll that had turned into a two-hour hike. When she came to take their orders, Miss Ann said that most of the guests had already had breakfast and were out enjoying the beautiful fall morning.

Griffin prayed today's investigation went smoother. Though he had yet to spot Haywood and the Markums, maybe, just maybe, Kate could get them together for a down-to-earth discussion.

Ann served Finley her Belgian waffles and had started to slide Griffin's plate before him when a horrific shriek echoed down the corridor. The same corridor where he'd overheard Haywood and the Markums arguing. Ann jumped, dropping the plate, the china shattering on the hardwood floor.

"I'm so sorry." She bent to pick it up.

"Please don't worry about it. I'm going to go see what's going on."

"Yes, please do, Detective McCray."

Finley quickly followed, and they moved toward the open room door where a hysterical maid stood screaming and crying.

"Whoa!" Griffin caught her as her legs started to crumple. "What's wrong?"

"He's dead!"

"Who's dead?"

"Mr. Grant. In his bathtub."

Haywood was dead?

13

Tanner and Declan touched down in Houston, deplaned, and settled into their rental car—a black SUV. Why wasn't she surprised? He certainly preferred the government-issue style of vehicles. Simple. Understated. Resilient. Which suited him.

Declan punched Steven Burke's last known address into the GPS. It was a forty-minute drive from the airport, which would give them lots of time to either talk or simply be silent. She wasn't sure which she preferred. She just prayed he didn't give her *the* talk—the one about how foolish or rash his actions had been when he kissed her. Maybe he'd surprise her and not go all analytical.

The key to their future hinged on what happened next, on how Declan proceeded. Would he shock her and suggest they pursue a romantic relationship, or would he shift to his über-rational self and recommend they ignore what happened along with their more-than-evident feelings for one another? She wanted him to say *something,* to give her some indication of where his head was.

"So what did you learn about Burke?" she

asked as the SUV hummed down the highway. The silence was becoming unnerving, and she figured that was a safe topic to start with.

He shifted in his seat. "From all angles, Burke looks to have been a good agent—thorough, intelligent, and he solved more cases than not. There was one in particular that caught my attention."

"Oh?"

"Yeah. A kidnapping case from last December. A young woman from Houston. Eighteen years old. Taken across state lines to Louisiana. Found dead on the shore two weeks later."

Tanner frowned, not following. "You think that ties to our terrorism case somehow?" Declan was brilliant, so if he saw a connection, she trusted it.

"No." He shook his head. "But some of the particulars of the case remind me of Jenna's."

That jolted her. "Jenna McCray?" Griffin's sister, who had been murdered just shy of her eighteenth birthday.

"Yeah. Griffin's been spearheading the reopening of her cold case. We've been working it in our off time, and there's some-thing about Chelsea Miller's case that *feels* like Jenna's."

That's the second time in as many days that Declan had done or said something based on feelings. Had he always been this way and she was just now seeing it? Or was he changing? Growing?

"How so?" she asked.

"Chelsea was abducted at night, rather late, walking to a friend's house. She was raped and tortured in a similar manner to Jenna, and her body also washed up on shore several weeks after the attack. The main difference was that a neighbor saw a black van pull up and grab Chelsea, so it was reported as a kidnapping rather than a missing persons case, as in Jenna's situation."

Declan draped his right arm across the wheel, tapping it with his thumb. "I've always wondered if Jenna's killer was a mover, or a drifter, since we were never able to catch him. He didn't seem to have roots, so I believed he wasn't local."

"That makes sense."

"Yeah, but the frightening thing is *if*—and I say a big *if,* as it's only a gut feeling and a handful of facts—but *if* it is him, that means he's been operating for over seven years, as recently as last winter if Chelsea Miller and Jenna were both his victims."

"That's a terrifying thought, because my mind automatically wonders how many other women might have been killed in between."

Griffin sprinted into Haywood's bathroom, only to recoil in shock and stunned sadness at the sight of Haywood's body resting in a pool of red. Crimson water had splashed over the tub wall and splayed in puddles across the white tile floor.

Finley dashed in after him, and a rush of air escaped her mouth.

"Don't look, honey." He wrapped his arm around her and guided her to the main room. "Do me a favor, get Parker and Avery in here while I call Jason."

Unable to wrap his mind around the fact that Haywood was dead, he called his partner, Jason Cavanaugh.

Jason headed out while they were still on the phone, promising to bring a handful of officers from the squad with him.

Griffin was just about to hang up when a piece of stationery lying cockeyed on the floor caught his eye. "I'll see you when you get here."

"ETA fifteen," Jason said before disconnecting.

Griffin retrieved the paper and scanned the words scrawled across it.

It was a suicide note in Haywood's hand-writing. In it, he confessed to stealing from his clients and then murdering the Markums after they threatened to go to the authorities.

Shock piercing through him, Griffin raced out of the room as Avery and Parker entered.

"What's wrong?" Parker asked.

"Read the letter on the bed." He ran his

hands through his hair in frustration. "I'm hoping you have your equipment in your car because you have a crime scene to investigate."

After leaving the scene to Parker and Avery, he tracked down Miss Ann, learned the Markums' room was at the end of the same hall as Haywood's, and got her to let him in after no one answered when he knocked.

The door swung open, and he held his breath at the chaos frozen before him. Chairs knocked over, clothes tossed about the beds, and . . . was that . . . ? He bent down to examine the dark red substance trailing across the plush carpet.

He'd need Parker to confirm, but it certainly appeared to be blood. Had Haywood seriously murdered the Markums and then killed himself?

Declan pulled to a stop outside Steven Burke's apartment building, finding a spot in the visitors' section. He was just about to climb out and walk around to open Tanner's door when his cell rang.

"Grey."

"It's Park."

"What's wrong?" Parker's tone said something was *very* wrong.

Tanner frowned beside him.

"I hate to be the one to tell you this, but I

know you'd want to know." Parker exhaled. "Coach Grant is dead."

Declan's throat went dry. "W-what?"

"Found in his bathtub. It appears to be suicide."

"Coach Grant? No way!"

"Av and I are just beginning to process the scene. I'll keep you posted."

"Thanks."

"And, Dec . . ."

He had a feeling he wasn't going to like what came next. "Yes?"

"That's not the worst part."

How could it not be? His beloved coach, Haywood Grant, was dead.

"He left a suicide note admitting to embezzling funds from his clients and murdering the Markums—the couple who called him on it."

He nearly choked. Haywood, murder? "You can't be serious."

Tanner rested her hand on his arm, and her comforting touch felt soothing in a moment of utter shock and chaos.

"Have you found the Markums?"

"Griffin is in their room now and has called in a team to start searching for them."

"This is unbelievable."

"You're telling me. I see it with my own eyes, but I can't fathom it."

"Keep me posted."

"Will do."

Declan hung up and stared into the blankness before him. Haywood was dead. Had he stolen from clients, murdered two people, and committed suicide? His gut said no way, but what if it was true?

"What's wrong?" Tanner asked slowly.

"My first Little League coach, the one who's now my financial planner, just committed suicide."

"Oh no. At the retreat?"

Declan nodded, half thankful he wasn't there to see that, and half wishing he could be there to help. He never would have pictured Haywood capable of any of those crimes, let alone as a man who'd take his own life. Haywood was a Christian, and Declan had never seen the man depressed. Their relationship was strictly business, but he met with him regularly and saw him every year at the retreat.

This was going to burrow into his head and follow him throughout the coming days and weeks. That always happened when he couldn't wrap his mind around something. When a case didn't make sense—when life didn't make sense. He knew God was in control, but until he got to heaven, he'd carry a lot of questions. But he trusted God was good and one day it would all make sense, or he'd be so at peace that concerns of this world would simply fade away.

Tanner reached over, clasping his right hand, hers feeling soft and small against his palm. "I'm so sorry."

"I just can't believe it. It doesn't make sense."

"A lot of things in this world don't. I know it doesn't make it any easier, but I take solace that one day injustice, pain, poverty, sadness, and heartache won't exist. I know that to many people that can sound super trite, but it is what God's Word says, and I trust Him through it all. Even when I don't understand—like with Mira."

He brushed the back of her hand with the pad of his thumb. "I do too."

"Do you want to fly back?"

"Yes . . . but I also know Burke plays a key role in our terrorism case, and I can't just walk away from it."

She looked up at the apartment building towering over them. "Shall we?"

Luke watched through binoculars from his rental car parked on the far end of the lot. He'd known that Declan was in danger, had heard as much from Sayid and Jose's conversation back in Malaysia, but now that Declan was in Houston, digging deeper into Burke, the threat against him had skyrocketed.

Clearly Declan understood Burke played an important role, but once he discovered the true depth of it—and Luke had no doubt he would—Ebeid's Houston cell leader, Stan Stovall, would report it, and then Declan and that woman would be bumped to the top of Ebeid's kill list. They'd no longer be classified as targets but rather as priority assets, needing to be destroyed.

Luke needed to warn them, but he couldn't reveal himself. Not yet. It would jeopardize everything. He'd have to find another way to warn his friend of the extreme level of danger he had just walked into.

14

Griffin knew he had his work cut out for him—the investigation of Haywood's death and what was definitely looking like the Markums' murder, and then, of course, attempting to contain the frenzy the news would incite among the retreat guests when it began to spread. So far they'd been able to contain it to the owner, Ann, and the distraught maid, but as soon as Jason and the squad cars arrived, all bets were off.

He'd sent Ann to locate Lowell Brentwood, in the hope that together he and Lowell could reassure the guests they were in no danger. As soon as possible they needed to account for all the guests and question those who might have pertinent information.

Unfortunately, Miss Ann was old school and had no video cameras in her inn—*not one*. She did, however, have an alarm system, which monitored the opening and closing of doors and provided an alarm button in case of emergency, so they could at least track when doors opened and closed—if that helped any.

The Markums' cell phones were in their room, along with all their belongings, which was not a good sign, and as far as he could tell, the only things missing from the room were the blankets off the bed. Had Haywood murdered them, wrapped them in blankets, carried them to his car, and transported the bodies someplace? He'd taken a big risk carrying them out, if that's what he had in fact done, but the Markums' being the last room in the hall, next to the exit door, would have worked in his favor.

There'd been a towel cart in the alcove where Griffin had stood last night when the Markums walked by; he checked, and it was still there. Perhaps Haywood had used it to transport the bodies to his car. He'd have Parker run it for any traces of evidence.

The question bugging Griffin was, how did Haywood kill them and move them from their room without someone hearing at least some scuffle? Haywood's firm had booked the entire inn for the retreat, but they didn't need all the rooms, so they had placed the guests in alternating rooms for optimal privacy. Because of that, the room next door was empty, and there were no guest rooms on the other side of the hall, but it was still hard to imagine no one heard anything.

Perhaps Haywood had threatened Elizabeth to keep John silent, but how had he killed them? So far no murder weapon had been found. Just the blood, heel marks like a body had been dragged across the carpet, and various signs of disruption. He would talk with whoever was staying two doors down as soon as Jason arrived and he could leave the Markums' room secure.

The blood in the carpet was still tacky, so the murders couldn't have occurred too long ago. He'd seen the Markums at ten, and guests had still been milling around the inn well past midnight. Miss Ann said she had been up working by five thirty, so the murders and removal of the bodies most likely had occurred between one and five.

"You sure know how to pick interesting retreats," Jason Cavanaugh said in his southern drawl as he slipped booties over his shoes and stepped in the room.

Griffin stood from his crouching position. *Understatement of the year.*

"Sorry about your coach."

"Thanks." He nodded, still in shock.

Jason glanced around the room and released a long exhale. "So catch me up to speed."

"Rest of the team here?"

"Yep." His partner nodded. "Corporal Howe and his K9 just arrived, a second K9 unit is on the way. But I'm a little confused. Parker is in a room four doors down, working a crime scene."

"Haywood's body."

"So . . . the dogs are for?"

"Haywood's suicide note said he killed John and Elizabeth Markum."

"Who are, I'm assuming, the couple that was staying in this room?"

"Yes."

"No sign of them?"

"I have the owner searching for Haywood's business partner and Finley casually asking the guests who are up and about if they've seen the Markums, while looking for them herself. But we're trying to keep this under wraps for as long as possible. Though I'm sure people have figured out something is going on now that you all have arrived. As soon as Haywood's partner shows, we can put him in charge of calming his clients. Assign Jax to taking down everyone's name and contact information so we can get in touch with them as we need to."

"Sounds like a plan. And the Markums?"

"I don't believe they'll be found alive. But I'm hoping we can find their bodies so autopsies can be done and the case run fully through. Have Howe and his dog search the property starting from the east, and the second unit from the west, but since the Markums' bed blankets are missing and there are drag marks on the floor, I have a feeling the bodies were moved off site. After we work the room, we need to check Haywood's and the Markums' vehicles, which Finley said are both still in the lot. See if there's any evidence that Haywood transported the bodies." He couldn't believe the words coming out of his mouth—*Haywood* and *bodies*. It was all wrong.

"Sounds like a plan."

"Since you're here to keep an eye on the room, I'm going to check in with Parker." He'd been dying to see what Parker had learned thus far but wasn't about to leave a crime scene unmanned.

"Go ahead. I'll do a run-through while you're gone, and when you finish with Parker, we can head for the vehicles."

Griffin nodded and moved for Haywood's room at the other end of the short hall.

Avery's flash bounced off the burgundy walls of the colonial-style bathroom, Haywood's body in the drained claw-foot tub, the slashes on his body now even more apparent and gruesome.

He eyed the straight shaving razor open on the floor beside the tub.

Parker looked up at him, a grim expression on his face. This was hitting them all hard.

"I let Declan know," Parker said, slipping a vial of what Griffin could only assume contained the liquid contents of the tub into his evidence case.

"How'd he react?"

139

"The same as us—shock."

Griffin surveyed the body once more, as well as the room. "Anything stand out?"

"Other than the fact that the suicide was staged? No."

Griffin's jaw went slack, his eyes widening as that blow landed. "What?"

Tanner and Declan walked across the parking lot of Steven Burke's apartment building. It was only a half hour from the federal building where Steven had worked, which would make for convenient travel if Steven's ex-partner agreed to meet with them. Griffin wasn't holding his breath, as yesterday's conversation with Chuck Franco hadn't gone well, but he still held out a slim hope.

Despite being early in the day, Houston was already a sunny eighty degrees, and Declan loved it. Griff was all about fall; Parker loved both summer and winter, which seemed a great contradiction; and Luke had preferred spring; but Declan was all about summer. Summer meant board shorts, flip-flops, and going out in the boat with his dad on the weekends he was home visiting his folks.

As they entered the generously sized lobby, he wondered about Steven Burke. About his home, *his* parents. How were they taking his death? Losing a parent was one thing, a friend another, but a child, no matter the age . . . *beyond horrific.*

They stepped to the chest-high marble counter and greeted a gentleman wearing a navy-blue suit. He was working the desk and also clearly monitoring access to the building's elevators, which were to their right.

"Hi. Special Agent Declan Grey." He showed his badge. "And my federal associate, Ms. Shaw."

"How may I be of assistance?" The man was mid-twenties, well-groomed, and professional. He'd been trained well.

"We have a warrant to search Steven Burke's apartment." During yesterday's phone conversation, Chuck Franco had said Burke's apartment was still vacant. Declan hadn't gotten much more out of the man because Chuck claimed his and Steven's superior, Tony Henshaw, had no patience for conversations and speculation about what Burke had been doing aboard the *Hiram.* But he vehemently insisted that it had not been an FBI-sanctioned operation. Had Burke really gone rogue? If so, why?

"Just a moment," the young man behind the counter said, turning his back to them as he placed a phone call. He kept his voice low, but Declan was able to make out *federal agents . . . search . . . Stevie's place . . . now.*

The man hung up and turned back to face

them. "The owner will be down to escort you to Mr. Burke's apartment."

"Thank you," Declan said, certain they could locate Burke's apartment on their own, but without a key, they'd have to kick in the door, and there was no sense in that when the owner was willing to let them in.

His mind raced as they waited. He still couldn't believe Coach Grant was dead.

Moments later, a couple he guessed to be in their late sixties stepped off the elevators and approached them. The man, tall and slender with wispy gray hair and steely blue eyes, spoke first. "I assume you are the federal agents."

Declan stepped forward. "Special Agent Declan Grey, and this is my associate, Ms. Shaw."

"And Eric said you have a warrant?"

"Yes, sir." He handed him the piece of paper.

"Very well. This way." He gestured toward the elevators.

"That's it?" The woman strode behind him—five-four, one-thirty, curly brown hair that bounced just above her shoulders. There was something familiar about her profile and also about the man's blue eyes. He'd seen that color before. They were the same as Steven Burke's.

Were these his parents? Is that why the apartment was still unoccupied?

"They have a warrant, Muriel. They're here to help."

"Sure they are. Just like the agents who took my Stevie's things."

That shook Declan. He looked to Tanner. "Someone took Steven's belongings?"

"We don't know it was them," the man said, turning to Declan. "We had a break-in right before the FBI came to search Stevie's apartment."

"It was them. I just know it," Muriel protested. "I'm his mother. You think I don't know these things?"

So, yes, the building owners were Steven Burke's parents. No wonder his apartment had been kept as-is. Well, as close to as-is as possible, given the apparent break-in and theft, which Chuck Franco curiously enough had neglected to mention.

"What was taken during the break-in?" Declan asked as the elevator doors opened and they all stepped in.

"Stevie's external hard drive—and his computer was wiped clean. All his pictures were on there. So many of us and the family . . ." Muriel's brown eyes welled with tears.

"Now, Mar." The man enveloped her with his right arm, pulling her to his chest.

Muriel dabbed her eyes on the handkerchief he offered.

He exhaled. "I'm Jacob Burke, and this is my wife, Muriel. If you haven't guessed already, we are Steven's parents."

"And you own this building?"

"Yes. Both our children live—well, lived—in it."

"Samantha still does," Muriel whispered. "At least God left me one child."

"Come now, Mar, these agents don't need to hear about our life. We can talk upstairs."

"Why? You think I care what they think? They're probably no better than the crooks from Stevie's office who got him killed and took his things. Do they take an ounce of responsibility for my Stevie's death? No. Zero responsibility. Said Stevie left without their permission, but I don't buy it. I think they put him undercover on that ship and it got him killed and now they want no part of it."

"As you can imagine this is a trying time for our family," Jacob Burke said at his wife's heated emotions, which given the circumstances were understandable. She'd lost her child, and there appeared to be no clear answers for anyone's questions.

"Of course. We'll do our best to get our job done as quickly as possible and with as little stress to you as we can manage," Tanner said.

"Humph." Muriel expelled a burst of air as the elevator stopped on the fifteenth floor—

second to the top. They stepped off and followed Mr. Burke to apartment 1510. He produced the key while Muriel clutched the large pendant necklace around her neck. Jacob opened the door and stepped in, gesturing for them to follow.

A Baylor sweatshirt lay across the back of a lounge chair, a daily paper opened to the sports section lay next to a coffee cup.

It begged the question: How long before Steven left for the ship did he know he was going? It looked as if he'd run out for milk and anticipated returning home straight after, not like the apartment of a man who planned to be away from home for months.

"Did Steven leave everything like this or has someone else used the apartment since he left?"

"No. This is how he left it." Muriel's eyes welled with tears. "We cleaned out the refrigerator, but otherwise, I didn't have the heart to change anything. Not yet."

"He left perishables in the refrigerator?"

She looked at him as if she thought he had a screw loose. "Yes."

"And he didn't tell you he was leaving to go on a merchant ship?"

"No."

"If you don't mind my asking, where did you think he was?"

"A day after he left, he sent a postcard stamped in Galveston, saying he'd been invited last minute to join a friend on a cruise and that he'd be back in a few weeks."

"Did he say where the cruise was going?"

"No, but I assumed the Caribbean. That's where the cruise ships heading out of Galveston's port go."

"And a few weeks later . . . ?"

"We got a postcard from someplace in Asia. Said he and his friend were traveling. I started thinking his friend was a female friend and the two were off on some whirlwind romance. That is, until a month later. Chuck, his partner at the FBI, showed up at our door with the news of Stevie's death on a merchant ship. I don't care what he says, I prefer to think of him on that whirlwind romance."

"Please, Ma," a woman said from the doorway. A younger version of her mother, curly brown hair and all. "You don't still believe that."

15

"You want to run that one by me again?" Griffin swallowed, the sensation of knives jagging down his throat.

Parker stood and pulled the bathroom door shut, closing them in. No one else needed to hear this. At least not yet. "I've finished my examination of the body, and I don't believe Haywood committed suicide. It's my professional opinion that Haywood was murdered."

"Murdered?" Griffin gaped.

Parker nodded. "I'm afraid so."

"The evidence?" If Parker made such a statement, Griffin trusted he had the evidence to back it up.

"The slashes are downward thrusting and deep. Suicides are typically on the wrists and sideways or lightly upward. Just enough pressure to get it done. The cuts on Haywood were deep and look as if they were made in anger and at a completely unnatural angle."

"If you're right that means . . ."

"We have a killer among us."

"No, I don't still believe it," Muriel responded to the young woman in the doorway, then blew her nose into the handkerchief with a honk. "But it makes me feel better."

"Our daughter, Samantha," Jacob said of the young woman. "These are—"

"Feds," she said, unimpressed.

"Agent Grey and . . ."

"Hi, I'm Tanner."

Samantha's dark brown eyes narrowed. "You," she said, sizing Tanner up with a steely stare, "aren't a Fed."

Tanner smoothed her white blouse. "I'm a crisis counselor with the Bureau."

"Oh." Samantha plopped down on the couch. "So you're here to shrink our heads?"

"No. Actually—"

"Samantha!" Muriel hollered before Tanner could finish her sentence. "Get off the sofa, and get your feet off the coffee table." She swatted Samantha's bare feet off the glass tabletop.

"Why? It's not like he's coming back."

Muriel swallowed. "What a dreadful thing to say."

"Apologize to your mother," Jacob said.

"For what? Stating the truth? It's time we moved back into reality. Stevie isn't coming back, and he wasn't off on some whirlwind romance."

"Oh?" Declan arched a brow. "What do you think he was doing?"

148

"He was on a case."

Interesting.

"What sort of case?"

Samantha hunched forward. "He didn't get into specifics."

"But he told you he was going to work a case?"

She nodded.

"Samantha, why didn't you say anything until now?" her father asked, irate.

"Because no one worth telling asked."

"Excuse me?" Jacob said.

"Stevie told me not to tell you. Ma would just worry, and you can't keep secrets from her. It's endearing in a sick-to-the-stomach sort of way, but these two . . ." She looked between Declan and Tanner. "They seem to actually care about what happened to Stevie."

"And his partner doesn't?" Jacob asked.

"Not really. I mean, I believe he's upset about Stevie's death, but I think he's mad Steve didn't trust him enough to tell him where he was going and why. But it wasn't a matter of trust. Steve knew Chuck would view it as a wild-goose chase and try to talk him out of it. Plus, he didn't want Chuck to have to keep secrets from their boss. He was *always* looking out for his partner."

"Chuck said Stevie called in saying he was taking a personal leave and ended the conversation there. No one in the office knew where he went or what he was doing," Muriel added, clearly distressed by the conversation.

"Chuck should have done more. A good partner *always* has your back." Samantha looked to Declan. "Am I right?"

He nodded. It was true. But it sounded like Steven didn't give his partner much opportunity—just called and took off.

"Samantha, can we talk alone for a few moments?" he asked, believing she might have answers to more of his questions.

"Sure, hunky." She smiled.

Her mother's eyes widened. "Samantha!"

"Come on, Muriel," Jacob said. "I believe Agent Grey no longer requires our presence. Let's go."

"If it's all right," Tanner said, "I'd love to continue chatting with you two."

"Of course." Jacob nodded. "However we can help."

She followed them to the door.

"You don't need to leave," Declan said.

"I think I'll just make sure Mrs. Burke is all right." She winked.

He nodded. She was going to find out what she could from the parents—what they probably didn't even realize they knew—while he spoke with Steven's sister.

"So what else can you tell me about the

case Steven was working?" Declan asked Samantha as everyone else departed.

"I told you," she said. "He shared a lot with me—especially his frustration with other FBI agents—but he didn't share specifics about cases."

"Did he mention *anything*?" The slightest thing could give them a lead.

"He said he had to go this one alone."

"Meaning without the Bureau's knowledge—or his partner's?"

"Yes."

"And you didn't find that odd?"

"Nah. Chuck and Stevie used to be tight, but things had started to shift since the new boss, Henshaw, took over. They grew distant. Stevie became more independent and less of a team player."

"Did Chuck or Henshaw tell him he wasn't a team player?" He needed her to be as specific as possible.

She thought for a moment. "He said Henshaw first . . . and then Chuck. Said the FBI was really big on team players. You should know that. They felt Stevie was moving away from that mentality and had become a lone wolf."

"Any idea why Steven felt this mysterious case was important enough to break from the team rules?"

"I don't know." She looked around the room,

then exhaled as if she had just come to a decision. "Don't let Ma know, but I think she might be half right."

He arched a brow. "About the romance?"

"Yes, but not in the way she's thinking." She shifted to sit cross-legged on the couch, her yellow toenail polish showing. "Before Steve left he'd been spending some time talking with a gal at some coffee shop."

"Did you ever meet her?"

"No. He was pretty secretive about the relationship, which was strange because we usually shared everything. He told me he was meeting a friend, and when I pressed, he said it was a woman."

"Did you ask why he was being so secretive?"

"He said they were just friends, so there was no point going into detail, but he did say she was new to the area and he was just trying to help her out. But one day she didn't show."

"Didn't show? He told you that?"

"He came back from the coffee shop early and in a panic. I asked what was wrong, and he said she didn't meet him and he feared something had happened to her. He wouldn't elaborate, just said she was gone. I'd never seen him like that—so frenzied. He packed a duffel and said he was going to investigate."

"Did he say where he was going?"

She shook her head. "I told him he needed

to tell Chuck, work with him, but Steve insisted the Bureau wouldn't back him on this, that Chuck would get in trouble if he helped him, that he had to handle it on his own." Tears filled her eyes. "And then he just left."

"And he never came back?"

"No."

"Any idea which coffee shop they met at?" If they could get the woman's name—or even a description—they could begin to search for her.

"Frank's is his favorite," she said. "It's more a diner than a coffee shop, but Stevie usually had his morning cup there. Sometimes he went to Beans & Buns—they have the best cinnamon buns—other times he went to Denton's."

"And he never let on which coffee shop he met her at?"

"Nah. Like I said, he was pretty secretive about the whole thing."

"I could be wrong, but you just don't seem the type to let things go that easily."

She smiled ruefully. "I tried following him once, just to get a glance at her, but he caught me right away. He was a stellar agent, after all."

"And he never let on why he was so worried about her? What made him believe she had disappeared, and not that she just hadn't shown up for some reason?"

"He seemed convinced she was in some sort

of danger. He was definitely fixated on something tied to her. I could see it in his eyes. He'd get this look whenever he was on to something. Only this time, he went chasing after whatever it was and it got him killed."

"According to the ship logs, it appears Steven was aboard the *Hiram* for close to two months."

"That's about how long he was gone before we learned of his death."

"Did you or any of your family members have any contact with him during those months?"

"He sent my parents the two postcards they told you about—one before he left Galveston, and the other a few weeks later—but those were just filled with fluff about the imaginary friend he was traveling with. He only sent those to keep them from worrying. He sent a couple postcards to me through the P.O. box he kept. I always checked it for him while he was away."

Interesting. So he sent his sister two postcards, but he went through his P.O. box instead of having them delivered to the apartment building. Was he trying to avoid his parents seeing them or was he worried about somebody else monitoring his mail?

"Any chance I could see the postcards?" he asked.

"Sure. Like I said, you and Tanner are the first people who actually look like you might be bright and eager enough to figure out what happened to Stevie."

"Thanks . . . I think."

"It was a compliment. Trust me." She smiled and stood, heading for the door. "I'll be right back. They're down in my apartment."

Declan looked around while he waited for Samantha to return. The apartment was good size—a living area, full eat-in kitchen, bedroom, and two baths—a half off the living room and a full off the master bedroom. There was a Lee Child book on the nightstand, a slip of paper holding Steven's spot. Declan picked it up, having really enjoyed *Die Trying*, and looked at the slip of paper—nothing but page numbers. They were probably just sections that Steven had enjoyed, but maybe—he could hope—they were clue notations to something he'd discovered. He'd ask Samantha if he could take both the book and the paper.

Samantha returned and handed him the postcards. Both from ports the *Hiram* had made late in the journey, according to his memory of the manifest. They appeared to be nothing but short notes to his sister, but Declan didn't think it was too much of a stretch to hope there was more to the postcards than what appeared on the surface.

"Does what he wrote have any significant meaning to you?"

"I thought maybe he was trying to tell me something, because they were sort of weirdly worded, so I kept rereading them, but I couldn't figure out what he was trying to tell me. I feel horrible that I didn't figure it out in time to keep him from dying."

"You can't blame yourself."

She exhaled. "It's hard not to."

"Would you mind if I borrowed them, along with the book on his nightstand? I'll be sure to take really good care of them and return them to you. I promise."

"If you think you could crack the postcards, then by all means, but why the book?"

"It has some numbers noted on a slip of paper. Probably nothing, but it's piqued my curiosity."

"Sure," she said.

He rested his hands on his waist and looked around, trying to decide if there was anything he'd missed. "So other than the hard drive, was anything else taken?"

"I think some notes he had on his desk went missing, but he kept his personal files at my place."

Jackpot.

"Let me guess," she said, before he could ask. "You'd like to borrow those too?"

"Yes, please."

"I'll go get them."

"Anything else he had you keep at your place?"

Might as well ask before she needed to make a third trip.

"Nope." She headed for the door. "I'll be back."

"I'll be looking around."

She nodded and shut the door behind her.

He strode once again through the living room, wondering what it was like to be Steven Burke. The local Feds had already processed the place, or at least made a sweep. How he'd love to get Parker down here, but he could only imagine the logistical red tape. Though if Burke's parents allowed it . . . perhaps they could do it under the radar. Steven may not have been killed at his apartment, but the break-in indicated he had information that a third party wanted.

Declan moved back into the bedroom and sat on the edge of Steven's bed, surveying the space, wondering what Steven's morning routine was like.

He reached to flip on the bedside lamp, and the room lit. He strode to the reading chair and flipped on the gooseneck reading lamp beside it, pausing as a shadow under the hood of the lamp caught his eyes. *Is that . . . ?* He bent and angled his head.

"Little bugger," he murmured, disengaging the listening device, inspecting it. It looked a lot like the ones Parker found in Mira's apartment. Coincidence? He didn't believe so. Too many things seemed to indicate Steven Burke was a link to their terrorist case in Baltimore. But how did it all fit together? He slipped the bug into a small evidence bag.

Samantha returned with a file box.

"Thanks so much," he said.

"Discover anything else?"

He held up the evidence bag with the bug.

She squinted. "Is that what I think it is?"

"I'm afraid so."

She shook her head. "I can't believe they had the nerve . . ."

"*Who* had the nerve?" Who did she think was listening in?

"I have no idea, but whoever it was sucks." She glanced around the apartment. "Are there more?"

"Not that I've found, but I still have the rest of the place to search."

"Can I help you?"

"That'd be great." Since Tanner was occupied, it'd help him move through the place quicker. "Put these on." He tossed her a pair of gloves.

"Now I'm a real CSI," she joked.

The two combed the remainder of the apartment but found no more bugs, only a small piece of wiring that had been left behind. He was betting whoever wiped the computer and took the hard drive removed the bugs in an effort to hide the fact they'd been listening. But they'd been sloppy and left one and a piece of one behind. The bugs definitely weren't federal issue, so he truly believed the party that broke in, whoever they were, were behind the listening devices.

When Declan was satisfied their search was complete, Samantha showed him to her parents' penthouse. Tanner was in the midst of having tea and cookies with Jacob and Muriel Burke. Muriel appeared to be in a much better mood, actually smiling and offering him some refreshments as he and Samantha entered. The penthouse was huge—stretching the full length of the building's top floor. He supposed when you owned the building those perks came with it.

He sat down next to Tanner, a cup of tea in hand. He much preferred coffee but didn't want to be rude.

"Muriel's been telling me all about Steve," Tanner said. "He's quite the man of accomplishment."

Muriel's cheeks flushed. "Oh, you're too sweet," she said.

"He was a track star in high school and college, graduated top of his class at the academy," Tanner said with a smile.

"That is impressive," he said, amazed at the change in Muriel's demeanor and at the woman sitting next to him.

How did Tanner do it? Get people to open up so readily? Get him to listen to his heart for once? It was terrifying but at the same time exhilarating.

Griffin watched as Haywood Grant's body was zipped up in a black plastic morgue bag, still in shock that it would be his last sight of the man he'd first met when he was just a kid and had believed was larger than life. How did this happen? Who murdered his coach and staged it to look like suicide? Who set him up to take the fall for the Markums' murder? What had the killer done with the Markums' bodies? Was the killer Lowell Brentwood? And if so, how were they going to prove it?

16

The search for the Markums was flatlining quickly. The K9 units covered the resort grounds and surrounding woods, but the only trail they picked up led from the resort's side door straight to Haywood's car. They'd checked the alarm record and found the exit door next to the Markums' room had opened during the night at roughly one o'clock, two o'clock, and finally at two twenty, not to open again until seven thirty.

Griffin and Jason found dried mud caked in Haywood's tires and looked in the trunk, where they saw what looked to be more blood, but they needed to wait for Parker and Avery to properly process the vehicle before examining it in greater detail. Parker and Avery still were in the midst of processing the Markums' room.

It was vital to Griffin that this case be worked to the letter, each piece of evidence photographed and catalogued. He *would* find Haywood's killer, and when he did, he wanted all the evidence in order. He just prayed God would equip him to restrain himself when Lowell Brentwood returned, given that Haywood's partner was suspect number one.

But at least they'd finally learned where Lowell was. One of the guests had seen him and Emmitt Powell heading out for a horseback ride early that morning. Surely they'd be back soon—and what a return they'd have waiting. Haywood dead, the Markums missing and presumed dead, and the remaining clients upset and scared. All of them were anxious to leave, and while a good number had been released once they had been interviewed and their contact information taken down, several had been asked to stay based on information they gave, their room's proximity to the crime scene, or the fact that they were one of the clients who were missing funds.

As they entered the inn, Griffin and Jason headed to check in with Parker as he finished processing the Markums' room. Griffin prayed his friend had found something—*anything*—that might aid in the search for the Markums' bodies.

Parker worked the Markums' room, trying to keep his focus on the minute details and the task before him, but his mind kept shifting back to Haywood slashed up in the tub—the metallic smell of blood, the feel of the cool water as he dipped his gloved hand in for a sample, the sound of the draining water.

The wounds on Haywood's body were deep

and purposeful. Not the marks he usually found on suicide victims. Those were shallower, jagged even—the body fighting not to cut itself despite the person's intent. And the handwriting on the suicide note was too shaky, like he was at great struggle within himself. The tentativeness of the note and the purposefulness of the cuts didn't match—unless Haywood suddenly got very angry at himself for killing the Markums. The autopsy would show conclusive proof of what had happened and provide the evidence they needed to confirm his belief, but he *knew* Haywood had been murdered. The question was, by whom?

Lowell?

That made the most sense.

Avery stood above him as he worked to get a decent blood sample without any carpet fibers and then a carpet sample with blood on it. "I'm done photographing the room and items you noted."

"Thank you," he said, finishing his task.

She rested her hand on her hip, yoga pants on. They'd packed for a relaxing weekend, where they'd planned to hike and enjoy the scenery at Oregon Ridge Park, so they didn't have their professional clothes with them. It felt strange working a crime scene in casual clothes . . . but he didn't mind seeing Avery in yoga pants.

"You think they were killed here?" she asked, gazing about the room. Chairs knocked over, items strewn around the small table, blood on the carpet, heel marks through the carpet, as if someone had been dragged . . . "Maybe he dumped the murder weapon wherever he dumped the bodies."

Murder weapon . . . Parker looked up at her, eyes wide.

Avery's brow furrowed. "What? I know that look. You're on to something."

He got to his feet. "We're searching the wrong room."

"If they were killed here . . ." she began.

Parker shook his head. "I have all the evidence I need here, but whoever killed Haywood obviously wanted to set him up, hence the suicide note. The killer most likely forced Haywood to write the note and then killed him, staging it to look like a suicide. I bet you the weapon that killed the Markums is stashed in Haywood's room to further set up his appearance of guilt."

"If the killer wanted to make Haywood look guilty, why not just leave it out in the open?"

"Too obvious. That would make it all too easy, and any cop worth their salt knows cases are never that straightforward."

"So . . . back to Haywood's room?"

"You got it."

• • •

"Was Samantha helpful?" Tanner asked as Declan held the apartment building door open for her with his back, his hands full with the file box and a smaller box with the items he'd taken with the Burke family's blessing.

"Very," he said. "And her parents? Seems like you were able to break through to Steven's mom in spades."

"She's a sweet lady."

"How do you do it?"

"Do what?"

"Connect with people so easily? Get them to let down their guard?" She was a master at it, and yet her approach was in no way manipulative, but exhibited pure caring and compassion that reached the hearts of people.

"I don't know." She paused, her eyes narrowing. "I think . . . No, never mind."

"What? I'd like to know."

"I think it's just how God made me. Like a gift." She grimaced. "That probably sounds silly or boastful."

"Not at all. I believe God gives us all gifts to use for His glory."

"You do?"

"Absolutely."

"And yours is brilliantly putting puzzles together when it looks like the pieces don't fit," she said as they approached their rental SUV.

165

He smiled. "That's how you see me?"

"Part of you."

His smile deepened. "And the other part?"

"You're strong, loyal, protective . . ."

"You mean annoyingly smothering."

She bit her lip. "I'm sorry I said that. I was frustrated. I know you were just trying to help. You didn't know my background and were trying to look out for me. And while I don't show it often, I do appreciate it."

"I would have acted much differently if I'd known how well you can take care of yourself. But even so, I went overboard. You just made me nervous."

Her nose crinkled. "Nervous?"

"You seemed so reckless . . . from my unenlightened perspective, and I felt helpless to get through to you."

"I'd say you did a very good job getting through to me the other night."

His face grew warm.

And she laughed. "Did I actually just make Declan Grey blush?"

When had he last blushed? Without a word he set the file box on the hood of the SUV, opened Tanner's door, put the boxes in the backseat, and strode around to his side.

When he climbed into the driver's seat, she was looking more serious. "Can I ask you a question?"

"Sure," he said. But he worried about what she was going to ask. Now might not be the best—

"Why were you trying to be so protective of me? I mean, why me?"

"After our kiss, I hoped you'd figure that one out."

"So even back then . . . ?"

He shrugged. Though not the best timing, apparently this conversation was happening. "I guess I have a lousy way of showing I care."

"You *care* about me?" She scooted closer to him, and he followed suit.

He ran his fingers through her hair. "You still have to ask?" He supposed he wasn't the best at expressing his feelings. Doing so made him vulnerable, and after Mandy in high school, and then Kate, and for a *long* while after, he'd given up being vulnerable.

"When?" Tanner asked.

He frowned. "When, what?"

"When did you start caring?"

"Oh . . . the day you came striding through my hospital door in that nurse's uniform, demanding answers. You were so determined, so fired up—I respected that."

"But you gave me such a hard time."

"Because I assumed I wasn't your type." His boorish behavior had been his poor attempt at trying to distance and protect himself. Not to mention, she did vex him like no one else. It was part of the attraction, but equally part of the frustration. She was so headstrong, which he loved, but it also gave him concern. One day, he feared her steadfast dedication and head-strong personality would get her in real trouble—it had nearly gotten her killed when she'd crossed the wrong man in Cambodia while working for the Global Justice Mission.

"Not my type?" She laughed. "That's ridiculous."

"Grumpy, straight-laced . . . Let's see—what else have you called me?"

"I'm sorry. I felt there was so much more there below the surface, but you kept putting on the by-the-books-agent façade, and I didn't understand why you wouldn't let me see beyond that—to see the *real* you. I concluded you didn't want me to."

"I'm curious. Who do you think the real me is?"

She shifted sideways to face him better, resting her head on her hand as she propped her elbow against the headrest. "I'm just learning, but for starters, you like medieval literature—as do I—you were on the rowing team in college, you love your family deeply, and you are an aggressive rugby player. I thought you were going to kill someone during that pickup game I watched."

"That's kind of the point," Declan said. "Put it all out there."

She smiled. "Let's see. What else? Oh, you love mint chocolate chip milkshakes. You thrive off adrenaline. You're passionate and, if I may say, an exquisite kisser."

"Exquisite, huh?" His smile deepened. Just that quick she had his guard slipping. Sooner or later he needed to make a concrete choice: pull back like he always did, or dive in head-first and risk getting his heart smashed again.

She leaned in. "Very much so." She pressed her soft lips to his, tentative at first, and tasting of banana lip gloss.

Giving up his restraint, he passionately returned her kiss, his heart thumping in his throat, his ears.

What was she doing to him, and where had his steadfast logic over emotion gone?

Blissful moments faded away as realization hit. Restraining himself, he pulled back and glanced over Tanner's shoulder.

She blinked, her lips still pink from kissing him. "What's wrong?"

He scanned the parking lot. "We're being watched."

She turned and studied the lot as well. "Are you sure?"

"Pretty darn. We better get going."

She nodded and shifted back in her seat,

pulling her seat belt across her body and clicking it in place.

They pulled out of the lot, the eerie sensation they weren't alone refusing to leave him.

Luke pulled back to a seated position behind the wheel of his rental car after Declan and the woman he'd just learned was Tanner Shaw drove past. Luke was trained to be invisible, but Declan had sensed him. *Impressive.* He was clearly on top of his game. Maybe it would be enough to save him and the woman who, it appeared, had come to mean very much to him.

17

"Where you headed?" Griffin asked as he and Jason swerved to avoid Parker and Avery jetting past them in the hall.

"Back to Haywood's room," Parker called over his shoulder.

They turned and followed. Had Parker forgotten something? Found something in the Markums' room that led them back to Haywood's?

Hope sprung inside. He prayed they had found *something*. Something that would answer at least one of the hundreds of questions dancing a jig through his mind.

He waited until they were inside Haywood's room with the door closed before asking, "What's up?"

"We're looking for the murder weapon," Parker said, scanning the room as Avery searched the closet.

"Another bit of 'evidence' to make Haywood look guilty," Griff said. "Smart, Park."

"I have my moments."

"Any idea what kind of weapon?" Griff asked as he rifled through the dresser drawers and

Haywood's clothes. Jason looked under the bed and pulled back the sheets.

"I'm thinking something quick and quiet," Parker said.

"But the room showed signs of a struggle," Avery said. "Wouldn't the neighbors, even a room removed, have heard something and reported it?"

Jason tossed the bedclothes on the floor and said, "Maybe they weren't in their room at the time of the murder."

"True. They could have been out on the patio late or going for a stroll."

"It's possible, or perhaps the neighbors are very sound sleepers."

"Either way we need to talk with whoever is in that room," Griffin said. "I told Jax not to release anyone staying in close proximity to this area, and we haven't allowed anyone back in this hall, so they have to still be here."

He paused, his mind going back to another dangling thread in the investigation. "We have to find Lowell Brentwood. If he and Emmitt—"

"Got it!" Avery said, pulling a .22 with a silencer from the wall air vent.

"Good job, love." Parker grabbed an evidence bag and, after taking a moment to examine the gun, dropped it in the clear bag and sealed it up. "I need to run it at the lab to be certain, but it looks like it's been fired within the last twenty-four hours."

"So the chances the Markums are still alive just dropped tremendously?" Griffin said, knowing better than to rule anything out completely. "Let's keep this between us. I don't want to scare the guests any more than they already are."

"Of course," Avery said.

"We'll start processing the cars now," Parker said, gesturing between him and Avery.

"I'll tag along, if you don't mind," Griffin said, anxious for answers.

"Of course," Parker said, grabbing his kit.

"Why don't I go help with the interviews?" Jason said.

"Sounds great." Griffin followed Parker and Avery toward the exit door at the end of the hall, while Jason headed in the opposite direction toward the dining hall.

Parker took Avery's hand and gave her one of his charming Irish smiles. "Sorry our getaway weekend is ending this way, love. I'd really been looking forward to spending this time with you, but . . ." He raked his free hand through his hair. "I still can't believe this happened."

"I know. I'm so sorry. . . . And it's okay. I knew what I was getting into when I started dating you."

"Is that right?"

Griffin was beginning to wonder if they'd forgotten about him walking behind them, and just as he was about to give them a good-natured reminder, Avery leaned in to kiss Parker. But she caught sight of Griffin mere steps behind and blushed.

Griffin smiled, and she turned back around, heading outside.

"Thanks, mate," Parker said as they walked out the door.

"Anytime." It was the first nanosecond of relief from the shock and heartache of the morning. But before he knew it, Parker had popped Haywood's trunk and the bloodstained interior jolted the pain right back to the surface.

Steven Burke's partner, Chuck Franco, agreed to meet, but away from the Bureau building—which Declan found interesting, and possibly promising. Maybe Chuck had information he hadn't been willing to share during yesterday's call while he was in the Bureau office, under the watch of Henshaw. Or it could just be that it was a Saturday and Chuck didn't want to go into the office. Whatever the reason, Declan was eager for the meeting.

The hair-raising sensation of being watched still rippled along the nape of his neck, but he couldn't pin down the watcher. Until he did, he'd keep Tanner close and move forward with the investigation. It seemed a long way for Ebeid's men to come just to watch them, as they'd made no point of contact yet, but he supposed it was possible. Or perhaps Houston held more secrets than it first appeared.

He was leaning toward the latter and would remain permanently on guard until this case was solved. Who was he kidding, he was *always* on guard—it had been ingrained in him at Quantico. He certainly wouldn't have a moment's rest until Ebeid was behind bars and his network dismantled.

As arranged, he and Tanner arrived in front of the Ollie's hot dog cart on the corner of Carter Avenue and Memory Lane beneath a shady oak tree, its leaves rustling in the early afternoon breeze. Declan had to look at the street sign twice. It literally was called Memory Lane. It was quirky and corny enough he actually found it amusing.

"You guys like chili dogs?" Chuck asked, approaching them from behind.

"Who doesn't?" Tanner said, making Declan chuckle.

After they made introductions, Chuck walked to the cart. "Three howling dogs." He turned back to them. "Onions and cheese?"

"Of course," Tanner said.

"With da works," Chuck added.

Chuck was shorter than Declan. Maybe five-ten, probably one-seventy-five. Combed-back auburn hair with strands of gray. He reminded Declan of an eighties PI, tan trench coat and all.

The vendor handed Chuck each dog, and he in turn passed them out.

Declan inhaled the smell of the southwestern-style chili—minus the beans, of course. The red chili powder and red pepper flakes with small diced onions were just like you got at a ball game. Shredded cheddar cheese was already melting into the chili. He silently said grace, knowing Tanner would do the same, and then bit into the dog. "Mmm." He nearly moaned. "That is a thing of beauty."

"I told ya," Chuck said.

"New York?" he inquired of Chuck's accent.

"Long Island, born and raised."

"So what brought you to Houston?"

"The Bureau had an opening in the counter-intelligence division."

"Is that what you and Burke are—Burke *was?* Counterintelligence?" He'd assumed counter-terrorism, given Darmadi's presence on the *Hiram*. Perhaps that's how Burke blended in so well on the ship—he was a trained spy, of sorts, which made Declan wonder how Burke's cover was eventually blown or what caused Burke to blow it.

"Yes," Chuck finally responded between bites, wiping the chili from the corner of his mouth with a bunched napkin clutched in his right hand. "But as you can imagine we work very closely with counterterrorism on preventing spies from extremist groups and terrorist countries from entering the U.S. or uncovering them if they've already made it through."

"Have many made it through that you are aware of?"

"More than I'd like, but I'd hate it even if there was only one, so that's not saying a lot."

So there were others here. Declan knew it. "Was Burke good at his job?"

"Too good." Chuck took another bite.

"Meaning?"

After swallowing he said, "Meaning sometimes he latched on to things that weren't our division's concern and wouldn't let them go."

"Like the kidnapped woman whose body was dumped in Louisiana?"

Chuck shook his head. "Not going to ask how you know about that, but yeah. Burke kept on pressing, despite our old boss, Jenkins, and our new boss, Henshaw, putting a kibosh on that line of Burke's investigation."

"They didn't care about finding the killer?" Declan asked with a crisp edge of irritation.

"It wasn't that." Franco wiped his mouth. "Our focus is counterintelligence, not tracking some serial killer Burke blamed for every missing girl in the area."

"*Every* missing girl? There was more than the one?"

"Well . . . it appeared Burke had found a legitimate pattern, but again, that was not our job."

"Why was he so interested in missing girls, given you are counterintelligence?"

"Because he knew one of the girls—Chelsea . . . Miller, I think. Knew her dad, at least. They went to the same church. Went fishing together. After Chelsea was found dead in December, the dad just lost it. Ended up taking his own life."

"That's terrible," Tanner said.

"Yeah, Burke believed if the killer had been brought to justice, if there'd been some closure, that the dad—I forget his name—wouldn't have taken his own life."

"Possibly true."

"Either way, Burke started looking into the case, and once he did, he dove in, went looking for cold cases and never came back out."

"So your bosses—old and new—weren't happy with Burke's divided attention?" Sad, but understandable from a strictly professional point of view.

"Not happy in the least," Franco said. "When Henshaw arrived, he laid down the law, and soon after, Burke stopped talking about the missing girls' cases."

Declan doubted he'd stopped working them though. He and Tanner hadn't had a chance to look at Burke's personal files, but he was pretty sure what they would find when they did. "So he just walked away?"

"He acted like he did, but I know Steven. Once he had his mind fixed on something, there was no stopping him. He probably spent his pathetic free time on it."

Pathetic? "Doesn't sound like you liked your partner very much."

"We're just two different agents. I follow orders. Focus where the focus needs to be."

"And Burke?"

"He was an idealist—always hunting for the truth. Wanting to play Superman. To be honest, I half admired him for it, but we had a job to do. *Together*. Steven lost track of that."

But Burke longed to see justice done—Declan got that. Like Chuck, he admired it too, as long as it didn't detract from assigned work.

On that vein, Declan decided he needed to return to the possible link to the terrorist plan he was trying to uncover—the catalyst that sent Steven on board the *Hiram*. "Do you know anything about a woman Steven had been meeting at a coffee shop shortly before he took off?"

"Nope. Had no clue Steven even had a woman in his life."

"I don't know if it was that kind of relationship."

"Of course not." Chuck chuckled, tossing his empty chili dog wrapper in the trash can as they strolled past a park. "He was probably trying to save her too."

"Save her from what?"

"Who knows? An angry husband, crippling debt, a shady past, whatever." He stopped and turned. "Look, I didn't keep tabs on Steven's personal life—basically because he didn't have one. I got along with the guy well enough when we were on the job, but I didn't like the intensity of his focus on things that weren't within our scope of work. I don't know about any woman, don't know why Steven took personal leave, and sure as shooting don't know what he was doing on a merchant ship, but I can tell you it had nothing to do with our job."

Soon after his declaration, it seemed Chuck's willingness to talk dried up. Claiming he had errands to run, he walked away, cutting through the park.

"Well, he was cheery," Tanner said as they watched him leave.

"At least we learned more about Burke."

"Yeah. Funny how Chuck made it out to seem

like negative stuff, but in all honesty, I only admire Burke more."

Of course she would. Burke too seemed to have been devoted to helping the helpless. But Declan felt strongly that they needed to figure out the identity of the woman Steven was meeting, which coffee shop they met at, and why Steven felt she needed help. "Let's pay a visit to Frank's."

"Sounds good. You've got Burke's picture?"

"Right here." He patted his shirt pocket. Once someone recognized him, hopefully they could provide a description of the woman too.

Hopefully.

He could use a little bit of hope right about now, the shock of Coach Grant's death still haunting him.

18

"Well," Parker said forty minutes after starting to process Haywood's car. "The car is parked in the same spot as when we arrived, but it's clearly been driven overnight. It rained right around one, and there's dried mud caked in the tires. I've already tagged and bagged Haywood's keys, so I'll run them for prints. Maybe we'll get lucky and find another set of prints or a partial . . ."

None of them wanted to believe Haywood capable of fraud, let alone murder.

"And the notebook you pulled from the car?" Griffin had spent the majority of the time watching Parker and Avery work, watching the dogs search the expansive grounds, and keeping an eye out for any sign of Lowell and Emmitt's return from what was becoming an incredibly long horseback ride. A little too conveniently long in his opinion.

"Right. The notebook." Parker pulled it from the evidence bag with gloved hands. "I found it shoved in a makeshift compartment underneath the driver's seat." He opened it to show a printed-out Excel spreadsheet folded inside.

"It appears to be a record of the money skimmed from Haywood's clients."

Griffin swallowed. "Seriously?"

"It's a printout, so there's no proof it was Haywood's doing, but the notebook appears to be his, based on the handwriting inside."

"We should hand it over to Thatcher. It might help his investigation," Griffin said.

"I agree." Parker slipped it back into the clear plastic bag. "Should I call him and ask him to meet up with us at CCI this evening?"

Griffin nodded. "Definitely." His gaze shifted back to the tires. "Any guess on the source of the mud in the tires?"

"I'd have to examine it under the scope to give you a solid read, but I can tell you it is a gravelly reddish-brown soil, like what you find in Loch Raven's watershed near the Cockeysville Marble formation. I'd need to compare it to known samples to be certain, check its carbon content and such, but that's my best off-the-cuff guess."

"That covers a wide area—Merryman's Woods out to Warren Road—and that's just one section of it. Though that section is the closest to the inn and far more secluded than most of the trailheads," Griffin said.

"I think I'll send the K9 units over to take a sniff. Hopefully we'll get a lead."

Griffin conversed with Corporal James Howe,

and then he and the other K9 unit headed over to the Merryman trailhead.

Meanwhile, Griffin headed back inside to find out who had been staying in the room closest to the Markums.

He met Jax in the hall. "Have you learned who was staying two rooms down from the Markums?" he asked.

Jax's smile was grim—he looked beat. "As a matter of fact, I do know, and they are waiting to talk to you."

He nodded toward a nervous-looking Jenn and Jeremy Barrit sitting at a nearby table. "When Jason interviewed them earlier, they told him they'd seen the Markums arguing with Haywood last night. When he then learned they were the occupants of the room two doors down from the Markums, he decided to save them for you."

"Thanks, Jax. I'll talk with them now."

He strode over to the couple. "Mr. and Mrs. Barrit, would you join me in the kitchen, please?"

They stood and followed him into the stone-tiled room with wood-beam ceilings and a roaring fire in the hearth.

"Please take a seat," he said, gesturing to the table.

They did so, Jenn clinging to Jeremy's hand as she scooted her chair close to his.

After introductions, Griffin asked, "Could you tell me about the conversation you overheard between Haywood and the Markums last night?"

Mrs. Barrit looked to her husband, and he nodded.

She cleared her throat. "When we went back to our room to change before going out to the fire pit, we saw the Markums rushing out of the side entrance door looking very upset."

"Do you remember the time, Mrs. Barrit?"

"It was pretty close to ten o'clock."

About the time he had heard Haywood and the Markums arguing in the hallway.

"We changed quickly and headed out our patio door. Haywood came out of his patio door two doors down at the same time, crossed right in front of us as if we weren't there."

She turned to her husband and sniffled. "That is not like Haywood—he is usually kind and attentive." She sniffled again, but at her husband's encouraging smile, she continued. "My husband claims I am a busybody, and maybe I am, but after he ignored us, I just couldn't resist wanting to see what he was doing. He called to the Markums, who were standing in the parking lot, and they appeared to start arguing. I couldn't really hear what they were saying, but no one looked happy, and Haywood looked . . . agitated."

"Agitated? How?" Griffin asked, wondering

if Haywood had ducked into his room to grab something before following the Markums out via his patio door. It would explain how he'd missed Haywood in the hallway.

"He was gesturing with his arms, and his body language was, I don't know . . . very *off*."

Jeremy took his wife's hand as she started to sniffle again, looking as if she was about to cry. "At that point I felt we were snooping somewhere we didn't belong, so I insisted we head to the fire pit."

He and Finley had chatted with the Barrits last night by the fire, right around that time. If only the Barrits had said something then and there . . .

But how could they have known the possible importance of what they had seen? It was typical that people were hesitant to get involved in others' business. But most of Haywood's clients knew Griffin was a detective. Mentioning it to him would have been a logical choice.

As he was considering his next question, Mrs. Barrit's eyes widened and she put her hand to her mouth. Did she have more?

She looked to her husband, appearing a bit flustered. "I just thought of something. Some-time in the middle of the night I woke up to what sounded like shuffling."

"Do you know where it came from?"

"It seemed like it was down the hall, toward

the outside door. The Markums were the only ones down that direction."

"Could you describe the shuffling noise?"

"It sounded like someone was moving something around. I don't know . . ." She shook her head. "I was half asleep, was probably awake for less than a minute." She leaned onto her husband's chest. "If I'd known . . ." Tears pooled in her brown eyes.

"There's no way we could have known, Jenn," Jeremy said.

"Your husband is right," Griffin said. "You couldn't have known." But he did wonder what might have been prevented if she had investigated. Actually, though, they might now be dealing with another body. There was no way to know.

"There's more." Mrs. Barrit sighed. "A little while later I woke up again. I heard something like a door opening and closing, and then footsteps. It was muffled. I just rolled back over. And that's all I remember."

Griffin couldn't imagine what else they could tell him, so he decided it was time to drop his own bombshell. "Were you aware that Haywood—or someone at the firm—has been stealing money from your accounts?"

Mrs. Barrit gasped. Mr. Barrit lunged forward in his seat. "What?"

"I'll take that as a no."

Before he could add anything else, a commotion sounded outside the kitchen door.

"Excuse me a moment," Griffin said, heading for the heated voices on the other side of the door. He exited to find Jax holding off an extremely agitated Lowell Brentwood and a rather solemn looking Emmitt Powell.

Both were still dressed in riding gear—crisp white shirts, black jackets, tan pants, and tall brown riding boots. Brentwood's black felt-covered helmet was in the cradle of his left elbow, while Emmitt Powell's was in the cradle of his right.

"What is the meaning of this?" Lowell roared. "I hear you've been harassing my clients all morning."

Jeremy Barrit exited the kitchen behind Griffin, striding around him to meet Lowell head on. "The detective said Haywood or *someone* at the firm has been stealing our money!"

Lowell's cheeks flushed crimson, and he glared at Griffin. "You told him *what?*"

"I told him the truth. Maybe it's about time you did as well."

Lowell's jaw twitched. "What are you implying?"

Mrs. Barrit joined them in the hallway, and Griffin looked between the Barrits and Lowell. He understood the Barrits' frustration, but there were bigger matters at hand. "I'm afraid that discussion will have to wait." The real question was, why did he see no hint of concern on Lowell's part regarding his dead partner and the presumed dead clients?

"The heck it can," Mr. Barrit said, getting in Lowell's face.

"I understand you're upset." Griffin stepped between them. "But are we forgetting about Haywood's death and the fact that the Markums are missing?"

Lowell exhaled. "Of course, and I couldn't be sadder about Haywood. He was a mentor to me. I still can't believe he committed suicide or that he stole from his clients." Apparently he'd been quickly brought up to speed on the situation.

And now he was more than happy to admit *Haywood* had stolen from his clients. As long as the blame rested on his deceased partner.

"But the last thing my clients need is your harassment," Lowell said. "They've been through quite enough."

"I realize you've been gone all morning on a ride"—which he still found to be awfully convenient timing—"but we're in the middle of a criminal investigation. It is our job to interview those we feel are pertinent to the case. And that most especially includes the clients whom it appears Haywood stole from."

Lowell cocked his head. "*Appears?* You tell these people that Haywood stole from them, and you're not even certain he did it? This is ridiculous! I can't believe you've upset my clients over a hunch."

Interesting how quickly he switched to *my* clients when they'd clearly been Haywood's.

"We know the funds were taken," Griffin said, his gaze fixed on Lowell. "We just aren't positive by whom."

Lowell's light blue eyes widened, his ruddy appearance reddening more. "What *exactly* are you implying now?"

"Only that until the forensic accountant has finished his investigation of your accounts, we can't be certain of anything."

"This is preposterous." Lowell set his riding hat on the buffet table behind him and lifted his arms up in the air for what Griffin could only assume was dramatic effect.

"Thank you, Mr. and Mrs. Barrit," Griffin said. "You two are free to go."

"But what about the money they stole from us?" Jeremy Barrit asked.

"As I said, a forensic accountant is investigating. I can assure you he's the best, and we will be in touch as soon as he has news."

They didn't look one hundred percent pleased that that was the most Griffin could offer, but at this point, unfortunately, it was.

After a few angry words aimed at Lowell, Jeremy Barrit and his wife excused themselves.

Griffin took time to read both men their rights before any further discussion occured. "Now," he said, directing his attention to Lowell. "I can start by interviewing you or Mr. Powell. What's your preference?"

"My preference," Lowell stammered, "is that you stop this madness. You are going to destroy *my* company."

"*Your* company?" Griffin said, glancing at Emmitt, who remained remarkably stoic. "You're a partner in the firm," he continued, returning his gaze back to Lowell, "and are you forgetting Emmitt standing right behind you?"

"Emmitt is an *employee,* not a partner, and seeing how Haywood took his own life, it appears the company has fallen to me. He's left me with a huge mess to clean up, if he hasn't fully destroyed the firm."

"What makes you so sure the company is yours?" Griffin said.

"Haywood and I agreed the day we became partners that even if we left our share of the company to someone else, we'd leave acting control of the company to one another."

"And are you certain Haywood didn't change his mind?"

"He *stole* from our clients. Apparently, I didn't know him at all. So no, I'm not positive about anything other than the fact that *his* stealing is going to ruin the firm. I'm going to have to distance myself as much as possible from his name and start all over again. Haywood might as well have stabbed a knife in my back while he was falling on his own sword."

Griffin exhaled. The key was going to be getting underneath all Lowell's posturing to uncover the truth. First thing they needed to discover, after they concluded their interviews, was who Haywood had left his share and control of the company to.

Was it possible Lowell set Haywood up, killed the clients who were causing a fuss and could have destroyed everything he worked for, and then staged Haywood's suicide? It would take a stone-cold man to take those actions—or a really desperate one. It was time they started digging deeper into Lowell Brentwood's background.

19

Declan held the door for Tanner at Frank's coffee shop.

"Grab an open table," the brunette waitress walking by said, a coffeepot in one hand, three plates in the other.

Declan spotted an open table near the side windows, led Tanner to it, and pulled out the chair for her.

"Thank you," she said, taking a seat.

Declan moved around and sat with his back toward the wall, facing the front entrance. The place was comfortable—cherrywood walls and wooden tables, Texas memorabilia, and the scent of pancake batter wafting from the open short-order kitchen. The bell rang every few minutes, signaling another order was up and ready.

The brunette waitress grabbed an order, dropped it off, and then stopped at their table with coffeepot in hand. "I'm Darlene. I'll be your waitress today. Would y'all like coffee?"

"Yes, please," Declan said, flipping his over-turned cup upright.

"Me too." Tanner did the same.

"The special today is huevos rancheros."

"That sounds wonderful, but just coffee"—
Declan flashed his badge—"and a question."

Darlene cocked her head.

Declan pulled out Burke's photo. "We were told this man came in here a lot."

She studied the photograph. "He used to."

"Up until about four months ago?"

"Yeah. How'd you know?"

"I'm afraid he was murdered two months back."

"Murdered? That sweet man. How awful."

"We're trying to track down the men who killed him, but to do that we have speak to a woman he had been meeting with."

"Hmm. Only saw him in here with one woman, but I always thought she was his sister."

"Brown curly hair, about your height."

"Yeah, that's the one."

"You were right. That's his sister."

"I figured."

"Thanks for your help." They finished their coffee, and Declan left a generous tip on the table.

They crossed the street, walked the eight blocks over to the next stop, Beans & Buns, and entered to a totally different vibe. Millennial French pastry shop is what came to mind.

It was a counter-service place with an extremely limited menu of primarily coffee drinks and baked goods. Declan still had no room left to eat anything, but Tanner ordered a latte, and they got the opportunity to show Steven's picture. The woman behind the counter was a combination of rude and bored, but she hadn't seen Steven with any woman that she could recall. At Tanner's request the woman talked to the only other employee who waited on customers, and his answer was the same. Strike two.

Fifteen minutes and a refreshing walk later, they entered coffee shop number three, the last one on their list—Denton's. They moved to the counter and hopped up on two cushioned stools.

A twenty-something woman with long brown hair pulled back into a braid came over holding an iPad. "Hey folks. Can I get you something?"

"I'll take a mint lemonade," Declan said, and she swiped her finger on the iPad and turned to Tanner.

"I'm good, but thanks."

The server turned to walk away.

"Hang on a sec," Declan said, flashing his badge. "Can we ask you a question?" He pulled out Steven's photograph. "Do you recognize this guy?"

"Sure. Number five."

He followed her hand gesture toward the menu board and saw a numbered list of coffee drinks. "Great. So he came in here a lot?"

"Now and again since we opened last year, then almost daily, and then not at all."

"For the last four months?" Tanner said.

"Yeah." She shrugged. "Guess he got tired of number five with an extra shot."

"Unfortunately, he's dead," Declan said.

She scrunched her face. "Ohhh gross. Are you serious?"

"I'm afraid so."

"Poor dude."

"We were told he'd met a woman at this coffee shop not long before he left?" Declan said, leading the witness.

"Nisa. Yeah, she stopped coming around the same time. I assumed they'd left together."

Thank you, Jesus.

"What can you tell me about Nisa?"

"She liked to mix up her order, try a lot of different combinations. She was a nanny to a rich family who lived somewhere around here."

"Where was she from?"

"Somewhere in Asia. She told me once, I think, but I can't recall."

"Did you get the impression she was a recent immigrant?"

The server thought for a moment and then said, "I think so. Her English wasn't very good, but she was eager to learn, and it was getting better."

"What did she look like?"

"Petite, tan skin, fabulous complexion, dark hair, pretty eyes. She was sweet."

"And you haven't seen her in a while?"

"Nah, probably not for . . . four or five months, maybe."

"Any idea where we could find her?"

"Oh, so you can give her the bad news?"

"We want her to be aware of what's happened."

"Sure. I get that, but I have no idea where she lives, her last name, who she worked for. Nothing. Other than that she liked to talk with Number Five."

"Do you know what they talked about?"

"Not really. It wasn't like I could stand around and listen to their conversations." She put her hand on her hip and frowned. "Though, now that I think of it the last time I saw her she was crying—but not like they were fighting. She said something about 'they' were going to get her. And he kept talking about a ship, said he would help her get away, but she ran out, still crying." She looked around. "I only remember because she was so upset."

He raised his eyebrows at Tanner. It seemed that Nisa had been smuggled in on a ship— maybe even the *Hiram*—and whoever had brought her in was giving her trouble. "Okay. Thanks for your time."

"No problem. I'll be back with your drink."

Tanner held up her hand. "If it's not too much trouble, could I try a number five?"

The waitress smiled. "Sure thing."

"Number five piques your interest?" Declan asked.

"Nope. Method investigation."

He arched a brow.

"Like actors. You try and do the same things the victim or person you're looking for did, and maybe you learn something about them."

"In that case, I should get a number five too." He smiled.

She narrowed her eyes. "Are you humoring me?"

His smile deepened. "I would never." He swooped in and stole a kiss. "It's actually a good idea."

"Thanks."

The waitress brought their drinks and an address on an order slip.

"What's this?"

"It's where the short-order cook said Nisa lived."

"They're friends?"

"Nah, but they lived in the same building."

"Lived?" Declan took a sip of his mint lemonade—too sweet.

"He said the landlady told him Nisa just up and disappeared one day. Didn't take any of her stuff neither. Left it all for the landlady to clean up. Super rude, if you ask me. I wouldn't have expected that of Nisa."

"Thanks." Declan slid the address in his shirt

pocket. "We really appreciate it. And if it's not too much trouble, I'll take a number five to go."

"You got it."

"Thanks."

After leaving another very generous tip, they stepped outside with their number fives, and each took a sip.

"Delicious," Tanner said. "Tastes like dulce de leche."

"Yeah, like caramel sweet milk."

Tanner licked a drop off her lip. "Exactly, but with espresso."

"It's interesting," Declan said. "Not what I picture a fellow Fed drinking, but I suppose not everyone can handle the real stuff." He winked.

She smirked. "So plain black coffee is the real stuff?"

"Yep."

"I beg to differ."

"Of course you do. And what would your definition of the real stuff be?"

"Espresso with a dollop of whipped cream."

"Strong and sweet."

"Yep."

He smiled. "Rather describes you."

"I suppose I could say the same of your drink of choice."

"Oh? How do you describe black coffee?"

"Strong, no frills, and hot." She winked.

He nearly choked on his drink, but very ungracefully sputtered in bemused surprise. Tanner was going to keep him on his toes. He'd suspected as much early on, but this was at a far steeper level than before. The adrenaline coursing through him said he was in for an amazing journey at her side.

At her side? Wow. He was in far deeper than he'd realized, or perhaps just deeper than he wanted to acknowledge. Once he acknowledged it, everything became real. And once it was real, he could lose it.

20

"Mr. Brentwood, how about you go take a moment to compose yourself and calm down while I speak with Emmitt."

"I do not need to be told to calm down like I'm a child."

Funny, that's exactly what he was behaving like. A petulant child.

"I've concluded my other interviews," Jason said from the doorway. "Why don't you follow me into the library, Mr. Brentwood? We can talk while Griffin and Emmitt finish up in here."

Lowell's eyes narrowed. "Why can't we be interviewed together?"

"Procedural policy," Griffin said bluntly.

Lowell exhaled. "Very well. If you insist."

Jason started for the library, and after a moment of posturing, Lowell Brentwood followed.

Griffin glanced back at Emmitt, who remained pretty much where he had stood through Griffin's entire conversation with Lowell. "Please sit down, Mr. Powell." He gestured to the open chair across from him.

Emmitt nodded and took a seat at the kitchen table, the wooden chair legs scraping against the stone floor as he slid the chair back. He set his helmet off to the side. He was about Griffin's height and build and of partial Asian ethnicity. When he spoke, it was in a low and thoughtful tone. "How may I be of assistance?"

"Let's start with how you learned the news of Haywood's death."

"The Coveys came up to us as soon as we returned, demanding to know what we were going to do to get their stolen funds back. Apparently, they had just come from being questioned by your partner, and he informed them of the theft as well as Haywood's death."

"And how did Lowell respond?"

"He promised to get to the bottom of everything, and assured them they'd be well taken care of—that he'd see to it personally."

"How does he plan to do that?"

"I don't think he has a plan. He was simply reacting."

"He appears to be good at reacting." Griffin shifted his focus fully to Emmitt. "How long have you been at the firm?"

"Three years."

"And who hired you?"

"I met with both Haywood and Lowell, but Haywood officially hired me."

"And in your years working with Haywood and Lowell, have you seen or sensed any discord between them?"

"Not really."

Griffin rested his forearms on the oak table, the grain smooth and indicative of late nineteenth-century workmanship. "I need you to be completely honest with me. We need to know the truth."

Emmitt shifted uncomfortably, but after a moment he spoke. "They butt heads occasionally. It's not surprising. They both have . . . had . . ." He raked a shaky hand through his dark spiky hair, still messy from his riding helmet. "I can't believe Haywood is gone. . . ."

"None of us can."

Emmitt swallowed. "They were both headstrong. Lowell had a different vision for the firm. Modern. Techie. Sleek. Haywood was more of your good-ol'-boy, hardworking, no-frills type of guy."

"What about money? Did they ever argue over money? The firm's or how the clients' funds were handled?"

"They didn't let me in on that type of discussion."

"Sounds like you were kept at the outer edge, even after years of working with them?" That had to be a sore spot.

Emmitt shrugged. "They're partners. Like Lowell said, I'm just an employee."

"Does that bother you?"

"It doesn't make me feel good, but it's the top firm in the area, and I've learned so much. Haywood really mentored me. I still can't believe . . ."

"Do you believe that Haywood was capable of stealing from clients?"

"I never would have believed it."

"But?"

"If he didn't, why did he commit suicide?"

"Any chance Lowell could be the one behind the theft and was just making Haywood the patsy?"

"Lowell?" Emmitt tucked his chin in. "I can't see either of them stealing."

"But someone definitely did. If it wasn't one of them . . . ?" Time to put some pressure on.

"Whoa!" He held up his hands. "First of all, I don't have sufficient access to mess with the client accounts, but even then, I would *never* steal. I pride myself on my work ethic and on my faith."

"Your faith?"

"I'm a Christian. Stealing is one of the big ten."

That was one way to put it.

"Okay. Then between Lowell and Haywood . . . ?"

He inhaled, thought about it, and exhaled. "If I had to pick one . . . I would have said Lowell, but with Haywood's suicide, it sure makes him look guilty."

"Yes it does." But perhaps that had been the point all along.

21

Declan held the smudged glass door of the run-down apartment building open for Tanner. He preferred she not even go inside, but this was Tanner. No way was she waiting outside. They found the landlady behind a glass window in the office cubby at the base of the narrow stair-well.

Please, Father, let her be helpful. Help us find out what happened to Nisa or where she is. If Burke believed her to be in danger, I worry something bad may have already happened to her. Even if this doesn't lead us to evidence of our terrorism case, I can't just walk away without checking. It wouldn't be right. Please help us.

"Excuse me." Declan rapped on the glass with a smile.

The woman looked up with a frown, but took one look at Declan and smiled as sweetly as a grandma holding a newborn babe. She stood and leaned across her desk, sliding the glass window open. "May I help you?"

"We're looking for Nisa."

"She doesn't live here anymore. Crazy lady just took off. Left all her stuff behind."

"We'd heard that. Any chance we can see her room?" Declan held up his badge. He could get a warrant if necessary.

"Sorry. Someone else is living there."

"What about her belongings?"

"I could have thrown them away, with her just leaving them for me to deal with, but I didn't. I went out of my way. Boxed them up and put them down in the storage unit in case she came back. I can take you down there, if you'd like."

"That would be great."

"Wait right there. I need to grab my key." She disappeared from sight.

Tanner smirked. "Looks like someone else is smitten with the handsome Declan Grey."

Lindy, as she introduced herself, smiled a little less after seeing Declan had a companion, but she still led them down to the storage unit in the basement. "I think I put Nisa's boxes over here." She rummaged through a few printer-paper boxes and finally located the right ones. "Here you go. These three red ones."

"Three boxes. That's all she had?"

"Yep. The apartment was fully furnished, so she didn't move in with anything big."

He moved to the first, took the lid off, and began pulling out items one by one.

"I've got work to do," Lindy said, clearly

bored. "I'll be in my office. Just let me know when you're done so I can lock up."

"Will do. Thanks again," Declan said, turning back to the items.

"Looks like Nisa didn't have much," Tanner said as Declan eyed the tattered clothes, shoes, and a single paperback romance with *.10* marked in pencil on the top right-hand corner of the first page.

"But if this is everything she owned, it is hard to believe she would leave without anything."

"So she either left in a hurry or . . . ?" Tanner began.

Declan put the lid back on the box. "Or she didn't leave. She was killed."

"You think because she talked to Burke?"

"My guess is whoever paid for her on this end probably kept a close eye on his 'property' and when he saw her talking to Burke, he did some digging. Realized Burke was a Fed and took Nisa out before she could say anything to jeopardize him or his business."

Anger flushed Tanner's cheeks. "That's disgusting."

He swallowed. "At the very least."

"Now what?"

"Let's see if we can't get the local Bureau office to send over a sketch artist to Lindy and the cook from Denton's, and then try running

Nisa's rendering through as a missing person. See if we get any hits."

"Okay. And then?"

"Tomorrow we get on a plane and head back home. I need to pay a visit to Captain Randal Jackson."

Griffin and Jason concluded their interviews and ran a background check on Haywood and the Markums, discovering Elizabeth Markum was a prominent defense attorney. It seemed odd that she had not mentioned that last night, but she'd clearly wanted to keep their conversation as short as possible, excusing herself and her husband at the first opportunity. Parker and Avery had finished processing the known crime scene and collected all the evidence to be worked back at the lab. They were just about to pack up when Griffin received a call from K9 Corporal James Howe.

"Hey," Griffin said. "Have any luck over at Loch Raven?"

"If you consider finding a finger good luck," Howe said.

Within fifteen minutes, Griffin, Jason, Parker, and Avery were at the Merryman branch of Loch Raven Reservoir.

The late afternoon sunlight shafted through the red leaves above, casting a crimson glow over the reddish-brown soil of the trailhead where they met Howe.

"The two dogs picked up the Markums' scent here at the trailhead lot and led us down the trail branching to the left about two hundred feet in, and Knox, here"—he patted the German Shepherd with pride—"found the finger in some foliage near the falls' edge. Follow me and I'll show you."

Griffin watched as Parker knelt beside the foliage and Avery snapped pictures.

Why a finger?

Had the killer taken the time to dismember the bodies before dumping them into the deep water below?

He looked around. There wasn't enough blood, unless the rain had washed it away, but the rain had only fallen in the area for about an hour—from one to two, according to the local meteorologist Griffin had confirmed Parker's estimate with on their way over. That meant anything that occurred after that time would be muddy but not washed away. What blood surrounded the finger indicated the severing occurred post-rainfall, which could prove a huge win for them. It meant they could take shoe print and tire impressions. There'd no doubt be several for Parker to sort through at the trail-head lot—though Howe had been considerate enough for the integrity of the investigation to avoid parking the vehicles in the lot proper, and instead had parked along the side of the road.

Griffin prayed that Parker would be able to match at least one set of tire prints to Haywood's tire tread, confirming the body drop site, or at least the presence of Haywood's car. Parker would need to get a mud sample to compare to Haywood's tires.

"Has any more blood been found along the trail?" Parker asked, echoing Griffin's thoughts.

Howe shook his head. "Not that we've found. And I went in with Knox first and placed markers by the shoe prints present before we did our search."

"Excellent job," Parker said, examining the half dozen flags staked around them. It wasn't many, but even though it was a Saturday, Merryman wasn't a high-volume trail. Parker would have to compare the shoe prints found to everyone's at the retreat—especially Lowell Brentwood's.

"There is no sign of additional dismemberment based on the limited amount of blood we found," Parker reported and he and Avery worked the scene, taking print, tire tread, and mud samples. Sorting through all their shoe prints would be time consuming—having to go to each client's home, but thankfully that was Parker's area, not his.

"And?" Griffin said, hoping they had some answers.

"My guess is that the killer started to dismember the bodies and either determined it would take him too long or something spooked him and he dumped the bodies and rushed away."

"So we may have a witness to the dump?"

"Kids party in this area. Maybe the killer heard someone arriving or moving around. I can only conjecture."

And Parker hated conjecture. He was a man of facts and evidence.

"We're going to have to get divers in the water," Griffin said.

"I'll call it in." Cavanaugh lifted his chin. "But the search will have to wait until morning."

"Thankfully we have just enough light to finish processing the scene without bringing in artificial light," Parker said, always preferring to use what he termed "clean" or natural light.

Once finished at Loch Raven, Griffin returned to the inn to pick up Finley, who had spent the time they were away curled up with a throw by the patio heaters and fire pit, reading in the dying day's light. Kate had taken off around noon.

He regretted that he hadn't been able to join his beautiful wife for a restful weekend. Instead he'd found a man he'd admired almost all his life dead in a tub, and a couple's bodies were most likely submerged somewhere in the reservoir. This case was definitely going to push him to his limits.

Finley rubbed Griffin's arm as he reversed

out of the inn's parking lot, the spots where the Markums' and Haywood's vehicles had been parked, empty, the cars having been towed to the station's impound lot.

"You okay?" Finley asked softly as he pulled out onto the main road.

"Yeah." He shifted gears. "Just not an easy case."

"Never is when someone you know is involved."

22

Kate worked on digging into Lowell Brentwood's life at her front room desk at CCI, while Griffin tracked down Haywood's lawyer's name and contact information after paying a painful visit to Haywood's wife, Carol. Apparently the two were separated, but not yet divorced.

Kate didn't envy Griffin having to make that death notification visit. Carol and Haywood had been married close to thirty years prior to their separation, and Haywood's death under harsh and questionable circumstances had to be extremely difficult for Carol to hear.

Griffin said she'd cried, and he attempted to soothe her, but Kate knew when losing a loved one—even when you had no idea why you'd lost them or where in the world they were—the sorrow never subsided.

Kate shifted her gaze to the light emanating from under Parker's lab door as he and Avery worked the recovered evidence from the inn and reservoir.

Jason Cavanaugh sat on the sofa, taking a brief reprieve over a cup of coffee while they awaited Thatcher Grimes' arrival.

Kate would never hand over a significant

piece of an investigation to someone she didn't know without checking their credentials, so she had done some digging on the man. And she learned Parker hadn't been exaggerating when he said Grimes was the best forensic accountant in the field. His credentials were stellar—he had authored the premier textbook and handbook in use in both the field and in training schools. He was the Parker Mitchell of the forensic accounting world.

The door signaled someone's entry, and Kate turned to find what could have been Morgan Freeman's twin, twenty years younger. The man was tall, handsome, and genteel in mannerism.

"Thatcher Grimes," he said, taking off his hat and dipping his head.

She stood and moved to greet him. "Kate Maxwell. Thanks so much for coming. I'll let Parker know you're here."

He nodded.

"This is . . ." She started to introduce Jason, but he was already on his feet and moving to shake Grimes' hand.

"Detective Jason Cavanaugh," he said.

"Pleasure to meet you," Grimes said as she moved down the hall toward Parker's lab.

She opened the door to find him standing over the printer as pages slipped out.

"Find something?"

"A number of somethings."

"Mr. Grimes is here."

"Great. Griffin and Finley should be here any minute." He grabbed the papers out of the printer tray and, taking Avery's hand, headed out for the front room. "Thatcher," he said, greeting the man with a handshake.

"Parker, always good to see you. Sorry it's not under better circumstances."

"Thanks." Parker turned slightly. "This is my photographer and girlfriend, Avery Tate."

Grimes once again dipped his head. "Pleasure to meet the woman who finally wrangled this man's heart."

Avery smiled. "The pleasure is mine."

The bell signaled another entry, and Griffin and Finley walked in.

"Griffin, Mrs. McCray," Grimes said, "so nice to see you."

"Thanks for making this a priority."

"No problem a'tall."

"Shall we?" Kate said, indicating the seating area. "Mr. Grimes, let me take your coat."

"Thank you, young lady."

She hung his coat on the rack and joined the team, anxious to hear what Grimes had to share.

With a sigh, he pulled a portfolio out of a worn brown leather satchel. "I ran the preliminaries on the company. It's going to take several more days to sort everything out, but at this point it appears Haywood was the one stealing from his clients." He surveyed the room. "That, however, doesn't mean much."

"No?" Griffin asked with a twinge of hope.

"It's complex. The log-in used was Haywood's, and most of the clients affected were his."

"Most?" Kate frowned.

"It appears that he—or whoever was behind it—also siphoned from Emmitt Powell's clients."

Parker leaned forward. "Which to me would indicate Lowell Brentwood."

Grimes smiled. "That's where my mind went. Everyone's clients, but Brentwood's."

"And Haywood said Lowell had access to his log-in."

"Exactly. The warrant came through to access the firm's computers and paperwork. I'll be heading there with my team first thing in the morning."

"Wonderful. Please keep us posted," Kate said, anxious to know who was behind it all and praying for the guys' sake that it wasn't Haywood—despite how guilty he might appear.

"I most certainly will."

After Thatcher left, Finley moved to make a fresh pot of coffee, and Parker began sharing the results he'd found so far.

As he stood and moved to the whiteboard,

Kate scooted forward in her seat. It was weird working a case without Declan and Tanner—especially without Declan running the board. She'd be glad when they were back from Houston.

"First," Parker said, "the fingerprint from the dismembered index finger is a match for John Markum."

"Which would indicate a body dump," Griffin said, "or at least that the Markums were there and, if not already dead and being dismembered, under severe duress."

"Correct," Parker said with a sigh.

Griffin straightened. "What?"

They all knew that was Parker's "bad news is coming" sigh.

"One set of the tire treads we found matches Haywood's car, along with the mud sample from the trailhead matching the mud caked in his tires."

"Any other fingerprints on Haywood's steering wheel?" Griffin asked, again with hope in his voice.

"Actually, yes." Parker smiled. "Lowell Brentwood's."

"Finally, some good news."

"And there's one additional piece," Parker said.

"What's that?"

"None of Haywood's shoes match the imprints we took from the reservoir."

"So he wasn't there?"

"At least none of the shoes he had in the room were. There's always the possibility he tossed them somewhere along the way, as there was no mud on the floorboard of his car, but that could also indicate that whoever drove it to the trailhead either never got out of the car, covered their shoes in some way, or changed shoes before getting back in."

Tanner watched Declan meticulously spread Steven Burke's personal files in an order that suited him across his hotel room bed, then step back and assess what was before him.

"Where to start?" she murmured.

"Top left and work our way across and then down." He pointed in the shape of an upside-down L.

"You want me to take notes while you read?" she asked.

"Sure. That'd be great. But are you certain you aren't too tired? It's been a long day."

"Nah, I'm fine." The more time with Declan the better. Plus, she was intrigued by the case. She wanted to know what had happened to Steven Burke, why he'd been on that ship.

Declan smiled, his chin dimple hollowing. "You mean you're hooked."

She sure was—and not just on the case.

Declan looked amazing, and considering he

was simply wearing a yellow-and-green rugby jersey and a pair of straight-legged black sweats, that was saying something. She looked down at her yoga pants and very worn-in Towson sweatshirt, hoping she didn't look half the wreck she felt. She'd pulled her hair up into a lopsided bun, the annoying slips of hair escaping the band, but at least the majority was off her freshly washed face. It felt good to be casual, and if she and Declan ever really began a romantic relationship, it was better he saw the real her now rather than later. She was a firm believer in being true to who God created her to be and never pretending to be someone else. *Take it or leave it* was her motto. And she was pretty sure Declan shared a similar one.

He handed her a steno pad—she hadn't seen one of those in about a gazillion years—and a pen. Her tools in hand, she sat on the one chair in the room, tucking her legs beneath her. "Where are you going to sit?" she asked, assuming the edge of the bed, but with all the files, he hadn't left himself much room.

"I won't."

"Won't sit?"

"I think better moving."

"Okay. See, there's one more thing I've learned about you."

He smiled and grabbed the first file. "Case 1045. Since these are personal files, I'm assuming the case numbers were part of Burke's own coding system, but we'll see if we can find a pattern, or if there are references back to his work files."

They ran through the first three files, each clearly a cold case. All missing women. All in a similar age range. The three cases spanned the last five years, the most recent being Burke's personal file of the Chelsea Miller case. They took a few minutes to compare the file with her Bureau file, and they found the details to be pretty much the same.

Thanks to Franco, Declan now understood Burke's connection to the missing women—when a friend's loved one is kidnapped and killed, it heightens one's commitment to finding the truth. But he wondered how Burke had come across Nisa, and how he recognized she needed help.

Was there any connection between the three threads—the missing women from Houston, the smuggling of refugees and terrorists on the *Hiram*, and Nisa and the ship she and Burke spoke of? Or were they all separate cases Burke was juggling? And what was Burke's motivation for boarding the *Hiram*?

It was highly likely Nisa had been smuggled in through Galveston's port and entrapped in a situation like Max Stallings' victims were in Baltimore. Was Galveston's port and the city of Houston another branch of Ebeid's or was it like Max Stallings' network? Either possibility was terrifying.

"You're thinking Nisa might have been smuggled over as Mira had been, just in a different port?" Tanner asked.

"Yes." He glanced at the bedside table. It was already nine o'clock. Realizing they hadn't eaten anything since the hot dog cart, he placed a hand on Tanner's shoulder. "We still have five files to go. Are you sure you aren't getting too tired or hungry?"

"I could go for some room service," she said.

They perused the menu and Declan placed an order for two cheeseburgers and fries, and then they moved back to the files. The next two victims were very similar to the rest—young women, abducted in Houston and murdered.

He lifted the sixth file and read the case number. Tanner noted it, and he flipped back the cover, his eyes widening with shock.

"What's wrong?"

He turned the photo of the victim to face Tanner.

"Jenna?" Tanner stood and walked to his side, taking the file to better examine the picture of Griffin's younger sister, who'd been murdered more than seven years ago. "Why would Burke have a file on Jenna McCray? She was murdered in Maryland."

Declan skimmed the file. "Because the MO

is remarkably similar in all these files. Young women—ages sixteen through nineteen—dark hair, green eyes, petite, walking alone at night, and found washed up on shore a few weeks later, tortured, raped."

He rubbed his forehead. "Maybe he was a drifter after all. Maybe this is why Jenna's killer was never found—because he relocated to Houston."

"Are all the other victims from Houston?"

"So far, but we still have two files to go."

"So . . . do you think Burke found a link between all the cases—missing women, human trafficking, terrorism?"

"I can't be sure, but my gut says no—at least not intentionally. Burke picked up the missing women thread because of his connection to one victim's father. From there he searched cold case records and recognized a pattern. He developed a passion to pursue justice for all those women whose killer was still at large.

"But then Burke met Nisa. I am guessing they bonded and she shared what had happened to her. Their interaction drew the attention of whomever is in charge of a Houston ring similar to Max Stallings' in Baltimore. Someone figured out he was an FBI agent and that person silenced her.

"Burke knew she'd come through Galveston's port on the *Hiram*, so knowing the Bureau would not support his investigation, he headed to Galveston on his own and joined the *Hiram* crew. And then, in addition to his investigation of human trafficking, he stumbled upon the smuggling of terrorists into the U.S."

"That's crazy."

"That's criminal justice. You'd be amazed at the cases I work and the connections that are sometimes made."

"What about the last two serial-killer victims?"

"Right." Declan retrieved one file and then the other. "Both victims were young women, both fitting the profile, but both had been killed in Wilmington, North Carolina—one about six months after Jenna's murder, the other a year after that. Then . . ." He retrieved one of the earlier files. "The earliest Houston murder we have was about nine months after that. I think we may just have our first big lead in Jenna's case. The footprints of her killer."

A knock sounded on the door. "Room service."

Declan moved for the door, his hand on the butt of his holstered handgun.

Tanner smiled. "It's food, Declan."

He smiled back at her and opened the door to a room service attendant, his hands on the cart's edge.

"Come in," Declan said, stepping back.

A split second later, a rush of movement blew past him, someone tackling the man to the floor. The room service attendant pulled a syringe from his pocket, trying to jab it into the other man's neck.

Declan and Tanner both pulled guns on the pair, but the wrestling didn't cease.

The man on top, his back to Declan, overpowered the room service attendant and injected him with his own syringe, pumping yellow liquid into his neck. Within seconds, he spasmed, foamed at the mouth, and died.

The other man stood and moved for the door, but Declan grabbed his arm.

The man spun around, gun aimed at Declan's face, Declan's aimed right back at his. Shock ricocheted through Declan. "Luke?"

23

Luke paced the room, trying to settle the adrenaline coursing through him. "I'll clean this up."

"That's it?" Declan said as Luke crammed the man's body onto the lower tray of the room service cart, covering it with the draped-over tablecloth. "You disappear without any word and reappear over seven years later, killing a room service guy . . ."

Luke cocked his head.

"Okay, clearly he wasn't a real room service guy," Declan said. "But a little explanation would be nice."

"A little explanation will only put you in deeper."

"Deeper into Ebeid's network?"

"I knew you'd figure it out, but he's not Ebeid's man. Not directly."

"Then whose man is he? The guy who runs the Houston branch of Ebeid's network?"

"I've already been here too long." Luke raked a hand through his hair and slipped his ball cap back on.

"Are you coming home?"

"I don't have a home anymore."

"Sure you do. You're at least going to see Katie, right? She's been searching for you this whole time."

"I know. I made her PI in Malaysia."

"Is that why you came back?"

"For Katie? No." He wished, but he'd left that life, left *her* behind. She might have been looking for him, but she couldn't possibly still hold feelings for him. "And you can't tell her."

"What?"

"You can't tell anyone."

"Why not?"

"Because he'll kill her. Kill you all. It's a wonder you and Tanner aren't dead already." He grabbed the room service cart and moved for the door.

Tanner's eyes widened at the mention of her name. Declan hid his surprise better, but Luke still sensed the shock.

"She still loves you, Luke."

Luke paused, his grip tightening on the cart's edge. "That's impossible."

"I'm telling you, she does."

Luke swallowed. "It doesn't matter."

Declan took a step back. "Who are you?"

"A ghost," he said, shutting the door behind him.

Two hours later Declan was still processing what he'd seen, or rather *who* he'd seen—Luke

Gallagher in the flesh. Kate was right. Luke was alive, but she didn't know that he was in the States.

How did Luke tie to Ebeid?

Who was running the Houston branch of the terrorist network?

Had the hit man been sent because they'd touched a nerve today? If so, which nerve? Asking around about Nisa was his best guess. But, again, how did Luke fit into all this?

"You okay?" Tanner asked, as she slid under the bedcovers.

"Yeah." They'd switched hotels and with only king-size rooms left, he'd once again be taking the floor. But, after what happened—or *nearly* happened, thanks to Luke—he wasn't leaving Tanner's side for an instant.

Tomorrow they were on a flight back to Baltimore.

If the enemy planned to return for him and Tanner, he preferred to be on home turf.

Resting his weight on his forearms, he leaned over and kissed Tanner's forehead. " 'Night." He smiled, amazed at how intensely he cared.

" 'Night," she said sleepily.

He checked his watch. *One o'clock.* She had to be exhausted.

He, on the other hand, was filled with questions and adrenaline, which thankfully would help keep him awake.

Settling back on his blanket on the floor, he gazed at Tanner, only to discover she was already fast asleep. Since the light in the room was clearly not bothering her, he'd leave it on and get some work done while he waited out the remaining hours of the night.

He retrieved Burke's copy of *Die Trying* and opened to the slip of paper tucked inside, where two neat columns contained page numbers. Flipping to the first corresponding page number, he read the scene, hoping to find something, but nothing popped out. He did the same with the second column . . . but nada. Then, just as he was about to place it back in the evidence bag and cut the lights, an idea hit him.

What if the first column was the page number and the second column the number of the word on the page? Kind of like the Ottendorf cipher he'd learned about at Quantico but had never used in the field. And they used it in that adventure movie Tanner loved. What was it called? Something Treasure . . . *National Treasure*—that was it.

He flipped back to the key and started with page thirteen, word number forty-two. *Leader*. He continued through the list.

Luke surveyed the perimeter one last time before settling in his motel room. It was drafty and sparse, but it'd do. He'd disposed of Lark's body, making sure it would never be found. After taking a long, hot shower, he wrapped a towel around his waist. Swiping the steam from the mirror, he stared into it, Declan's question echoing through his mind.

"Who are you?"

Did he even know anymore?

It'd been months since Kate's contact, Hadi, had lost Luke's trail in Malaysia, and she wondered if Luke had moved on or if he had simply slipped under Hadi's radar. She'd spent years trying to find Luke, and now, after just a glimpse, she'd lost him all over again. Though not remotely prone to crying or getting overly emotional, she felt on the brink of a meltdown.

Why was this so hard?

Why couldn't she let go?

Because it was Luke, and no matter how much she wished otherwise, he held her heart. It belonged to him. If only he'd return so she could be whole again.

The question beating inside, the one that refused to lessen its stranglehold, was *where* had Luke gone, and what route had he taken to get there?

She'd been running a facial recognition program through the world's ports and airports ever since Hadi lost his lead on him. "Come on . . ." She *had* to get a hit soon. Her leg bounced as the images flashed by on the screen.

Exhaling, she pulled back her hair and then let it fall across her shoulders. The *Barefoot* bobbed in the harbor's waves. She glanced out the starboard porthole at the patrol car stationed up the metal ramp from her slip. It was there at Griffin's insistence after Declan and Tanner's nasty homecoming last night. While it was possibly overkill, she actually didn't mind the extra protection for once. The bullet holes peppering her boat were a vivid reminder of what could happen. She couldn't explain why, but she felt strangely vulnerable lately. Like something was coming she wasn't prepared for.

With a sigh, she let the porthole curtain fall back in place. Praying for a match, she glanced back at the program sifting through facial images by the nanosecond. A few possibilities had come up in the low ten percentiles, but she needed more. She needed a *match*.

Hours later, her laptop dinged beside her on the bed, rousing her from slumber. Rolling over, she fumbled to slip her glasses on and stared back at the screen, her heart thwacking in her chest as she stared into Luke's eyes.

24

Sitting straight up in bed, Kate rubbed the haze of sleep from her eyes and stared back at the image.

It was Luke, going through customs in Toronto.

His hair was a different color, and it looked as if his nose had been broken a couple times, perhaps his jaw too, at least once, but it *was* him.

Cross-referencing the security records with the time the picture was taken, she determined he'd used the name Brad Walsh. *Brad Walsh . . .* That had been the name of a star football player during their time at UMD.

Who knew how many aliases he had, but she finally had a lead. She'd start searching other athletes' names from their time at the university and see if any popped.

She prayed so, though now that she'd found him, she couldn't fathom what he'd been doing all these years.

Her Malaysian contact, Hadi, had told her that Luke was not a man to be trifled with, a man to avoid if you wanted to live. That wasn't the Luke she knew, but neither was the one who'd clearly abandoned her.

● ● ●

Declan's cell rang a little after three a.m.

Kate?

He answered, trying to keep his voice low so as not to wake Tanner. "What's wrong, Kate?" She *never* called in the middle of the night.

"I found him."

Declan rubbed his tired eyes. "Found who?"

"Luke."

"What?" Had Luke made contact after all? A weight lifted off his chest. He wouldn't have to bear the burden of keeping that secret from his friends.

"I got a facial recognition match of him coming through customs in Toronto. It was clear. No doubt."

Oh.

"What's wrong?" Tanner asked, as she sat up.

"Sorry, I didn't mean to wake you," he said with a wince.

"Oh. Sorry . . ." Kate said on the other end of the line, her voice drenched with shock. "Who *is* that?"

Surely she knew he wouldn't spend the night with a woman. Not like *that*. Not until marriage.

"It's Tanner. We had an . . . incident tonight. I wanted to keep her close."

Tanner smiled.

"Are you guys okay?" Kate asked. "You've had a dangerous couple of days."

"Yes, we have. But we're fine. How are you?" She now knew for certain Luke was alive.

"I don't know. I knew in my heart he was alive, but it still doesn't seem real."

"I can imagine." He'd *seen* Luke and it still didn't feel real.

"Sorry for disturbing you," she said. "I'll let you go. I'm going to give Griffin a call next."

"Okay. See you tomorrow."

"You're headed back?" Kate asked.

"Yeah."

"All right. See you then."

He hung up and stared at his phone.

"What's going on? What's wrong with Kate?"

Had she woken as soon as his cell rang, heard him say Kate's name, or had she simply assumed . . . ? "She found a clear picture of Luke at the Toronto airport."

"Wow. She's good."

"Yeah. It's only a matter of time before she learns he's in the country."

"Are you going to tell her?"

He raked a hand through his hair. "I don't know."

Hesitation clung to Tanner. "Do you . . . still *care* for her?"

What a fool he was. He should have explained his lack of feelings beyond friendship for Kate so much sooner. Had Tanner been wondering all along? "No." He shook his head. "Not for a long time. Not since you."

"Really?" She asked with a soft smile.

"Really."

She bit her bottom lip and lay back down, leaving it at that. But that was a conversation they'd certainly need to have in more detail, along with so much more. He needed to tell her *everything*.

He longed to move to her side and kiss her, to *show* her how deeply he cared for her, but it was the middle of the night. They were sharing a room.

When he shared the entirety of his feelings for her, he didn't want it to be while they were under duress, or because they were in such close quarters, or after she'd just asked about another woman. He wanted her to know his feelings were *all* about her and the life he prayed they'd start together after they made it through this case alive. But that was where his focus had to remain for now—keeping the woman he loved alive and keeping his country safe.

After calling everyone to update them about Luke, Kate knew better than attempting to go back to sleep. Her nerve endings were alive and tingling with shock. The same shock everyone had expressed—everyone except Declan.

He'd seemed off. Though, to be fair, it sounded like he was in über-protection mode, which was awesome. Well, not that he and Tanner had experienced danger, but that he felt *that* way about Tanner. She could hear it in his voice, and she couldn't be happier for him, for *them*. They deserved love.

But *she* deserved love too.

She swallowed as pain washed over her so fiercely it was blinding.

If Luke was alive and traveling freely, it meant he'd walked away, stayed away, of his own volition. She couldn't shake the thought. The harder she tried, the more it repeated, burning like a flame of truth over and over again in her soul. He'd *left* her.

Needing to abate the crushing agony so she could breathe, she pulled her MacBook onto her lap and began working Haywood and the Markums' case. She started by digging into Lowell Brentwood's life, and as dawn crept over the horizon, moved on to Emmitt Powell's.

25

The Markums' house was in the affluent Hunt Valley area, not far from the Gilmore Inn.

They certainly weren't hurting for money, Griffin thought as he stepped from his truck on the cool October morning.

Jason had headed with Parker and Avery to question Lowell Brentwood about his fingerprints being on Haywood's steering wheel, and to determine whether his shoes matched any of the prints found at the reservoir. Earlier that morning the coroner had confirmed that Haywood had been murdered—and that indicated the Markums had likely been murdered as well. With the most to gain and the most to lose, Lowell Brentwood appeared to be their top suspect.

Needing to pursue every viable lead, Griffin had obtained a warrant to search the Markums' property. The best way to learn about a victim—or in this case, victims—was to see where they lived. He wanted to check their home computers for any correspondence regarding the money being stolen from their accounts.

The Markums were a professional couple with no children, so as anticipated, he found the house empty and eerily still. He made his way through the glass, marble, and cherrywood entryway, mirrors lining the back wall above a marble cutout where the Markums' mail was piled in a neat stack. A gold tray sat beside the mail, a set of keys and a watch nestled inside. A large gleaming crystal chandelier hung from the two-story open cathedral ceiling.

His cell rang as he headed for the Markums' home office. "Jason. Give me some good news."

"Lowell said he borrowed Haywood's car two days before the retreat when his car broke down at the office."

Griffin scowled. "Verifiable?"

"Unfortunately for our case against him, it checks out."

"What?"

"Lowell's secretary, Margaret, confirmed the incident. So did the towing company that towed Lowell's car to the dealer that day."

"Great."

"And it gets worse."

"Seriously?"

"None of Lowell's shoes match any prints taken from the scene. Parker and Avery are moving on to the Coveys, as they live closest to Lowell. I'm going to head over to you and can always reroute if Parker and Avery discover a match."

"Sounds good. I'm getting ready to go through their home office."

"See you in twenty."

Griffin hung up, only to have his cell ring again. "McCray," he answered. It was going to be one of those days, but he expected no less with all the irons they had in the fire.

"Detective McCray, this is Daniel Caldwell."

Haywood's lawyer. He'd left a voicemail for the man after obtaining his contact info from Haywood's estranged wife.

"Thanks for calling me back."

"Certainly. I can't tell you how sorry I am to hear about Haywood. We worked together for close to twenty years."

"We're all in shock," Griffin said.

"Carol gave me permission to share any details with you. She was still listed as the executor of Haywood's will."

"Really?"

"After thirty years of marriage, I guess he assumed he could trust her despite the separation."

Interesting.

"What would you like to know?" Caldwell asked.

"A number of things, but most importantly, who did Haywood leave the shares and control of his company to?"

Caldwell cleared his throat. "Haywood left

the shares equally split between his children, his life insurance to Carol . . ."

Again interesting. For a man who'd separated from his wife, he still appeared to care a great deal for her well-being. But that was just like Haywood, always looking out for the people around him.

". . . and his control of the company to Emmitt Powell."

That rocked Griffin back. "I'm sorry. Could you say that again?"

"He left control of the company to Emmitt Powell."

"Lowell Brentwood said he and Haywood agreed to leave control of the company to one another."

"Yes, and it *had* been left to him until two weeks ago."

"Two weeks?"

"Yes. I was quite surprised myself by the change, but Haywood was adamant about it."

"Did he say why?"

"I couldn't help myself. I had to ask . . ."

"And?"

"He said he wasn't sure he could trust his partner any longer."

"Did he say why?"

"No, and I didn't press. I could see he wasn't going to share beyond that, so I let it drop. I made the requested changes and Haywood came by last week to sign the final notarized documents."

"Do you know if Lowell or Emmitt were aware of the changes?" Griffin asked.

"He said he'd informed Emmitt of the change but would not be informing Lowell."

"I can imagine not. Thank you, Mr. Caldwell. You've been extremely helpful."

"I'm glad to be of any help. Please don't hesitate to call if you require any further information."

"I appreciate that."

Well, that was a crucial piece of information Emmitt Powell had neglected to mention during their interview. He phoned Jason, redirecting him along with Parker and Avery, to Emmitt Powell's house—the young associate had some explaining to do.

Declan and Tanner found a church to worship at in Houston, and it was a particularly God-timed sermon on David and Goliath. In this case, they were facing plenty of giants. It was a comforting reminder knowing God was the one in control and that they just had to follow His leading.

Their flight left at two, so they headed straight from the church to the airport, only to discover their flight had just been delayed by three hours.

Heading through security anyway, they found a nice restaurant in the terminal to have lunch. While waiting for their order to arrive, Declan pulled out *Die Trying*, the list of numbers, and deciphered series of words. Though the words didn't reveal anything to him, they didn't feel random either. He couldn't shake the discovery from his mind and was anxious to share it with Tanner.

Given the nature of the words—*Leader. Glock. Handcuffed. Message. Wrists. Barn. Agent.*—he'd decided to wait until after worshiping God before shifting back to the case that was becoming more intricate and frightening with each new clue.

Tanner leaned across the table, studying the words Declan had written out. "Which of Burke's cases do you think these refer to?"

Declan shook his head. "I don't know. It could be any of them . . . or none of them. That's what we've got to figure out."

Griffin called as the waitress brought their drinks. "Sorry." He hated to answer during lunch, but given Haywood's case, he needed to take the call.

"No problem." She smiled.

He returned her smile and winked as he answered. "Hey, Griffin. What's up?"

"Coach's autopsy results came in this morning," Griffin said, his voice hitching.

Declan's chest tightened. "And?"

"Haywood was murdered."

He exhaled. "I don't know whether to be relieved or angry." He looked out the restaurant window at the sun gleaming off the plane at the nearest gate, trying to wrap his mind around the fact that his first coach had been murdered.

"There was no good outcome," Griff said. "Not under these circumstances."

"Who's your top suspect?" He'd feel far better once they had the murderer behind bars.

"We were looking at Lowell Brentwood—as Haywood claimed he was setting him up—but things have shifted, so we're shifting with them."

"I trust you'll catch his killer."

"I pray so."

"Keep me posted."

"Will do."

Declan hung up, still half in shock.

"What happened?" Tanner asked, slipping her hair behind her ear.

"Autopsy results are in. Coach was murdered."

"Oh, Declan." She clutched his hand. "I'm so sorry."

He sunk back against his chair, oblivious to the crowds swirling around him. Coach had been *murdered*.

Griffin hung up with Declan and reached to open the Markums' front door on his way out to join Jason at Emmitt Powell's, only to have it open from the other side.

A woman near his age, with dark skin and hair, wearing a bright red dress stared back at him. "Who are you?" Her voice was bold and bouncy.

He flashed his badge. "Detective Griffin McCray, and you are . . . ?"

"I am—I *was*—Elizabeth's paralegal."

"Oh." He looked at the manila folder in her hand. Was she dropping papers off at the house on a Sunday? "How can I help you?"

"You can arrest Samuel Arlow for murdering my boss and her husband."

26

"Excuse me?" Griffin said, gaping at the woman dressed in red.

She pushed past him into the house, dropping her cherry-red bag on the entryway table and riffling through the mail, while she continued, "I heard what happened when I called the inn after not being able to reach Liz this morning. I can *always* reach Liz. Doesn't matter what time of day or the circumstances, she *always* picked up. When I couldn't reach her, I called the resort and spoke to the owner, who informed me that they'd been murdered."

Wow. Real subtle, Miss Ann.

"We *believe* they've been murdered," Griffin clarified.

She narrowed her eyes. "What do you mean *believe?*"

"Their bodies haven't been found." The divers had gone into the water first thing that morning.

"That's not surprising."

"Why's that?"

"Because when a person deals with the kind of criminals Liz did and you make a mistake like she did—you disappear." She extended

245

her hand, nails polished red to match her dress. "I'm Pauline Harper, by the way."

"Nice to meet you, Pauline. So what kind of criminals did Liz work with?"

His phone rang yet again.

Jason this time.

He thought about returning the call after he'd finished talking with Pauline, but something told him to pick it up. "Excuse me one moment," he said.

"Take your time. I'm going to water the plants. Come find me when you're done." She disappeared around the corner.

She was an interesting sort, but he instantly liked her. Shaking his head, he answered the call. "Hey, Jas, what's up?"

"You're not going to believe this."

"I was about to say the same thing to you."

"Oh?"

Griffin explained the limited but intriguing conversation he'd had with Pauline.

"That is interesting. I assume you're going to dig deeper?" Jason said.

"As soon as we hang up. What's your news?"

"Guess who we found at Emmitt Powell's residence when we arrived?"

"Lowell?"

"Try his secretary, Margaret."

"What? Why would Lowell's secretary be at Emmitt Powell's house?"

"Given the state of dishevelment we found them in, I'll give you one guess."

"Seriously?" Margaret was married and had to be nearly a decade older than Emmitt. Adultery was definitely one of the "big ten" Emmitt had mentioned earlier.

"Afraid so, and there's more."

"I'm scared to ask after that disturbing bomb."

"Thatcher called. Turns out that all the theft transactions that took place with Haywood's log-in did so on Lowell's computer after hours and, as he mentioned the other night, involved Emmitt Powell's clients too."

"Okay."

"The interesting part is that the theft actually started with Emmitt's clients."

"You don't think he . . . ?" Had Emmitt used Margaret to gain access to Lowell's and Haywood's log-in codes as well as Lowell's computer after hours?

"That's where the evidence seems to be leading . . ."

"But why?" The theft had been going on well before Haywood made the change to his will.

"I'm going to take them into the station for questioning. See if I can't find out. But I'm wondering if Emmitt started stealing from his own clients and then, to cover it up, started skimming from Haywood's. When the Markums called Haywood on it, Haywood believed Lowell was the only other person with access to his log-in, so naturally assumed his partner was setting him up."

"Haywood probably didn't even bother checking Emmitt's accounts."

"He'd have to have gone back quite a ways to find any of Emmitt's accounts skimmed. Thatcher said Emmitt likely found Haywood's clients far more wealthy and the skimming more easily hidden. Plus the evidence would point to Haywood or Lowell as the patsy if anyone discovered what was happening."

"I'm not sure which is more unexpected, your news or mine."

"I'd say we're about equal."

"Let me know how the questioning of Emmitt Powell proceeds. Oh, and call Kate—see where she's at with digging into his private life and finances."

"On it."

Griffin hung up and found Pauline in Elizabeth Markum's office, watering the rhododendron hanging by the east window. "So you were telling me about Elizabeth's clientele and why you fear one of them murdered her?"

"Liz represented the worst of society."

"Such as?"

"William Merrell."

"The drug dealer who runs half of Maryland's drug trade?"

"That's him. Everything outside of Max Stallings' territory is basically Merrell's. She got him off his second rape charge with just probation and time served."

"Why on earth did she choose to represent a man like William Merrell?" As a private defense lawyer she would have had her choice of clients.

Pauline rubbed her fingers and thumb together. "Money, pure and simple."

"High character, then?" he remarked, unable to fully suppress the revulsion brewing inside.

"I'm not saying I agreed with her choices, but Liz paid well, and I have three kids to provide for. . . ."

"When you entered, you mentioned Samuel Arlow?" He was a Black Guerilla leader— seriously upper gang echelon. "Didn't he just go to prison for life?"

"Yep."

It hit home. "And Elizabeth was his defense attorney?"

Pauline tapped her nose. "Here's a record of the death threats she received." She handed him the manila folder she'd set on Elizabeth's desk.

He flipped through them. Was it possible the murders were unrelated to the embezzlement at Haywood's firm?

should pull back some until he expressed more of his feelings on the matter. Though, to be fair, she hadn't expressed hers either.

"I talked to Kate while you were grabbing your Dunkin' at the airport," he said. "I called to ask her to check Galveston's port logs and cameras to see if we can pinpoint Steven Burke boarding the *Hiram* the day he sent the postcard from there."

"Good idea, and speaking of postcards . . ."

He arched a brow. "Yes?"

"Can I take a look at them again?" Curiosity had been nipping at her.

"Sure." He retrieved them from the folder in his carry-on bag. "Why?"

"You found codes in his book. It just makes me wonder if we're missing something in the postcards, and I got to thinking"—she placed the postcards one on top of the other—"if these worked in a similar way . . ."

She read them both up and down, but nothing stood out. She tried side by side, but again, nothing. *Hmm.* Good thing she had a three-and-a-half-hour flight ahead of her.

27

Griffin knew Samuel Arlow by reputation but had never met the man.

Despite the fact Samuel was in for life, his business, according to Griff's colleague in the gang unit, hadn't decreased or slowed one iota. He was simply running things from the pen, much like Max Stallings was.

Griff had just gotten word from Jason that, under the fear of being charged with murder, Emmitt Powell had cracked and confessed to stealing from company clients, but he strongly professed his innocence in any of the deaths. In addition, Lowell's secretary, Margaret, was able to confirm Emmitt's whereabouts for the night of the murders, having spent it with Emmitt at the resort.

Suddenly this conversation with Samuel Arlow held a lot more weight than it had minutes ago.

The corrections officer escorted Samuel—five eleven, just shy of two hundred pounds with dark hair and eyes and skin the color of a Hawaiian tan—into the lounge and cuffed him to the ring on the table.

"I don't think that is necessary," Griffin said.

The more relaxed he could make Samuel feel, the more likely he was to talk.

The officer disconnected the cuffs from the ring and exited the room, leaving him and Samuel Arlow alone.

"Who are you?" Samuel asked with a lift of his chin as he gave him the once-over. He was a few years younger than Griff, and if his "business" hadn't been extremely illegal in nature and of great harm to others, it would have been impressive for a man of his age to be running such a large and lucrative venture.

"Detective Griffin McCray," he said, eyeing up Samuel.

"Detective?" Samuel's shoulders squared.

"I was hoping to talk to you about Elizabeth Markum."

After a few choice words describing how he felt about Elizabeth Markum, Samuel finally cut off that thread and said, "Why? You here to charge me with something else? I'm already serving life thanks to her."

"So you admit to the death threats?"

He shrugged. "Just words, man."

"I got ya, but here's the problem," Griffin said. "She and her husband are missing."

Samuel leaned forward, his dark eyes narrowing. "What do you mean missing? She's supposed to be working on my appeal."

"Considering she wasn't able to keep you

out of prison and you've been sending death threats to her, why on earth would you want her handling your appeal?"

"Because I paid her well, and she owes me. The death threats are just incentive to make sure she sees the appeal through—that she works hard enough to get me off this time."

Shockingly, Griffin believed him. Samuel's body language and tells all indicated he was telling the truth. Which eliminated him from the suspect list.

"When you say they went missing . . . ?" Samuel prodded.

Griffin ran through the pertinent details.

Samuel shook his head. "I smell a rat. If she thought I was serious about my threats, I'm thinking she found a patsy and skipped town. That . . ."

Griffin ignored the string of expletives as he considered the man's theory.

When the Markums believed Haywood was the one stealing from them, they might have seen him as their way out of a dangerous situation. But that would mean they had killed Haywood in cold blood and then staged their own deaths. That was pretty extreme, but if a man like Samuel Arlow held your life in his hands and Elizabeth feared there was a chance she'd lose the appeal . . .

"Let me ask you something," Griffin said.

"Shoot, detective man."

"Do you think Elizabeth Markum or her husband is capable of murder?"

"I don't know the husband, but Elizabeth does whatever she needs to. That woman is cold. Why do you think I hired her?"

Griff sat back. Now they needed to reexamine the evidence in a totally new light.

A frustrating three hours after takeoff, Tanner finally lined the postcards up in what appeared to be the proper way, or her eyes finally opened to what had been right in front of her.

"Anything?" Declan asked.

She exhaled. "Maybe. Do you have a pencil?"

"Sure." He pulled one from his bag.

"May I?" she asked, holding it over the postcard.

"Sure. It's in pencil, and you aren't changing anything."

She set to work circling words and then scribbling them on her paper napkin. Going back, erasing, and reworking until she got the right words in the right order, and her napkin finally read:

> If I don't return tell Chuck it's because I
> did what he told me not to and they know.
> Really bad villain. Port at Baltimore soon.
> Tell good guys to meet us there.

Declan leaned over her shoulder as they touched down in Baltimore. "Brilliant, Tanner."

Warmth shot through her at his nearness, at his compliment, or perhaps both. . . . It didn't matter what it was, she just enjoyed his closeness and certainly didn't mind the compliment.

"I can't believe you got that from . . ."

If I don't have a lot to say it's because I'm so busy, but it's good guys here. They know me too. I think we're docking into the port of Baltimore soon. Meet there and bring my stuff.

"And . . ."

Return the DVD or tell Chuck to, though he'll just lecture me because I did what he told me not to and forgot to return it. The movie was great. Really bad villain, but the police get him at the end. Remember to tell Chuck so I don't get fined.

It'd taken her the entire flight and her love of word puzzles, but she'd cracked it. It felt good to be useful. "So it sounds like Burke knew Darmadi, or whatever alias he was traveling under, was either a terrorist or someone extremely dangerous, and Burke was hoping to get Samantha's attention to have Chuck and the Bureau meet them at the port when they docked in Baltimore."

"But Samantha didn't figure out the message in time."

"And they probably monitored incoming and outgoing mail, especially if they were on to him, which it sounds like they might have been since he said 'they know me.' "

"And that's why they killed him?"

"I'm guessing, or when they got close to port and Burke realized no one was there to help, he tried to detain Darmadi by himself, thinking he could enlist the captain's help."

"Not knowing the captain was corrupt and well aware of who he was smuggling."

"Right. Darmadi knows Burke's an agent or some kind of law enforcement, so while Burke's talking to the captain, Darmadi approaches from behind and shoots him. The first mate freaks out and Darmadi shoots him too, then conks the captain over the head, stages the scene, and flees in a fast raft. All speculation, of course, but it fits with the findings Parker collected and the scenario he presented based on gunfire trajectory and evidence on the scene. We can run it by him when we return."

"Great idea."

He prayed the answers came fast.

"You know . . ." She shifted to face him

better. "Burke's message seems to indicate Chuck knew what he was planning to do."

"True. Did Chuck lie to us about knowing, or when Burke tried to tell him, maybe he told Burke to focus on their job, meaning he wasn't interested in finding out what Burke was onto, so Burke didn't go into details?"

"I'm going to give him the benefit of the doubt and say the latter. Given the dynamics between the two, it wouldn't surprise me if that's how it went."

"I'll give Chuck a call and see what explanation he has."

28

"Well?" Tanner asked after Declan hung up with Chuck Franco and they'd settled back into their SUV.

"He said he knew Burke was headed out, but he told Burke to focus on the job. *Their* job. He had no idea Burke was boarding the *Hiram*, only that he was following another lead not related to their job."

"So Franco believed it had nothing to do with counterintelligence or counterterrorism."

"That's right, and it wasn't tied directly to any of their cases."

"So you believe him?"

"I think so."

"Did you tell him you're hoping to send Parker to run Burke's place?"

"No. Burke's folks agreed to allow Parker to process his apartment, so we're looking at it as an unofficial family request. If he finds anything of note, maybe I'll share it with Franco."

"Speaking of sharing. . . ." She intertwined her fingers with his as his right hand rested on the console between them. "Are you thinking of telling Kate about Luke?"

"I don't know how I can't, but Luke said it would put her in more danger, and I don't want any of us in more danger."

"Let's pray for guidance and see what God says," Tanner suggested as they pulled into CCI's lot and parked.

Declan appreciated the suggestion. He desperately needed the Lord's leading.

He poured out his heart, asking God for direction, and after Tanner prayed, he felt confident Luke was telling the truth. Anyone who learned of his presence was at risk in a war that was further reaching and far deeper than Declan ever imagined.

But how on earth was he going to look Kate in the eye and not tell her that he'd seen Luke? Talked to him? How Luke had taken out a hit man sent to kill them?

"You okay?" Tanner asked, clasping his hand.

He nodded. "I just pray I'm doing the right thing by not telling Kate."

"That's your call. I trust your decision."

"Thanks." He squeezed her hand before climbing out of the car and moving around to open her door. She stepped out, and the confidence shining in her eyes as she looked up at him, grounded him.

Taking a steadying breath, he held the glass door to CCI open and she stepped inside. He followed quickly behind and heard a round of greetings, but none more exuberant than Kate's as she held Luke's facial recognition picture out to him. It *was* Luke. Kate had found him. The image didn't exactly match the man who had been in their hotel room last night—in the photograph he had black hair, but in Declan and Tanner's room Luke's hair had been brown.

Declan squinted. And were those colored contacts? Luke's eyes had been blue, but in the photograph they looked green.

"Can you believe it?" Kate said.

He swallowed, praying again for guidance, and once again feeling the need to protect Kate and everyone else present, at least until he understood the full magnitude of what they were dealing with. "It's crazy," he said.

"Now I just have to find where he went from North Dakota," Kate said.

"North Dakota?" He frowned.

"Yeah. I ran with UMD athletes' names from our time there as possible aliases and got a hit. Luke crossed from Canada into the U.S. at North Dakota's border as Devin Clarke. Now I just have to figure out where he went from there."

"I have no doubt you will." When Kate set her mind to something . . . which meant sooner or later she'd realize they'd both been in Houston. Luke should have known better than

261

to return to the States if he didn't want to be found by Kate. She was too good.

"Thanks." She smiled, and he felt even more like a heel for not telling her about Luke.

Griffin eyed him curiously.

Great. The best "reader" in the room knew he was purposely omitting information.

"So, Park," Declan said, shifting, or at least hoping to shift, the attention, "how would you feel about a trip to Houston?"

Parker arched a brow.

Declan went on to explain everything they'd learned about Burke and how he really would love for Parker and Avery to run Burke's apartment.

"Of course," Parker and Avery said nearly in unison. "We need to finish helping Griffin rerun the crime scenes tomorrow, but we can head out Tuesday morning."

"Awesome. Thanks."

"Food's here," Kate said, grabbing the bags from the delivery man with Tanner's help.

Parker squinted. "Those don't look like pizza boxes."

Avery winked, moving to help in the kitchen. "Great observation."

"Chipotle?" Griffin said. "Whose call was that?"

"You like Mexican," Finley said. "You were all talking, so we made the call."

Griffin lifted his chin. "Who's *we?*"

"Us," Kate said, indicating her and Avery.

Griffin laughed. "I told you they're going to gang up on us every chance they get."

They all grabbed plates of tacos and burritos, and settled on the U-shaped sectional and surrounding chairs—except Parker, who took his food to the lab to continue his work. Once he started on something, it was nearly impossible to get him to stop.

"What's the latest with Coach's case?" Declan asked.

"We're having to reexamine the evidence in a whole new light," Griffin said.

"Why? What's up?"

Griffin explained everything through his interview with Samuel Arlow.

Declan sat back. "That's crazy."

"Yeah." Griffin sighed. "But my gut says it's the right direction."

"Speaking of directions," Parker said, stepping out from his lab with the bug Declan had brought back from Steven Burke's apartment in his hand.

Declan straightened. "Yes?"

"It's a match for the bug removed from Mira's apartment."

"Meaning?"

"Meaning both Russian, the same design, make, and model."

So Houston and Baltimore were almost certainly connected, and Declan bet Ebeid controlled both.

Still in shock from the conversation at CCI, Declan settled on the floor of his living room, his back to his couch as he replayed all the threads of the case through his mind, trying not to let Coach's case seep through. Of course he cared, but he needed all his energy focused on the case at hand. The last two days had been exhausting. He was tired to his bones.

Gaining a glimpse into Steven Burke's personal life, seeing Luke, learning that Houston and Baltimore were tied together—both most likely under Ebeid's control . . .

It made him wonder exactly how vast and far-reaching Ebeid's network was.

Kate finally reached the point of exhaustion and headed home. The guys would kill her for not calling Declan or Parker, who both lived close by, to walk her home. There were threats all around them, and she needed to be careful, but she was never one to bend to intimidation.

And she craved the solitude, the still of the night, the sound of the water lapping against the ships' hulls. She waved to the patrolman Declan had stationed in the main lot and headed down the metal grate path to the third row, noting the light outage three rows over. She'd have to let Caleb, the maintenance manager, know. The wind shifted slightly, and a scent caught her attention. Aftershave, perhaps?

She squinted in the darkness. *Is someone there?*

"Hello?" she called, slipping the hair from her eyes. She pulled it back into a quick bun, but the wind kept whipping strands across her face.

No answer.

Maybe whoever it was had already gone inside or had their portholes open, sending the woodsy, citrusy aftershave on the salty breeze.

She waited a moment longer, saw no movement, heard no sound, so she turned down her row and climbed on the *Barefoot*.

Stepping inside, she glanced at Tanner's dark room. Tanner was bunking in Declan's guest room until the case was over. She smiled, loving how protective he was of her. She'd just pray Declan stayed out of his own way. He tended to overanalyze, to try to bring logic to something that was beyond logic. Love was the most powerful emotion in heaven and on earth. God sent His own Son to die for humanity out of His great love. Jesus willingly went to the cross out of love. Love defied logic, defied hatred, defied division. She'd seen it over and over again. Her love for Luke defied all logic.

He'd been gone more than seven years now, and she still loved him as strongly as she had the day he left. What a fool she was.

She grabbed a Snapple tea from the fridge, closed the door, and leaned against it. She gazed out the window and thought she saw the slightest movement. Probably just a flag moving in the wind.

She set her Snapple down and pulled the curtains.

Go to bed, Kate.

Luke had promised himself he wouldn't do it—he wouldn't go see her—but he couldn't help himself. Declan's comment had given him an ounce of hope that she might still hold feelings for him, but she didn't know the monster he'd become, what he'd been ordered to do time and again.

He turned away, his back to the wind. He was being ridiculous and endangering Kate at the same time. He'd lectured Declan about bringing Kate into his sphere, but here he was, practically at her front door. If he truly still loved her, which he believed with all his might he did, the best thing he could do was walk away.

29

On Monday morning, Declan approached Professor Malcolm Warner's office on the campus of his alma mater—the University of Maryland, College Park. Tanner had kindly offered to stay at the Bureau office, wade through their paperwork, and update their boss about their time in Houston, along with their case progress. They needed Alan to approve their moving forward with the investigation, and she had a natural way with people that made her more than capable of that task. He greatly missed her at his side, though, and now wondered what it would feel like once Lexi returned and he and Tanner were no longer partners.

His chest constricted. He loathed the thought of Tanner not being at his side.

She'd become an integral part of his life. While he might not be able to continue working with her as his partner, he *could* pursue a relationship with her, and the conscious decision to take that next, concrete step forward with her filled him with joy. He wouldn't *just* express his feelings and hope for the best—he'd ask her to stay by his side from now on. Because the

handed Declan his, and took a seat in one of the chairs opposite him. "So tell me about these cases."

"Before I get to that, I should tell you . . ." He still couldn't believe it. "Kate found Luke."

Malcolm choked on his coffee, spilling it on his arm.

Declan grabbed a napkin from the desk and handed it to Malcolm. "Sorry, I should have waited until you'd finished your sip before I dropped that bomb."

Malcolm's eyes narrowed. "What do you mean Kate *found* Luke?"

"She hired a contact overseas and got proof of life from him a little less than two months back." Had it really been that long since he'd last visited Malcolm?

"Luke's alive?" Color flushed Malcolm's cheeks.

"I know." Declan raked a hand through his hair. "I can hardly believe it." He so wanted to tell Malcolm everything, but Luke had asked him not to tell *anyone,* so instead he stuck to sharing only what Kate had learned.

"Where is he?" Malcolm asked, dabbing the coffee from his sleeve.

"He was in Malaysia, then Toronto, now in the States."

Malcolm's eyes widened. "He's here?"

"I don't know if he's actually *here* in

Baltimore." Though he had a strong suspicion it might have been his next stop after Houston.

Malcolm set his cup down and leaned forward. "You seem upset."

Declan swallowed. "Just wondering *why* he's been gone all these years . . . and why he's back now." It's the question that had plagued him ever since he looked into Luke's eyes in Houston.

"Of course. How could we not wonder? But let's move on to your cases. Tell me about them," Malcolm said, shifting topics rather abruptly. Especially considering *who* they were discussing, but he supposed they did have two cases to discuss, and Malcolm did have a meeting after lunch, which meant limited time.

An hour later, the office door closed and the one Luke was behind opened. "You let her find you?" Malcolm seethed.

Luke stepped out into the office, thankful Declan hadn't said anything about Houston. Malcolm would have killed him. Quite literally. If only Declan and the gang knew the truth about Malcolm . . . "I can't help it if Katie's persistent."

"You are too good to let some bloodhound she sent locate you." His eyes narrowed. "Did you want to be found?"

"Of course not. It was a heated time. I had greater concerns."

"Than them *knowing* you're alive?"

"Is that such a bad thing?" He was tired of the silence, of the lies, of not living a real life.

"Oh, please don't tell me you've gone soft after all these years."

"I'm here to do my job." What happened afterward was up for debate.

"Then do your job and let this nonsense about your friends die. Just as your friendships have."

Luke prayed that wasn't the case, but how could they not have after what he'd done to them?

"Let's run the scenario as if the Markums did as Samuel Arlow suggested," Griffin said as he, Jason, Parker, and Avery stood in the Markums' guest room at the Gilmore Inn on Monday morning. The rooms had been cordoned off as crime scenes until the evidence had finished being processed.

Until Griffin had learned what Elizabeth Markum did for a living and the type of clientele she represented—particularly the one she'd let down—he never would have anticipated the Markums being the murderers rather than the victims. However, taking all the factors into play, frighteningly enough, it *was* a viable option. And at the moment, it was their best one. He just prayed the rest of the team didn't think he was crazy.

"Okay, so what are we looking for?" Parker asked.

"Hear me out on this. Elizabeth Markum failed to get a major gang leader acquitted. He's been threatening to kill her if she didn't get him off at appeal. Maybe she feared she wouldn't be able to do it. Soon after, she and her husband discover they are being robbed by their accounting firm. They believe Haywood is the one responsible. They confront him. He purports innocence, but they assume he's lying and so they set plans in motion. . . ."

"To stage their own deaths and frame Haywood," Parker said, thankfully following his logic.

"But they couldn't leave Haywood alive, because he'd claim he was innocent of their murders, and there was the chance the truth could come out," Avery continued.

"So they killed Haywood and staged their own murders," Jason concluded. He paused. "That's cold."

"If that's the case, then why the finger at Loch Raven?" Avery asked.

"Finding that actually makes more sense in light of this scenario. Think about it. If you wanted to prove you were dead, that your body had been disposed of even if it was never found . . ."

"Ewww. He cut off his own finger?" Avery's face scrunched.

"Or his wife did it," Griffin said, not putting a thing past her at this point.

"So where are they?" Avery asked.

"That's what we have to figure out," Griffin said. "Let's rework the room with this scenario in mind."

"All right. . . ." Parker rubbed his hands together. "So the Markums go to Haywood's room after everyone is asleep, probably pretending they want to work things out. But as soon as Haywood lets them in, they hold him at gunpoint"—Parker exhaled—"having fired the gun earlier in the evening so as to make it look as if it had been used to kill them when we ran the gunpowder residue test. They couldn't risk firing it in Haywood's room, or anywhere else in the hotel, because it could leave conflicting evidence behind."

"Right," Jason said. "So they hold Haywood at gunpoint, force him to write the suicide note admitting to murdering them, put him in the tub, and cut him to make it look like a suicide—but they didn't consider that they needed to slice in the correct direction and angle."

"Or the amount of pressure," Parker added.

"Then . . . they stash the gun in his room and return to theirs, staging it to appear as if Haywood killed them before disposing of their bodies and committing suicide."

"I imagine they drove Haywood's car to the hiking lot with John riding in the trunk, at some point having cut off his finger—hence the blood and trace evidence we discovered," Parker said. "They placed the finger where it would suggest they'd been dumped over the falls and drove Haywood's car and one they must have stashed at the trailhead back to the resort, leaving Haywood's, and taking off in the stashed car."

"Both cars registered to the Markums are accounted for," Jason said, scrolling through his case notes on his iPhone.

"I'd bet they bought a getaway car for cash somewhere," Griffin said.

"Okay," Parker said. "Now the big question is . . . where'd they drive it to?"

"I'm guessing they wanted to disappear quickly," Griffin said. "Driving to Canada or Mexico takes time and affords a lot of opportunity for them to be seen at motels, restaurants, traffic cameras . . . and the airport has much higher security."

"So what are you thinking?" Parker asked.

"Let's check the cruise terminal. If a ship left Saturday, they could have used fake IDs, maybe even changed their appearance before boarding the ship. The popular routes out of the Port of Baltimore take them to Canada or the Caribbean. I'd put my money on the Caribbean."

"Why?" Avery asked.

"Because from there they could arrange transport to South America or Mexico," Griffin said.

"Perhaps even Cuba," Jason added. "Non-extradition treaty and all."

Griffin nodded. "Exactly."

"If that's the case, their getaway car would still be in the cruise terminal lot," Parker said.

"So they have been planning this for a while," Avery said.

"I can't believe I'm saying this, but that's how it's looking." Jason shook his head and pulled his phone out of his pocket.

"So we run every car in the cruise terminal lot?" Griffin said.

"Not necessarily," Parker said. "I have tire tread marks from the trailhead lot. That will help narrow the number down, and provide a match when we find the right one."

"We're going to need a warrant, and we'll need to talk to the authorities at the terminal," Griffin said. "If we get lucky, they might have used their real names, but I expect the Markums are traveling under false identities."

"I just checked," Jason said, lifting his phone. "A Carnival cruise ship headed for the Caribbean left the Port of Baltimore Saturday at noon."

"I bet that's it," Griffin said, feeling it in his

gut. "Send the Markums' pictures over to the terminal and the cruise ship, though I'm sure they have altered their appearance. They've taken too many careful steps to neglect an easy one like that. Let's get started with requesting the warrant, searching the cars in the lot, and sending the Markums' pictures to the ship's captain—alerting him that there may be some cosmetic variations."

"I'll also send out a full alert to all traffic cameras, airports, and bus terminals," Jason said. "Just in case they went a different route. But I think you've nailed it with the cruise ship."

"It's just the easiest way out of the country. Cruise agents are far less scrupulous about checking identification than TSA agents at the airport." But it was good to cover all their bases. If the Markums had murdered Coach— which the facts were strongly indicating—Griffin *would* catch them, no matter how long it took. He wasn't giving up until Haywood's killers were behind bars.

30

Declan waited in the meeting room for the guard to bring in the former captain of the *Hiram*, Randal Jackson. He was thankful Tanner hadn't accompanied him for this visit. He didn't want Jackson anywhere near her. He did not doubt she could easily hold her own, but Jackson didn't deserve to breathe the same air as her. He was a pig.

Finally, the guard escorted Jackson into the room in shackles. Committing treason by smuggling a known terrorist into your own country came with stiff penalties—not to mention the human trafficking charges on top of it. Jackson had copped a plea on the smuggling and human trafficking. What else could he do? They'd caught him red-handed. But he still claimed he hadn't known who Anajay Darmadi was.

Jackson appraised Declan with the same smug look he'd had the day of his arrest. "Agent Grey, how nice of you to visit me where you put me."

"*I* put you? You put yourself here by committing treason and human trafficking."

"Same old story, I see."

It took all the restraint Declan possessed not to lunge across the Formica table and throttle the man. "The truth doesn't change." He'd learned that invaluable lesson as a youngster in Miss Barb's Sunday school class.

Jackson laughed. "That's a good one. Please don't tell me that's why you're here. Do you think I'll change my statement—that you'll get something out of me?"

"I'm here because of Steven Burke."

Jackson rolled his head back. "Seriously? When are you going to let this go?"

"When I have the truth."

Jackson leaned forward, resting his cuffed hands on the tabletop. "When are *you* going to realize that *isn't* going to happen?"

"Why? Because whoever hired you to smuggle Darmadi into this country will have you killed if you talk?"

The truth of it washed over Jackson's face, but he continued his oppostion. "What does Darmadi have to do with Burke?"

"Burke knew about Darmadi—at least that he was extremely dangerous—and he tried to get the word out."

Jackson shook his head. "No, he didn't."

"Let me guess, you monitored everyone's correspondence?"

Jackson didn't respond, but he didn't have to. Once again, his face said it all.

"Well, he got a message out," Declan said.

Jackson snorted. "A lot of good it did him."

"Let me ask you a question . . ." Declan leaned forward, his forearms resting on the table. "When did you figure out Burke was a federal agent?"

Jackson leaned in, looked around, and then lowered his voice. "You really think I'm going to admit to knowing anything of the sort?"

"You might not, but Burke's bunkmate probably knows a lot more than what he said when we first questioned him. And guess what? He's living in Baltimore. Seems after your crew was dissembled, several decided to make Baltimore their home port."

Upon Malcolm's wise suggestion, Declan had checked up on the whereabouts of the *Hiram*'s crew, and it turned out to be a great one. He'd found Burke's bunkmate, Carlos Santali, and a number of other crew members to be quite within his reach.

A small vein in Jackson's right temple flickered. "Carlos won't tell you anything."

Declan sat back with a smile. He'd hit a nerve. "We'll see about that."

Panic flashed across Jackson's face.

Now he just needed to get to Carlos Santali

before any of the men Jackson was working with got a warning call from Jackson.

"Make sure Jackson doesn't make any calls out," he said to the guard as he stood.

"You can't do that. It's my right." Jackson tugged against the guard's hold as he hauled Jackson to his feet.

"You'll have to take that up with the warden," the guard said to Declan, wrangling Jackson back under firm control and out of the room, letting the door close behind them.

Declan rushed to speak with the warden, who agreed to suspend Jackson's phone rights for an hour. Just long enough for him to reach Carlos Santali.

Carlos Santali lived in a run-down apartment building owned by none other than Max Stallings. Max really was a piece of work, and the knowledge that the man housed crewmen who had smuggled Stallings' "refugees" gave Declan even more leverage on him.

A guy smoking out on the stoop directed Declan to Carlos's door. A lean, short, dark-haired Carlos Santali opened the door, took one look at Declan, and tried to shut it fast.

"Not gonna happen," Declan said, jamming his foot in the opening and shoving inward. Santali's small frame was no match for Declan's sturdy build.

"They'll kill me just for you being here," Carlos said, his eyes as panicked as his tone.

"Then get your stuff. Let's go."

Hesitation and anxiety mingled in Carlos's dark eyes. "Go where?"

"Someplace safe. You have my word."

Carlos hesitated, and then moved to pack a duffel. He flung it over his shoulder, and they headed for the door.

Lennie Wilcox was waiting for them at the bottom of the stairs, no doubt tipped off by the guy on the stoop. Carlos turned to run, but Declan grabbed ahold of his arm. "I've got you," he said firmly under his breath, and Carlos stilled in his hold.

Lennie's eyes narrowed. "Where you taking him?"

"In for questioning."

Carlos wisely remained silent.

Lennie's jaw shifted slightly to the right, his piercing gaze darting to Carlos, who looked down at his feet.

Declan boldly moved forward, leading a trembling Carlos past Lennie and his thugs, out to his SUV, praying no one shot at his vehicle or passenger.

He'd lost one witness, Jari Youssef, from the Islamic Cultural Institute, two months ago. He wasn't about to lose another one. He'd taken measures to ensure that.

He loaded Carlos into the backseat and climbed into the driver's seat. Locking the doors, he started the engine and pulled away.

"It's going to be okay—I promise," Declan said, reassuring Carlos.

"Why are you taking me in for questioning? I didn't do nothing."

Declan glanced in the rearview mirror. "I need to ask you about your last bunkmate aboard the *Hiram*—Steven Burke."

Sweat beaded on Carlos's brow. "They'll kill me for talking."

"That's why we're going to set you up someplace nice where they can't find you. Give you a fresh start—a far better job and a decent home."

"You mean like that witness program?"

"Yes. Witness protection. You tell me what you can about Burke, and I'll call the U.S. Marshals. You'll be on a plane to a secure location before the night's out."

"And Jackson, Stallings, Lennie . . . and the man in charge won't find me?"

"The man in charge?"

"The Egyptian dude who comes to meet with Stallings—or did before Stallings went to prison."

"He came to your apartment building to speak with Stallings?"

"Yeah. I overheard Lennie saying it was a

secure place for them to speak. There were multiple entrances in and out of the building and a soundproof room in the basement. I know because it's my job to clean the lower level daily when I'm not out to sea."

"And when you are at sea?"

"I'm a crew member. I do whatever the captain orders. Some trips I'm on the ship. Other ones I'm here."

"Which captain are you working for now?"

"Captain Jose Augero of the *Bainbridge*."

So Max had corrupted another captain. Sad, but not surprising. "What about Augero? Is he from Baltimore?"

"No. South America, but I think he's an American citizen."

"Is the ship's home port Baltimore?"

"Yes."

"Let me guess—it primarily runs between southeast Asia and Baltimore?"

He nodded. "And sometimes Galveston."

"Galveston?" Declan sat forward, adrenaline sparking inside. So they *were* connected.

Carlos nodded.

"And does he smuggle refugees and terrorists in?"

Carlos hesitated. "You promise you will get me away from here?"

"Yes, Carlos, you have my word. Just tell me everything you know."

He shuddered, as if forcing himself to speak. "It's different based on location."

"How so?"

"Galveston gets people and drugs. Baltimore the same, but also the higher-ups and merchandise."

"The higher-ups?"

"Men like Darmadi."

Terrorists. "And the merchandise?"

"Weapons."

Declan's chest squeezed, though he shouldn't have been surprised, given the men they were dealing with. "Weapons?"

"I helped load crates of them last time."

"What kind of weapons are we talking about?"

"IEDs and line charges in the crate I packed. There was also a different kind of weapon I didn't recognize that went into the last two crates—or maybe it was just parts to something. I didn't get a good look."

"How many crates total?"

"Six on that trip."

Declan's jaw tightened. "And the weapons only come to Baltimore?"

"On all the trips I've been on, yes."

Declan swallowed. A local growing extremist cell armed with extensive weapons—*beyond terrifying*.

They needed to locate the terrorists and

weapons, or at the very least determine their target or targets and their planned deployment date and time. Otherwise they were mice waiting for a cat to pounce. "How does the ship pass customs with that sort of cargo?" It didn't make sense unless they were dealing with corrupt MPA officers, and he prayed that wasn't the case.

"I don't know, but it always does. They're good at hiding the cargo."

No one was *that* good if the ship was thoroughly checked.

He pulled into the Bureau's garage, thankful for a trip without incident. Either Lennie wasn't worried about Carlos talking, or Max didn't order hits on federal agents' cars. He guessed the Egyptian whom Carlos mentioned was Dr. Khaled Ebeid, head of the Islamic Cultural Institute of the Mid-Atlantic. He, on the other hand, would have no qualms about trying to take out Carlos.

But apparently Ebeid was not aware Declan had Carlos—or hadn't had time to accomplish an ambush attempt. It was possible they believed he had nothing worrisome to tell, but Declan suspected otherwise.

The question was, were Stallings and Ebeid working together or simply side by side?

He'd have a great conversation starter for Max Stallings when he visited him at prison later today or tomorrow, depending on when he and Carlos wrapped up.

He needed to show Carlos Dr. Ebeid's picture. See if Carlos could identify him as the Egyptian man who visited Stallings. Even if he did, it didn't necessarily prove anything illegal, but at least he would know if Stallings and Ebeid were in business together. Then he could determine which way to move forward with the investigation. If Carlos identified Ebeid, he'd be paying Dr. Ebeid another visit. He could only imagine how much Dr. Ebeid would love that. Declan was the thorn in the man's side, and he couldn't have been prouder of the fact. He'd be as much of a nuisance as he could until he had Ebeid behind bars.

Declan moved around and opened Carlos's door, but Carlos hesitated, his gaze darting about the parking structure. He must believe Stallings' or Ebeid's reach was extremely far if he was worried they'd get him inside the Bureau's garage. "It's okay," he said.

Carlos swallowed and stepped out.

"Carlos, how many 'higher-ups' were transported on your last voyage into Baltimore?"

Carlos thought for a few seconds. "Five that I saw."

Declan's stomach dropped. Five more terrorists in Baltimore.

286

"You want to find who killed the Markums, check into Samuel Arlow."

Did the Markums' deaths have nothing to do with Haywood and everything to do with Samuel Arlow? If that was the case, then who killed Haywood, and why frame him for the Markum murders?

Or had someone beat Arlow to the punch?

His brain raced in a thousand directions, trying to put each piece of the murky puzzle in place.

Tanner settled into the middle seat for the return flight home, insisting on giving Declan the aisle seat. That way, once everyone was seated, he could stretch out his long legs.

He was such an attractive man, and she wasn't just thinking physical attractiveness—which he had in spades—but who he was, the *real* him she was finally getting to see after a year of struggling to get him to let down his guard. She wasn't sure why he'd chosen now, but she'd take it. She was falling hard for Declan Grey. The only question was, did he feel the same?

Sure, he'd kissed her and expressed a level of caring, but certainly not to the depth she was experiencing. Part of her, the cautious part, which was silent the majority of the time, popped to the surface and wondered if she fact was he couldn't imagine life without her anymore.

Reaching Malcolm's office, he knocked on the closed door, hoping the professor was in. He should have called ahead.

"Declan," Malcolm said, opening the door a moment later. "I didn't expect to see you today."

"Sorry for the intrusion."

"Nonsense. Come in. You know you are always welcome. How are the rest of the guys?"

"Doing well. Busy with a case."

"Ah, so you've come to talk through a case?"

"Cases, actually."

"Well then, good thing I don't have a meeting until after lunch. Please," he said, gesturing to the sofa, "sit down."

"Thanks."

"Cup of coffee? I've got this new K-something machine."

"Sure. That'd be great."

The room was a typical college professor's domain. Oak cabinets, shelves brimming with textbooks and reading material, a cluttered desk, a couch, and two chairs. Apparently, becoming head of the department had its perks—a larger office for one. Professor Warner had been a mentor to Declan—to all the guys—during their years at UMD. Declan had always loved dissecting cases with him.

Malcolm made them both a cup of coffee,

Father in heaven, what are they planning? I desperately need your help. Equip me to solve these cases and protect this city. Amen.

31

It took less time than anticipated to check the cars in the cruise terminal lot. The cruise personnel had permits in their windows, which eliminated a fair number of vehicles, and the majority of passengers had been dropped off by taxis or hotel shuttles, which left only a few dozen cars of non-cruise personnel in the lot. Based on tire treads recovered from the trailhead, they knew they were looking for a medium-size car, not a large truck or SUV.

Beginning at one end of the lot, Parker worked his way systematically through, while Griffin and Jason ran the plates.

An hour later, Parker stood by a silver Toyota Corolla. "I think we have a winner. The tire tread is a match for one taken at the Merryman trailhead."

"Well, I think we all know why the divers came up empty-handed," Griffin said, having received a call that the search had been discontinued.

Jason checked his notes for the vehicle plates they'd run. "Let's see . . . that one was registered to Lyle Manning at AutoSource."

"Why am I not surprised?" Griffin said. While AutoSource appeared to be a legitimate auto dealer on the surface, it had a reputation for being a chop shop.

"I'll pay Lyle a visit. Show him the Markums' photos, and see if he recalls selling them a vehicle," Jason said.

Griffin nodded. "Keep me posted."

"Same," Jason said with a lift of his chin.

An hour later, Parker and Avery finished processing the car. They had fingerprints and several hair samples, the lower four inches of each were synthetic—all of them dark, unlike Elizabeth's shoulder-length blond hair. If any portion of them were identified as Elizabeth's, it would prove that she'd dyed her hair and added extensions, as Griffin surmised.

Returning to CCI, Parker was able to confirm a strand taken from the car matched DNA in the hair strands found in Elizabeth's brush at the resort. He also matched fingerprint sets in the car as both John and Elizabeth Markum's. Now knowing the new color and length of Elizabeth's hair, they could alter the photo they'd sent to the ship. And after Jason assured Lyle Manning that he was at AutoSource only to find out who purchased the Corolla, the man ID'd Elizabeth Markum as the woman he'd sold the car to for cash.

Carlos had already provided Declan with more than enough vital information in the case—

he not only *needed* to be in witness protection, he *deserved* to be. Upon entering the office and after getting Carlos settled in an interrogation room, Declan contacted the U.S. Marshal's office, and then headed to grab them both a cup of coffee. The Marshals were processing the transfer and would send a team over to take possession of Carlos as soon as Declan was finished questioning him.

He passed Tanner in the hall, his hands full of steaming mugs.

"Hey." She smiled. "Saw you brought a suspect in."

"More like a witness. You want to join me?" Tanner would be a soothing element for the remainder of the questioning. Plus, she had a gentle way of garnering answers that highly impressed him.

"Absolutely. I've about had all the paperwork I can handle."

"How'd it go with Alan?"

"Surprisingly well. He said to just keep him posted."

"Awesome. I knew you'd do a great job." He longed to lean in and kiss her, but the Bureau office was most certainly not the place.

"How'd your day go?" she asked.

He brought her up to speed as they made the long walk down the far hall to the room Carlos was sequestered in.

Horror filled her eyes at the information Carlos had provided, and he wished he could provide comfort, assure her he'd get the terrorist cell before they could carry out whatever they had planned, but there were so many unknowns at play. He was reminded, yet again, of how desperately they needed God's help and guidance.

They relieved Agent Tim Barrows from his post guarding the interrogation room door and stepped inside. Carlos's wary eyes darted to Tanner.

"Hi, Carlos," Tanner said.

"This," Declan said, setting down a cup of steaming coffee in front of Carlos, "is Tanner Shaw. She's a counselor with the Bureau."

Carlos looked skeptical. "Counselor?"

"She's been working this case with me."

"Oh right. You were with the refugees on the *Hiram*." The hesitancy on Carlos's face eased slightly. "I thought you looked familiar."

"Is it okay if I join you two?" she asked, letting Carlos feel a bit in control.

Carlos thought it over a moment, and then nodded.

"Thank you," she said, taking a seat next to Declan.

Declan pulled a handful of sugar and creamer packets from his trouser pockets and dropped them on the table. "I wasn't sure how you took your coffee," he said to Carlos.

"Always black," Carlos said. "They don't bother with sugar or cream for the crew."

Of course.

Declan looked to Tanner. "Can I get you anything?"

"No, thank you. I'm fine."

"Okay then," Declan said. "We were discussing the five men who were recently brought over from . . . Malaysia, I'm guessing, as you said southeast Asia."

Carlos nodded.

"You also said they were treated as Anajay Darmadi had been—receiving special treatment as highly honored guests on the ship."

"Yes. Except whenever we made port, then they hid in the special cargo hold."

"And when you reached Baltimore . . . ?"

"They disembarked onto a fast raft when we were still a ways out, and then the fast raft was replaced after we were in port."

"Replaced by whom?"

"Lennie Wilcox and some men."

"And that didn't draw suspicion?"

"Not to the customs officials who always were attached to our ship."

"You always had the same customs officials?"

Carlos nodded.

The ones Stallings or Ebeid had in their pockets. Knowing how the port ran, Declan figured it was more likely Stallings' influence.

He would also need to get a sketch artist in for Carlos to provide a description of the customs agents. Even if Carlos didn't have direct contact with them, he should be able to at least give a basic description—but that could wait for a moment. He wanted to finish the current vein of questioning first.

"How far out were you when they left in the fast raft?" Declan asked.

"About a dozen nautical miles, I guess."

He'd have to pinpoint where that would be and what was in the surrounding area, but he was pretty sure they'd chosen to come ashore somewhere far more remote than Anajay Darmadi had. And yet, Dr. Ebeid blamed the entire connection with Darmadi on his murdered assistant, Jari Youssef. With Jari dead and no contrary evidence, there was no way to charge Dr. Ebeid with smuggling terrorists. It was sickening and frustrating, but one day Dr. Ebeid wouldn't be so lucky, and today might bring them one step closer to that day.

"Any idea where they went after reaching shore?" Declan asked, before taking a sip of his coffee.

Carlos shook his head. "I think the Egyptian handled those men and the weapons. Stallings seemed to handle the refugees and the drugs."

"Speaking of the Egyptian . . ." Declan pushed a picture of Dr. Ebeid across the table.

Carlos flinched.

Asking didn't seem necessary, but Declan did anyway. "Is this the Egyptian you saw with Stallings?"

Carlos nodded.

"Can you respond verbally?" Their interview was being recorded.

"Yes. That's him. He didn't always come himself. Sometimes he sent another man— younger, taller. But when important matters were to be discussed—at least when everything was tense in the building and I was sent to clean the lower room—the Egyptian showed up."

"His name is Dr. Khaled Ebeid," Declan said. "He's the head of the Islamic Cultural Institute of the Mid-Atlantic. Did you ever hear any of your shipmates or building mates mention that?"

"No."

Well, at least they'd obtained eyewitness confirmation that Dr. Ebeid and Max Stallings were both involved in the smuggling and trafficking, and in it together, at least on some level. Declan would be paying them both a visit once Carlos was safely with the Marshals.

He'd also pay Lennie another visit. What were Stallings and Lennie thinking? They were working with a man smuggling in terrorists and weapons of destruction. Did they not care about their country at all?

He shook his head. Men like Lennie and Max only cared about money.

"Let's shift back to Burke for a minute," Declan said. "There were items we took as evidence out of your and Burke's bunk room."

Carlos nodded.

"One area that was communal was the desk. Were the items on the desk—magazines and maps, if I recall correctly—yours or Burke's?"

"They were mine. I liked to see where I was spending time. Thought of relocating a time or two. You know, pretend I had a different life. Like somehow I could escape the cycle."

"The Marshals will do just that for you, Carlos. And I can give you some pointers before you leave, if you'd like," Tanner said.

Carlos didn't really seem interested, but he clearly liked Tanner, so he nodded, smiled, and said, "Okay."

"So everything on the desk was yours?" Declan needed to be certain.

"Yes, but Steven read through it all. He was especially interested in Baltimore, as that's where we were making port. He read that Chesapeake magazine I'd gotten at one of those free tourist boxes my last trip in. He read it over and over. Studied the map. I just assumed he was trying to familiarize himself with the place."

Maybe he had figured out that Baltimore was where the cells were building. Maybe he knew that's where the attack was going to occur. Declan needed to go through those magazines and maps with a fine-tooth comb, check to see if Burke had made any notations or markings.

"Did you ever notice Burke writing in the magazine or on the maps?"

"Yeah. A couple times. He asked if it was okay. I said I didn't mind. He made marks so small and faint I couldn't even find them. He went out of his way to be a nice bunkmate."

"Did you ever write or mark in them?"

"No. I just read them."

So anything they found marked inside could only be attributed to Burke.

"Do you know what happened the day of Steven Burke's death?"

Carlos swallowed. "He got caught going through Darmadi's berth."

"Did he find anything in Darmadi's berth that you're aware of?"

"All I saw when I stopped by after hearing the commotion were a couple brochures on the floor of his room, but it couldn't be over them. If he found something, it must have been something else."

"How come?" Declan asked.

"Like I said, it was just brochures. One about a bridge and another about tunnels."

Declan swallowed. "In Baltimore?"

"I think so, but I barely got a glimpse at the

bridge. The brochure was folded, so it was only a section."

"Was the bridge metal or concrete?"

"Metal . . . I think."

"And the tunnel? Did it have a name on it?" There were so many tunnels in the Chesapeake Bay region. The Bay Tunnel, the Harbor Tunnel, the Fort McHenry Tunnel . . . the list went on and on.

Carlos shook his head. "It just showed cars moving through a tunnel—it was such a brief glance. I peeked in later after Darmadi was gone, but the brochures were gone too."

Was a bridge in Maryland their target—the Key Bridge in Baltimore or the Bay Bridge in Annapolis? Or was it in D.C.—the Woodrow Wilson Bridge? Was that what the IEDs, line charges, and other weapons were for—to blow up a bridge or a tunnel?

"And then what happened?" he asked.

"Two crew members hauled Burke up to see the captain. I knew something bad was going to happen. Darmadi rushed after them, and within seconds, there were gunshots."

"What happened next?"

"Darmadi grabbed his stuff and left in a fast raft. A bunch of us went up to see what happened on the bridge, and we found Burke and Joseph, the first mate, dead, and the captain knocked out and slumped on the floor."

"Why didn't you report any of this while we were on the ship?" He knew it was a foolish question, and Tanner thought so too by the roll of her exquisite brown eyes—the color of his mom's homemade sea salt caramels.

"I was afraid."

"Of course you were," Tanner said.

"I understand," Declan responded, but they could have saved so much time, made so much progress, if Carlos had just talked earlier. He believed, however, that God had His timing, and ultimately, Declan trusted in that, in Him.

He just prayed they weren't too late.

Tanner continued chatting with Carlos until the Marshals arrived and Declan signed off on his transfer.

As soon as Carlos was gone, Declan headed for evidence.

"Going to get the magazines and maps?" Tanner asked.

"Yeah. I meant to grab them out of evidence earlier, but haven't had a chance until now. I'm really praying we find some of the notes Carlos said Burke made. I'm sure they are in code just as the postcards were, but Burke might have found a way of noting his thoughts without it being obvious to a casual observer."

Tanner joined him after he returned with the

evidence in question, and together they sat on the black leather couch in Declan's office and began combing through each magazine, brochure, and map, looking for any hint of a notation.

They certainly had their work cut out for them.

32

Declan roused himself, his eyelids heavy, his right arm asleep.

Please tell me I didn't fall asleep in front of Tanner.

His heart in his throat, he glanced to his right and found the reason for his numb arm—Tanner's head resting on it while she was fast asleep. Not wanting to wake her, he took a moment to look around, rubbing the sleep from his eyes. The magazine, brochures, and maps still surrounded them, his notebook with markings, scratched-out markings, and more notations lay open on the coffee table by his socked feet.

Tanner's legs were curled up beneath her on the sofa, her hand resting softly on his abdomen.

He swallowed and, blinking, looked at the clock on his office wall. *Midnight?*

Last he'd looked it had been seven.

The puzzle they were attempting to put together had just been too inviting to stop midway.

He inhaled, the smell of coconut and vanilla lingering in the air. Tanner's shampoo.

How long had they been asleep, and who had

seen them? He looked to find his office door closed. He frowned. Had Tanner shut it, or one of his colleagues? If the latter, he'd never hear the end of the ribbing.

He hated to wake her, but he needed to get her back to his guest room so she could get a good night's rest. Yesterday, he'd insisted she stay in his guest room until the case was over. Thankfully, she hadn't fought him on it, which was both surprising and encouraging.

He moved his arm slowly, the blood rushing painfully to the numb limb. Her head lolled, and her eyes fluttered open. Confusion marred her brow. So she hadn't closed the door.

She sat straight up. "What happened?"

"We fell asleep."

She stretched, planting her feet on the carpeted floor. "What time is it?" Her eyes lifted to the clock. "Midnight?"

"If you're too tired to head to my house, we can stay here. You can have this couch, and I'll take the one in Barrows' office, but I'd rather you get a good night's rest."

"Thanks, I appreciate that. Let's head to your place." Knowing Tanner, she was probably more worried about the sleep he needed than her own, but they headed down to the garage. The temperature had dropped, and Tanner wrapped her coat more tightly around herself.

"I'll crank up the heat," he said as he held

the passenger door of his vehicle open for her. "It should kick in soon."

"I'm fine."

He climbed into the driver's side and started the engine. She was shivering. He looked at the temperature display on the dash. Thirty-seven degrees. Not even close to the afternoon temps of sixty-five. October was the month of temperature swings in Baltimore.

The car warmed quickly, and soon Tanner relaxed, even unbuttoned her coat partway.

His house was a half hour drive from the office, but at this time of night they wouldn't hit any traffic. He pulled onto 695, another SUV pulling on after him, and another, and another, and finally a fourth one—the four spreading out. Two in the lane to his right, one to his left and one behind.

Declan pulled his gun from his holster. "Grab the gun out of my glove compartment. We've got company."

He watched her assess the situation as she pulled out the gun, and he hit the accelerator, but it was going to do them no good. They were about to be boxed in.

Declan punched the Bluetooth button on the dash. "Call Griff!" he yelled, explaining the situation in as few grunted words as possible when Griff picked up. Declan floored the gas pedal—the dark SUVs accelerating in turn.

Then, just as he'd anticipated, the front SUV in the right lane sped up and tried to pull in front of him. "Fire at his tires before he can box us in."

He powered down Tanner's window just enough for her to aim the gun out of it, and she shot the car's rear driver's side tire out. The vehicle swerved, but the driver regained control. Declan accelerated to give her a better angle, and she shot the front tire out. The SUV wobbled and screeched to a stop, the other three vehicles maintaining pursuit.

"Nice shooting," he said, rolling up her window as the windows of the SUVs on either side of them powered down. "Get down." He shoved her head toward the floor. The bullets ricocheted off the bullet-resistant glass he'd had installed after Jari's execution.

She tilted her head sideways. "Bulletproof glass?"

"Bullet resistant," he said as a round cracked the glass. Praise God it hadn't penetrated it. He accelerated, but not before a round made contact with his rear driver's side tire.

He swerved, bullets ricocheting through the night air, one pinging off his bumper, another landing in his rear passenger tire. He was now riding on two rims. Sparks shot out from the rims rolling at high speed along the asphalt. The two SUVs slammed into them from either side at the same time as the one on his bumper rammed them from behind.

Tanner's head whiplashed forward and back.

"Hang on tight." He hit his brakes, the two side SUVs flying past, the one behind swerving slightly.

Declan's heart dropped as the SUV behind them angled just right and . . .

"Hang on!" Declan roared as the driver rammed their back corner with the front of his SUV at just the right speed and position, sending Declan's Suburban flipping end over end. They landed upside down and skidded along the pavement.

Please, Father, let me see police lights.

They spun sideways, the brake lights of the SUVs that had flown past now frozen thirty feet in front of them as they rocked to a stop.

He looked over at Tanner and his heart squeezed at the blood dripping from her head. She appeared unconscious, but her hair hung long as she remained pinned upside down by her seat belt, so he couldn't tell how severe the wound was or exactly where on her head the blood was oozing from.

Please, Father, let her be okay. You know the love I have for her. Forgive me for waiting so long to tell her.

The SUVs reversed, and men piled out. Declan reached for his gun, but his arms were pinned.

They kicked the window in and hauled him out through it. His heart clenched.

Please don't take Tanner.

Thankfully, for whatever reason—probably the emergency lights drawing near—they left her. Shoving him into the back of the SUV, they pulled away as the sirens blared closer.

Thank you, Father. At least Tanner would be taken care of. *Please let her be okay.*

Waiting for the opportune moment, he slammed his elbow into the man's face beside him, knocking the gun from his hand, only to be cracked across the back of the head. Everything went black.

Tanner roused to consciousness, to see Declan being shoved into an SUV. She painfully craned her head left as the SUV sped away. Declan was gone.

A few seconds later a police officer knelt by the window beside her.

"Ma'am, can you hear me?" the officer asked, his flashlight shining in her eyes.

She blinked. "They took him."

"Took who?"

"They kidnapped Federal Agent Declan Grey."

33

Declan woke to blood rushing to his head, a rhythmic swinging motion pulling him back and forth, back and forth, as he was *upside down?* His head hung several inches above a cracked concrete floor. He followed his naked torso to his legs and up to the ropes that tied him to the wooden beam just inches below the low ceiling, his feet bare.

Who had him and what did they intend to do to him?

The room was practically barren. An old steel conveyer belt ran the length of the concrete wall on his left. A few tattered bags that once might have held grain had all but been chewed through until only shreds of burlap remained.

Some kind of deserted warehouse, he guessed.

His shoes, shirt, and belt were flung over a rickety metal chair, leaving him only in his trousers.

A man he didn't recognize entered the room, strode to a small table about ten feet from Declan, and unrolled a leather case. The flash of steel instruments caught Declan's eye as he swung to the right.

Thank you, Lord, they didn't take Tanner.

"Agent Declan Grey," the man said, his voice muffled.

He got a better look as the man approached—tall, slender, black hair sprinkled with gray, deep caramel-colored skin. One of Ebeid's men? If so, it was the first time he'd seen him. Which made sense, as Ebeid wouldn't want to send someone Declan could easily tie back to him or the Institute, if they were not planning to kill him—or if the Lord provided a means of escape.

The man held a six-inch serrated blade in his left hand. "I see you are no stranger to pain." He took a moment to assess Declan's scars. "That could delay our time frame," he said to one of the guards. "I can already see this one's willpower is strong."

Wrong. Not willpower—his confidence in God. In *His* power. The Lord's disciples had faced insurmountable and at times excruciatingly painful odds—having been hunted, imprisoned, and tortured, but God gave them the strength to endure with grace. God might not choose to alleviate the pain he was about to suffer, but Declan trusted God would give him His strength to endure it.

"Now, let's begin with what you know," the man said.

"What I know about what?" Declan wasn't giving up anything.

"So you are going to prolong the inevitable? Then let's dive right in." The man sliced Declan's upper chest.

Unwilling to give the man the satisfaction, Declan bit back the urge to grunt in pain.

Please, Father, give me dignity, strength, and endurance for what lies ahead.

Luke stood at a grimy window of the warehouse. He'd followed one of Ebeid's men there and found them holding Declan. Malcolm would say it wasn't his job to intervene, but he was done listening to Malcolm. He was doing what was right—and that meant saving his friend. Or at least the man who had been his friend through his entire childhood.

Crouching low, he made his way along the side of the building, adrenaline burning his limbs.

He found a patched opening in one of the broken windows and quietly pulling back the cardboard, looked inside.

They had begun their torture. He needed to move fast.

Declan grunted back the pain. They could punch and slice him all night, but he wasn't talking.

Movement near a window caught his eye.

Luke?

Luke held a finger to his lips, and Declan

forced his focus back to the man before him.

Within a minute one of the guards slumped to the ground on the outer edge of his peripheral vision. Mustering all the strength he could, Declan waited until the man approached with a new instrument of pain and swung upward, knocking the man to the ground. Luke opened fire, and Declan pulled up to his feet, working to untie the bonds that held him. After a moment, he dropped to the floor and staggered to his feet. The world swam for a minute, but Declan shook it off.

Luke tossed him a gun, and he joined the fight.

Soon only he and Luke remained standing, and he'd only gotten off a couple shots. What had his childhood friend become?

"Ebeid's men?" Declan asked.

Luke nodded as he searched the bodies.

"I need to call this in. We need a full team on this. And Griff, of course."

"I understand," Luke said, rifling through the last man's wallet. "Can't believe he was stupid enough to keep this on him, though the ID is definitely fake. Make your call," he said, lifting his chin. "Just don't mention me."

"What?"

"Just say some unknown man showed up and then disappeared."

"Seriously? You think they're going to buy that?"

"Do what you have to do, but if you bring my name into this, you'll blow years of casework, not to mention further endanger the country we love."

"So you *do* work for our country?"

Luke looked at him like it should have been completely obvious. "Of course."

"Which agency?"

"I could tell you," he said, climbing back up to the window where he'd come in. "But . . ." He smiled. "You know the rest." And then he was gone.

Declan shook his head. *Great.* He sighed, surveying the bodies around him. *How am I going to explain this?*

Tanner's heart raced as the nurses wheeled her gurney into an ER room.

She fought them in an attempt to stand.

"Tanner, you have to let them treat you," Finley said. "Griff, Jason, and the local precincts are searching for Declan, along with the Bureau's agents. Trust me, they'll find him, but it'll do neither of you any good if you ignore a possibly serious head injury."

"I want to help search." She couldn't just lie in a hospital bed when the man she loved was in extreme danger.

"He wouldn't want you to endanger your health," Finley countered.

Finley was right, but Tanner didn't have to like it, or agree.

"Listen to the woman," Avery said as she entered.

"Let me guess—Griffin sent you both to make sure I stay put?" Tanner asked.

"And me," Kate said, popping around the privacy curtain.

"I appreciate your concern, but you all should be out there looking for Declan, not baby-sitting me."

"We're here to make sure *you're* all right too," Kate said, and she held up her laptop. "I can help just as easily from here."

Tanner struggled to sit up, but her swirling head knocked her back against the thin hospital pillow.

Frustration blistered inside, sending hot tears streaking down her cheeks. "What if they don't find him?" Her lip quivered. "What if they're too late?"

Finley grasped her IV-free hand, and Avery moved to sit by her other side.

"They'll find him, honey," Finley said.

"It's what they do," Avery added.

She swallowed, praying they were right.

Her cell rang as the room swirled.

Please, Lord, let it be good news. "Grab it!" she said, frantically.

"On it," Kate said, digging through Tanner's jacket pocket. She handed it to her.

Tanner didn't recognize the number. "Hello?"

"Hey, sweetheart. It's me."

She sat up, ignoring the swimming of her head. "Declan." *Oh, thank you, Lord.* "Where are you?"

"A warehouse in Sparrows Point, according to the trace Tim Barrows ran off this cell."

"Whose cell is it?"

"One of the men who took me."

"But you're okay?"

"I'm fine."

"How . . . ?"

"Our friend from Houston."

Thank you, Luke.

"How are you, honey?"

She smiled. He floored her. He'd just been kidnapped—and she hated to imagine what he might have endured before Luke showed up—but he was worried about her. "I'm fine."

"Let me talk to your nurse."

"She's not here right now. Trust me, I'm fine."

"You at GBMC?"

"Yeah."

"I'll be there as soon as I can. Tim, Griff, and both teams are on their way. I already hear a helicopter circling overhead."

She nodded, tears of relief tumbling down onto her lap.

"And, sweetheart . . . ?"

"Yeah?"

312

"I love you. I'm sorry for not saying so before now. But I do. I love you with all my being."

She swallowed, her heart overflowing with joy. "I love you too."

She'd barely hung up, and the ladies pounced.

"What happened?" Kate asked.

"Declan's okay?" Finley said.

"Are the guys with him? What about Parker? Is he okay?" Avery asked.

"Parker went too?" Tanner said.

"Of course," Avery said. "He joined Griffin and Jason."

"Well, Declan is alone right now. It sounds like the cavalry is just arriving."

A few seconds later Finley's cell rang. "It's Griff. Probably updating me about what he knows." She stepped out of the room to take the call, as Avery, in turn, did the same when Parker called too, leaving Tanner and Kate alone.

"What happened?" Kate asked.

Tanner bit her bottom lip. "He . . . didn't go into detail. Just said he was okay and would be here as soon as he could."

34

A door slammed open, and fellow agent Tim Barrows and his team flooded into the musty warehouse. Griffin, Parker, and Jason entered as ambulance sirens whirred toward them. Declan just needed to make sure the ambulance took him to GBMC, because as soon as he explained—or came as close to *explaining*—this mess as best he could, he was going to be at Tanner's side, even if he had to stagger there.

She'd said she was fine, but he feared she was simply saying that to make him feel better. She'd taken a serious knock on the head.

His friends strode straight for him as agents began working the scene.

"What happened here?" Griffin asked.

Declan leaned in, lowering his voice. "I can't tell you, not *exactly*."

Griffin's brows arched.

Declan glanced around. "Not here. Not now."

"To say I'm intrigued is an understatement," Parker said.

"I understand, but I need you all to trust me."

Declan proceeded to brief Barrows while

the paramedics set to work cleaning and bandaging his wounds.

"And you didn't recognize the man who came to help you?" Barrows asked again.

"He was dressed in black. It was dim. It all happened so fast." Which was all true. It just wasn't the full truth. To say he was struggling with the precarious position he was in was no exaggeration, but there was a bigger game at play. He'd glimpsed enough of it to know Luke was telling the truth. There was a terrorist attack coming to U.S. soil, and according to Luke, if his presence was made public, it would destroy all the work he'd done to combat what was brewing. If keeping Luke's identity and presence hidden from the terrorists and whomever they had on their payroll was key in stopping those attacks, Declan had no choice but to remain silent.

Griffin joined Declan in the back of the ambulance headed for GBMC, while Parker and Jason followed in Griffin's car. Barrows and his team remained to process the crime scene. Unfortunately, all the men involved in his abduction were dead, so there'd be no questioning. But Declan believed that was part of Luke's plan. If there were no survivors to question, it assured Ebeid and whoever else was involved that the FBI and local police hadn't garnered any pertinent information about their plans. They were too close to catching Ebeid to spook him now.

Otherwise, Ebeid would move on, plan another attack, another location, and they'd have to start their case from scratch. It would delay Ebeid's impending attack, sure, but what was to say they'd ever get this close to catching him again? They were playing with fire, but they had no choice. Ebeid needed to believe his plans were safe, and that he could move forward with the attack as planned. They just had to catch him before it occurred. It was going to come down to the wire. Them against Ebeid in a race that held thousands of lives in the balance.

"All right," Griff said, moving to his side as the paramedic moved up into the passenger seat of the ambulance, shutting the door and allowing them a modicum of privacy. "Let me hear it," he said as he balanced on his haunches, bracing himself against the gurney.

Declan prayed for guidance. Luke *couldn't* be on the records, but Griffin could be trusted, as could Park. It was time for him and Tanner to stop carrying this burden alone.

He indicated for Griffin to lean in and whispered. "Luke."

Griffin moved to jerk back, but Declan clutched his arm, keeping him pinned in place.

"There's far too much risk if that information leaves our group, and only you and Park can know."

Griffin's brows arched.

"Kate's safety rests upon her not finding out about Luke."

"Why?"

"Luke said if his enemies discover she's digging into his whereabouts, or they learn he cares about her, they'll take her out."

"And us?"

"They'll kill us too if Ebeid discovers our connection to Luke."

"You're assuming we actually matter to him," Griffin said.

"He's saved me twice. Why bother if he doesn't care?"

"Twice?!"

Declan winced. "Houston."

"I knew you were holding back something about Houston."

"Sorry. Luke made me promise."

"Luke? Our 'friend' who's been gone for seven years? You felt the need to protect him over us?"

"No. I didn't say anything because I believed I was protecting you all, especially Kate."

Griffin exhaled. "It's hard to even fathom. . . . I mean, I can't believe you saw him, *talked* to him. How is he?"

"The better question is *who* is he? He's not the same Luke we knew."

"Meaning?"

"The guy's like Jason Bourne on steroids."

"Luke?" Griffin whispered, shock infusing his tone. "You're kidding?"

"I'm dead serious. He's in deep, and I have no clue which agency. It's no wonder we haven't been able to find a service record for him. Whatever agency he works for must have him ranked at a highly classified level—or completely off the books."

"Off the books, as in black ops?"

"I pray not, but . . ." At this point it wouldn't surprise him. He had no idea who Luke had become.

Tanner's hospital door slid open, and the privacy curtain pulled back to reveal Declan. His shirt hung open, his chest covered with bandages and scars—scars she'd first seen when she'd stitched him up and had gotten so sidetracked by his tattoo and rippling muscles. That day seemed a lifetime ago, but in reality, it had only been a matter of days.

So much had happened, so much had changed, and while most of what had occurred had been terrifying, the rest was the best thing that ever happened to her. Declan was *the* best thing that had ever happened to her, and she hadn't stopped thanking God since he'd uttered those three words. Declan Grey loved her.

He knelt at her side. "Hey, sweetheart." He brushed the hair gently from her bandaged forehead and placed a soft kiss to the side of it. "How are you, *really?*"

"You're covered in bandages, and you're asking how *I* am?" The man was crazy.

"Why don't we give these two some privacy?" Avery stood and collected her things.

"Good idea." Finley followed Avery's lead.

"You okay, Grey?" Kate asked.

He looked at Tanner and smiled. "I am now."

Everyone disappeared, leaving them alone, and Tanner couldn't have been more grateful. It wouldn't be long before a nurse or doctor appeared for another exam, but she'd treasure the brief moments they could steal. She had Declan back, and he loved her. She wished she could say they'd come through the worst of it, but she feared the worst was waiting right around the bend.

Luke listened in to the surveillance equipment he'd placed on Dr. Khaled Ebeid's cell phone. To this point, the man had been careful and hadn't provided much concrete information about his plans, but Luke wasn't giving up.

"What?" Ebeid asked, enraged when notified of the failed abduction.

"They're all dead."

"Any signs of torture?"

"No. Double taps. One to the center mass, one to the head."

"On all of them?"

"Yes."

Ebeid exhaled. "At least they didn't have time to give anything up. We can move forward as planned. Only we don't know what they learned from Grey."

"No, sir."

There was a long pause.

"We've worked too hard for this to stop now. Everything's in order?"

"Just waiting for Stallings to arrange for the trawlers. Otherwise, we're set."

"And the transport?"

"Happening on schedule."

The call disconnected, and Luke sat back, his head resting against the paneled wall of his motel room. The day after tomorrow whatever they planned for Baltimore was going down—and that was when the transport was scheduled. The distraction attack, which he prayed Declan would figure out, no doubt would occur slightly before or at the same moment. He hated the thought of a disaster occurring so close to home—or what had at one time been his home. Now that he was back, he craved for it to be again. But could someone like him really go back to a normal life?

Now was not the time to ponder what would happen after. He had to focus and make sure there was an after, that Ebeid and his men didn't succeed on either level—the transport or the diversion attack.

Luke shook his head. Who would have thought that Declan Grey would be working the other thread of this investigation?

Please, Father, let Declan discover the location of the distraction attack. Help to reveal what Ebeid has planned. There are so many lives hanging in the balance.

Intel pointed to it being local, and they had confirmation weapons had been transported in, but that was the extent of their knowledge. He couldn't personally shift any more attention to that detail though. He had to focus on intercepting the transport—otherwise what might be a thousand lives lost could easily turn into millions.

Flipping on the TV, he turned to the news channel, anxious to see how the raid had been reported, what was being shared with the media, and praying his name didn't come up. Declan had promised, but how could he expect anyone to keep their promises after what he'd done? After all the promises he'd broken?

He pulled Kate's creased picture from his inner shirt pocket and smoothed it out. She'd been so beautiful in college. It was hard to believe she was even more beautiful now.

He looked at the door, knowing better but unable to stop himself.

Within a half hour, he was watching her houseboat, battling the urge to enter. It was late. She would be sleeping.

It was too dangerous, but she was *so* close.

He yearned to feel the soft touch of her skin, the silky strands of her blond hair, the warmth of her in his arms.

He clenched his teeth.

He was such a fool.

As if, after what he'd done, she'd welcome him with open arms? He was delusional to even think that a remote possibility.

He stiffened, his limbs tensing as something, or rather someone else, garnered his attention.

There was someone else present.

It took him a moment to lay eyes on the man. He zoomed in on his binoculars.

Xavier Benjali. Ebeid's right-hand man—watching Kate.

Adrenaline pulsed through him.

Why was Benjali watching Kate? Had she hit upon something that flagged them? Or had they discovered his connection to her?

Fear flashed through him for the first time

in years. Actual fear. It'd been so long since he'd experienced the unsettling sensation. Now he understood why Malcolm said attachments were a vulnerability an agent couldn't afford.

Benjali moved toward the houseboat, climbing aboard, gun with silencer in hand.

Luke had no choice. He was going in.

35

Kate woke to a gun aimed at her head. Terror pierced her as a gun retorted. The man froze, then fell forward. Another man stood behind him, his silhouette outlined by the light emanating from the kitchen lamp she'd left on.

He turned to go.

"Wait!" It was the same aftershave she'd smelled on the docks. There was something familiar. *Something* . . . Her chest tightened. "Luke?"

His shoulders slumped, and he turned back around to face her as she switched on her bedside lamp.

It was him. After all these years, all her searching, Luke was standing less than ten feet away. She leapt from the bed and rushed for him, engulfing him in her arms.

He dropped his gun on the dresser beside them, wrapping her in his arms and kissing her with a passion she felt to her toes.

An unexpected emotion rushed over her alongside the passion—blistering anger. Seven years of waiting for Luke to return, and now he stood in her room, passionately kissing her and emotions completely opposite to how she pictured this reunion going festered inside. She'd envisioned running into his strong arms as she had, and all the pain of his disappearance evaporating. It was probably naive and a bit foolish, but it was the reunion she'd fantasized about for all the years he'd been gone. And, while she felt that longing, that instinctual pull to him, the yearning to stay in his arms and never leave, she also felt sorrowful anger. She wished the last seven years could be wiped away, but, unfortunately, time and wounds didn't work that way. Time didn't disappear, and wounds apparently remained raw.

Luke shook, physically shook, as he poured everything he'd been holding back for over seven years into the woman he loved. Still loved. Always loved. And she was kissing him back. She was in his arms. It was like a dream come true. Nothing else mattered. Everything else faded until . . .

Kate pulled back, staring up at him with wide eyes blinking, then she hauled back and walloped him across his face with such force that a red handprint had to be visible on his throbbing right cheek.

He stepped back, rubbing his jaw. "I deserved that." He deserved so much worse.

"Where have you been?"

He took a deep breath and studied her now

that she was right in front of him. She'd changed over the last seven years. Her face was thinner and her hair was shorter, cresting her collarbone rather than falling halfway down her back. And . . . she seemed a little taller.

In other ways, though, she hadn't changed at all. She still walked around with fuzzy socks or barefoot, proving she still hated wearing shoes.

She still pulled her blond hair up in a ponytail while she worked on her laptop, sticking a pencil in it so she always had one handy while taking notes.

She still licked her beautiful lips when nervous . . . exactly as she was doing right now.

"Well?" she asked, stepping closer again. She smelled of shea butter—the body cream she swore she would never stop using when her mom gave it to her for her nineteenth birthday— the same birthday he'd bought her the starfish ring. And to his amazement, she was still wearing it. Which meant she either loved the ring or, beyond all hope, she still loved him despite the monster he'd become. But she didn't know. Knowledge would change everything.

"It's a really long story."

"Fine." She indicated her reading chair with the tilt of her head. "Take a seat and start talking."

How he wished they could go back to kissing, but the fact she hadn't kicked him out straightaway was far more than he'd anticipated.

In all their years together, he'd never seen her cry. But Mack Jacobs, his friend from agency training who kept him informed about his loved ones back home, told him that Kate had cried almost nonstop for weeks after he left. It had killed him to know, but not knowing was worse. At least in the beginning. Then the distance between his past life and the life he had chosen became too painful.

"Professor Warner came to me before graduation . . ." he began.

Kate still couldn't believe what Luke had shared so far. It was Jack Reacher meets Jason Bourne.

"So let me get this straight. You're telling me that boring old by-the-book Professor Warner recruited you to be a *spy?*" She still couldn't wrap her mind around that. He had been a mentor to all of the guys. She had never really gotten that connection, but how could he just rip Luke from their lives like that? And, worse yet, how could Luke have purposely left them without a word?

There was so much she wanted to ask him, but would his answers be enough to dull the pain throbbing through her?

"Yes," Luke said, "Malcolm Warner is not what he seems."

Interesting, but regardless, it all came down to

why he'd left, and the truth was he'd chosen to go.

Luke continued, "Malcolm's a plant at the University of Maryland. There to recruit promising students into the program and agency."

"What program? What agency?" He'd been frustratingly vague when it came to those details.

"It's better if you don't know."

"Why?"

He tilted his head in that way that told her she'd hit a roadblock. He wasn't going to budge, and it drove her nuts. After more than seven years without a word from him she *deserved* to know why.

"Because it's safer that way," he finally said. "You've already caused quite a stir by hiring Hadi to locate me."

"How do you know about Hadi?"

"I knew someone was trying to track me down, so I did a little recon of my own."

So he'd known all along that Hadi was searching for him.

"When he photographed me, the boss decided it was time I left Malaysia, so he shifted me to a lead that brought me back to the U.S."

"And what lead was that?"

"It's adjacent to the case Declan's working."

"With the terrorists that were smuggled in?"

Luke nodded. "Yes, and Declan's doing a great job, but there's much more at play."

"Such as?"

"You know I can't tell you."

"Wait a second . . . how do you know Declan's doing a great job?" Her eyes narrowed. "You've got to be kidding me. You're the mysterious man who saved him?" She stood and paced the room, her anger fueling hotter. "Declan knew it was you and lied to me?"

"I told him he had to."

"And he just listened to you after you've been gone for over seven years? He doesn't even know you anymore."

Air jutted from his lungs as if he'd been gut punched. "He trusted me."

"Why? How can any of us trust you after what you did? After how you left?"

All she'd wanted was for him to return home, to pull her in his arms and kiss her. Now that he was sitting in front of her, nothing felt like she'd anticipated it would. Instead of wholeness and elation, all that filled her was a horrid mix of sadness and anger.

Luke had chosen to leave. He'd *deserted* her. How could she ever forgive him? How could she ever trust him again? And more importantly, did she even know the man seated in her bedroom chair? She thought her world would fall back into place if he just walked through her door. But it didn't.

He stood. "I can see this was a bad idea. I shouldn't have come."

She knew she should thank him for saving her life, but the words would not come. She just stared at him.

He turned to leave, and started, almost as if he had forgotten about the body lying in her doorway, then shook his head. "Sorry." He bent and hefted the body over his shoulder.

She wondered how he would get it past the policeman watching her boat from the marina parking lot. She sighed. What was she thinking—he was Luke Gallagher.

Tears streamed down her cheeks as he walked out her sliding door and shut it behind him. He was gone again. For how long this time?

36

The group met up at CCI the following morning before Parker and Avery left for Houston to process Steven Burke's apartment, and Griffin and Jason to Jamaica after finally getting a positive ID of the Markums from the cruise liner. They hoped to arrive before the ship docked.

Everything was falling into place . . . and then Kate entered the office.

A harsh silence filled the room as she glared at Declan.

He swallowed. *She knows.*

He stood. "Katie, I'm sorry."

She held up her hand. "Don't bother."

"Luke needed us to keep his secret," Griffin said. "For your safety."

She whipped around. "You knew too?"

Parker cleared his throat.

"Great." She swept her arms upward. "So you all knew."

"Just us guys and Tanner," Declan said.

"And Finley," Griffin said. "Sorry." He looked at Declan. "I can't keep secrets from my wife."

His wife, who was at work, was missing a really uncomfortable conversation.

"And Avery guessed," Parker said.

331

"But he refused to confirm it," Avery said. "Which actually told me I was right."

"Lovely." Kate practically threw her laptop on her desk and headed back to her office— her actual office at the end of the hall, which she never used.

They just stared at one another, trying to determine who was the best choice to go after her, when her office door slammed.

"Okay." Declan exhaled. "So apparently Luke changed his mind about contacting her."

"Maybe she was in more immediate danger," Parker said.

"My thoughts exactly," Griffin added.

"I'll ask him next time he decides to show up. *If* he decides to," Declan said, frustration filling him that Luke hadn't bothered to give them a heads-up he'd seen Katie. But, then again, it was Luke—the friend who'd left them without a word for seven years. No wonder Katie was angry.

"As fun as this party is . . ." Griffin said, "I've gotta pick Jason up in five."

Fortunately for him, Jason lived pretty much around the corner.

"Keep us posted," Declan said. "I hope you get 'em."

Griffin nodded and ducked out the door.

"We should be going too," Parker said, lifting his leather duffel over his shoulder and grasping

Avery's purple carry-on in his left hand. "We've got a flight to catch."

"Again, keep us posted," Declan said.

"Will do."

Parker and Avery headed out too, leaving Declan with Tanner and a very angry Kate.

Tanner took a step back. "Looks like you're up, slugger."

"Slugger?" He arched a brow.

"Seemed appropriate at the moment." She offered an awkward smile.

"And why me? You're the counselor."

"Because you've been her friend far longer, and you know her relationship with Luke, or at least what it was at one time."

Declan took a deep breath and exhaled, shaking out his hands. These kinds of talks were not his forte, but Tanner was right. Kate deserved an apology and an explanation.

He rapped on her door.

"Don't bother," she called.

He entered slowly, most likely to his detriment or very possibly bodily harm. Katie had a mean right hook and practiced at the boxing gym three days a week—though he'd never seen her hit someone outside of the ring. He prayed that held true today. "I'm sorry," he started.

She dropped the pen she'd been writing with and swiveled around on her desk stool. Her eyes were bloodshot and puffy, tears still lingering.

"Oh, Katie." He moved to her and engulfed her in a hug. "I'm sorry. I believed him when he said you'd be in danger if they connected you to him."

She sniffed, swiping at her tears. "He probably wasn't wrong."

Declan stepped back, dipping his head to look her in the eye. "What do you mean?"

"Someone tried to kill me last night. Came onto my boat and—"

"What?"

"Luke shot him before he could."

"And you didn't think to lead with that?"

She shrugged with a sorrowful laugh. "It wasn't top on my mind." She exhaled. "He's been gone over seven years, and he still . . ."

Has her heart.

"If he didn't still care, he wouldn't have worked so hard to protect you," Declan said, hoping it would offer her a modicum of solace. He couldn't imagine how she must be feeling. He felt betrayed, and he hadn't been massively in love with the guy. Katie had been—still was, if he was reading her right.

"Yeah." She blew a stray hair from her forehead. "If only things were that simple."

"Right now, everything . . . well, almost everything is about as complicated as it can get."

Everything except how he felt about Tanner.

That was as simple, pure, and true as anything he'd felt in his life.

Kate smiled. "I'm happy for you two."

"I'm sorry. I didn't mean to bring . . . to say . . ." He fumbled for words. Now was not the time to express how happy he and Tanner were. Not when Kate was in massive pain.

"Stop falling over yourself to apologize. You didn't say anything wrong. It's more than obvious that you two are in love, and I couldn't be happier for you both."

"Thanks." It'd been a long time coming, but Tanner was by far worth the wait. Suddenly God's timing seemed so perfect. All the obstacles, tests, and trials finally made sense. He'd been keeping him for her.

"Now, go on. You two have terrorists to stop. I think that's way more important than worrying about me."

"You gonna be okay?"

"Always am."

For the first time, he wasn't sure he believed her.

Luke had been at the center of her focus, but now that he was back, all the hard facts surrounding his leaving had to be difficult for her to swallow. Not to mention the reality of the man Luke had become—whoever that was.

There was so much about him that seemed like the old Luke, and yet there were moments when he felt like a total stranger—at least watching him work.

Even Luke seemed to grapple with it—a deep sadness occasionally showing through his steadfast, hardened gaze.

37

Wind whipped through Tanner's hair as it flowed out of the motorcycle helmet. She savored the warmth of the sun on her face and the feel of Declan as she wrapped her arms snuggly about his waist.

Until Declan's requisition for a new car came through, which sometimes took hours but occasionally took days, they'd be riding his Moto Guzzi motorcycle. No wonder he'd shown such skills on the motorcycle after Mira was killed.

While he'd initially expressed concern that riding the bike and going with him to interview Max Stallings might be too much for her after just being discharged from the ER, she quickly reminded him that *he'd* just been discharged too. It was an argument he epically lost.

They reached the prison, found a parking spot, and were about to walk in when a call came through. Declan put it on speaker. Tim Barrows reported that the two customs agents Carlos described had been identified—Marcy Cushman and Gregory Pyle.

"You want me and Greer to interview them?" Tim asked.

Declan exhaled.

Tanner knew he liked handling every aspect of a case, particularly the interviews, but after a moment's hesitation, he surprisingly said, "Yeah, go ahead. Just give me a call when you're finished."

"You got it." Barrows disconnected the call.

"You're letting someone else handle an interview?" she asked, surprised.

Declan clutched her hand. "I have a feeling we're going to miss something big if we don't get all these interviews done today. It's like we're on a countdown we can't see, teetering on the precipice of falling dangerously behind."

She'd been praying all morning about their interviews, praying about the entire case, including the fact that Lexi would soon return from leave and her one-on-one work time with Declan would be over. She hated to give up working with him, but their *relationship*—as he put it—didn't rest on the amount of time they had together. Rather it rested on the foundation of their relationship with Jesus and one another. They had a lot of talking to do, a lot of growing ahead, but she'd never felt more peace in her soul, other than when she accepted Christ into her life. This was where she belonged—at Declan's side.

"What?" he asked with a smile as they walked down the cold, dingy white corridor to the lounge.

"Just thinking."

He laughed. "That's dangerous."

She smirked. "You have no idea."

The guard ushered them into the lounge, and she could see Declan wanted to continue the conversation, but the door on the opposite side opened and another guard led a shackled Max Stallings in. His orange jumpsuit had 409 numbered in black, his head was shaved—not that he ever had more than a thin film of gray hair, but now he was completely bald. It made him look harder, though a crook like Max Stallings hardly fazed her.

"Nice of you to pay me a visit, Agent Grey," he said as he settled into his seat. Stallings shifted his gaze to Tanner and smiled. "And I never mind seeing someone like you, darling."

"I wish I could say the feeling was mutual," she said, trying not to gag.

"A tough one you got here." Max chuckled.

Was he implying he knew they were a couple now?

It wouldn't be impossible. Stallings had eyes everywhere, but Max knowing would probably freak Declan out. He'd want her safe, and she just prayed he didn't pull back in any way now that it seemed Max knew.

"You don't know the half of it," Declan said with pride.

He was proud of her. Proud of her background.

Proud of the changes she'd made and the chances she'd taken. He respected her and she loved him for it.

"Now, let's get to you, Max," Declan said, leaning forward. "We've had a nice chat with one of your employees, if you can call them that. *Servant* comes to mind."

"Oh, blah, blah. If you're here to lecture or give me some sob story about my people, I'm not interested."

"How about we chat about the fact you're in business with Dr. Ebeid, smuggling not only drugs and refugees, but weapons and terrorists."

That got his attention. "I don't know where you heard that, but—"

"It's true," Tanner said, "and we all know it, so why not just cut to the chase? How long have you been in business with Dr. Ebeid?"

He smiled, his crooked teeth showing. "You are a sight to look at, darling, but if you really think I'm going to tell you two anything about my supposed business dealings, you're crazy."

"You cooperate and we can get a lighter sentence for you," Declan said. "You don't help and choose to be an accomplice, you're going to be spending the next twenty to twenty-five in here. That'd make you, what? Seventy-five when you get out?"

"I ain't no accomplice. Ebeid does his dealings, I do mine."

"Using the same ship, with the same captain."

"The ships I use aren't mine. They are run by the captain. He chooses what cargo to carry and deliver. I ain't got no control over that."

"What about Ebeid visiting you at your Ashton building downtown?"

"I don't know nothing about that."

"Really? Because we have an eyewitness who says otherwise."

"Then he's lying."

"Let's put it this way," Declan said, getting straight to the point. "We believe the terrorists Ebeid has brought over are going to attack soon."

"And you think that because . . ."

"Because of Anajay Darmadi's last words—'The wrath is here.'"

Max chuckled. "Well, that has an ominous ring to it."

"You find the possibility of a terrorist attack on U.S. soil amusing?"

"No. Of course not."

"Well, if there is one and we know you are tied to Ebeid, you'll be charged as an accomplice," Declan said, before standing and turning to Tanner. "Let's go. I've had enough of this scum."

Tanner stood to follow, but Max said, "Wait a minute."

Brilliant. Declan was brilliant in negotiations.

He knew just the right buttons to press, and he did it so calmly.

Declan turned. "Yes?"

"What do you want to know?"

Declan and Tanner retook their seats.

"What does Ebeid have planned?" Declan asked.

"I don't know."

"Come on, Max. You're going to have to do better than that."

"I seriously don't know. I've never wanted to know."

"Why did Ebeid meet you in one of your apartment buildings?"

"Because we have a joint asset in the captain and the ship we use. When you started investigating the *Hiram* and put Jackson in prison, it put us in a tough spot."

"Good."

"Well, not for us and our business. Since we'd shared the same ship and captain before, we decided to do so again."

"So you had to find a captain who'd be willing," Tanner said.

"As well as the customs guards you turned," Declan added. "I'm guessing that was all you?"

"How'd . . . ? Never mind. They aren't important."

"Did you find a new captain and ship?"

"Yes, but you already know that, don't you?" Max said, his gaze narrowing.

"We're here to discuss what you know. Not what we know."

"Fine. Yes, we found a new captain and ship, but before I give up any more, I want your offer for a reduced sentence in writing."

"You know it doesn't work like that," Declan said.

"Well, go work it however you have to and come back. I'm not talking without a statement that if I cooperate I won't be charged as an accomplice and that I'll get my sentence reduced."

"How long is it going to take to get the papers he's asking for?" Tanner asked as they exited the prison.

"Longer than I'd like."

Declan placed the call, and when he was finished, hung up. "Okay, now we wait. In the meantime, let's not tip off Ebeid that we're on to him. Let's see what Max gives us first."

"What about Lennie?"

"Same thing. If we question Lennie, he'll get word to Max that we've still been poking around—and he could potentially tell Ebeid too."

"So what do we do now?"

"Let's head for the office. The customs agents

are there. We can see what Barrows and Greer got out of the agents and go ahead and interview them again if we need to. Might even give us more leverage with Max if they admit he was the one who paid them to look the other way."

Tanner climbed on back of Declan's Moto Guzzi and wrapped her arms around his waist.

He wished they could put the entire case behind them and just take off for a long ride—hit the back roads and see where they ended up. He could use a day like that with Tanner. A day with just the two of them alone and away from the madness. But there was too much at stake. The safety of their country was hanging in the balance.

38

Jason and Griffin learned upon arrival in Kingston, Jamaica, that the cruise ship was already in port and the Markums had disembarked about a half hour earlier. They considered returning to the airport to see if anyone recognized Elizabeth and John from their picture or if the couple had booked a flight to Havana or perhaps Caracas, Venezuela, using the aliases provided to Griffin and Jason by the cruise captain. But since the Markums had avoided airports in the U.S., they decided to assume the couple would look for another escape route, most likely to Cuba. Most likely illegally.

As they walked the docks, showing the Markums' picture, Declan prayed he and Jason weren't too late. They finally found a man who said his employee had left with the couple less than a half hour earlier.

"Headed for Cuba?" Griffin asked.

"Sí, señor."

"Any chance you have a boat that's faster?"

The man smiled widely, two of his bottom front teeth missing.

• • •

Declan and Tanner entered the Bureau's offices. He'd already spoken with Tim Barrows and got his and Greer's take on the agents, but Declan wanted to interview them himself, and now he had the time to do so.

Bob Matthews, head of the Maryland Port Authority, was waiting in the lobby to greet him. "Declan, good to see you again." His gaze shifted to Tanner. "And Miss . . ."

"Shaw," she said, extending a hand.

"Right. You helped with the refugees on the *Hiram*," Bob said.

"Yes."

"You did a fine job." He looked between Declan and her. "Are you working with the Bureau now?"

"I am."

"Congratulations."

"Thanks."

Bob tapped the manila folders in his hand. "I can't believe this. Can't believe two of my customs agents were willing to look the other way." He handed Declan the folders. "As soon as I heard, I pulled their personnel files for you."

"Thanks, Bob," Declan said. "I appreciate it."

"Anything I can do to help."

Declan watched Bob walk away, his patent leathers tapping along the linoleum floors. He looked to Tanner. "You ready?"

"Yep."

Declan opened the door to Gregory Pyle's room first, and they stepped inside.

"Gregory Pyle," Declan said, skimming the man's personnel file as he pulled up a seat. "I see you've been with the Port Authority for fifteen years. That's a long time to throw away."

"My kid needed braces."

"Oh, yeah, I can see that's a great reason to sell out your country," Tanner said.

"Sell out my country? What are you talking about?"

"What exactly did you think you were letting into the country?" Declan asked, tapping the folder in his hand.

"Drugs. Not like a few shipments were going to make much difference. We've got our fair share here already."

"Well, unfortunately, Mr. Pyle . . ." Declan dropped the file on the table. "You were also allowing in terrorists and weapons."

"No. That's not right. Lennie said it was just drugs and some people."

"People?" Tanner said, leaning forward. "Slaves would be a more appropriate term."

"No. They were being rescued from impoverished countries and brought here for a better way of life."

"You really think Max Stallings provided them with a better way of life?"

"Lennie said that was the deal."

"And you just believed him?"

"No reason not to."

"Well, that's the easy way," Tanner said, not bothering to hide her disgust.

"Look, I needed the money. I had no idea . . ."

"Well, you can hope a judge buys that, but you're responsible for what you let in," Declan said. "And let me tell you—the prison time for human trafficking is bad enough, but aiding terrorism is far worse."

"Dude, that's not fair. I had no idea."

"It doesn't work that way. You neglected your duty, and now we're dealing with the threat of a terrorist attack on U.S. soil."

Gregory raked a shaky hand through his thinning brown hair.

"Tell us about this man with Lennie." Tanner slid a picture of Lennie and Xavier Benjali across the table.

"He came with Lennie once in a while. I never dealt directly with him."

Declan looked at Tanner quizzically.

"So you're saying he worked with Lennie Wilcox?" Declan asked.

"Yeah. When he came it was with Lennie. I mean he drove his own storage truck, but they came together. This one . . ." He pointed at the picture. "He never spoke with me."

"What did he put in his storage truck?"

"Several crates."

Weapons. They'd offloaded the terrorists in fast rafts, but the weapons would be too heavy, so Xavier came with Lennie to collect those at the terminal.

"Were there any markings on the storage truck he drove?"

"Nah. Just an unmarked white truck like Lennie drove."

So he probably used one of Max's vehicles. Apparently Stallings and Ebeid were in deeper together than Max had let on.

The crisp saltwater sprayed across the bow of the powerboat Juan had rented to Griffin and Jason for an ample sum of money. As he drove at top speed, Juan's grin continued to widen. He was having fun as they sped over the waves, leaving a trail of wide-spreading ripples in their wake.

An hour into their pursuit, which had Jason looking green, they finally spotted the yellow boat Juan's employee had taken with the Markums.

Juan opened the throttle to full capacity, and within minutes they closed in on the other boat.

Sheer panic registered on the Markums' faces when they recognized Griffin racing after them.

Elizabeth hollered at the driver to speed up,

but Juan ordered his employee to stop and the man did.

Griffin and Jason boarded, guns aimed at the Markums, and produced handcuffs. John had his hand wrapped where his finger had been cut off, along with a long scratch up his forearm. He'd clearly taken the brunt of the difficult parts of the staging.

Thank you, Lord, for letting us capture them just in time.

39

Parker called as Declan and Tanner headed back to continue questioning Max Stallings with the agreement he'd requested in hand. It'd taken long enough to get, but they'd finally received the agreement that would benefit both parties, and as much as Declan hated making a deal with Max Stallings, it was the lesser of two evils. To stop a terrorist attack, he'd work with the man.

"Hey, Park. Please tell me you've got something?"

"Well, it definitely looks promising."

"Oh?"

"Got a significant hit off one of the fingerprints we lifted from Burke's condo."

"Yeah?"

"Stanley Stovall. Charges of larceny, racketeering, assault . . . I called Franco on the number you gave me, and according to him, it sounds like Stovall is Houston's equivalent of Max Stallings."

"Is that right?"

"Yeah, and there's more. Stovall also controls the docks down in Galveston. Franco said Vice and Customs have been trying to nail him for years on drug and human trafficking."

"Carlos Santali said the ship he signed on to after the *Hiram* also brought drugs and people to Galveston. Send over a picture of Stovall, and I'll get the Marshals to run the image by Santali. See if he recognizes the man or any of his known associates."

"Will do. Franco seemed really keen to look into the guy."

"Maybe he'll finally do his partner justice."

"We can hope. He said he'd keep us up to date."

"Great job, Parker."

"No problem. We've got about another hour left here at the apartment, and then we're going to take the late flight home."

"See ya in the morning, then."

"You got it."

Declan brought Tanner up to speed as they made their way back to Max's interrogation room.

"I've got your paperwork right here," he said, laying the agreement down in front of Max.

Max took his sweet time reading over the paperwork but finally signed it.

"Great," Declan said, taking the papers back and sliding them into his folder. "Now, talk."

Max sat back and linked his arms across his chest. "What do you want to know?"

"Ebeid. Where does he fit into all this? We

know he's smuggling terrorists and weapons, but how does it work?"

"He arranges for his cargo. I arrange for mine. It comes in. Lennie goes to collect ours and provides the transportation for Ebeid's man, Xavier, to retrieve his. I don't ask what his cargo is and he doesn't ask what mine is. It's very simple."

"And you have no problem bringing terrorists into your own country?"

Max shrugged.

"As long as you make a profit, right?" Tanner said.

Max didn't respond, which was answer enough.

"How long has your little arrangement gone on?" Declan asked.

"A few years."

"Years?" Tanner said, shaking her head. Exactly what Carlos had said. How many terrorists had Ebeid smuggled into the country during that time?

"Any idea what the terrorists' target is?" Declan asked.

"Nah. Like I said, we kept it simple, but he did have me arrange two trawlers and two cars for him."

"Trawlers? What for?"

Max held out his hands, palms up. "Again, I don't ask."

"And the cars?"

353

Max shrugged.

"Why not just get his own cars?" Probably because he didn't want them traced back to the cultural institute.

"What do you think?" Max said.

"What kind of cars?" he asked, gritting his teeth. It took all the restraint he could muster to remain steady, and to not lunge across the table and throttle the super smug Max Stallings. They were talking about a terrorist attack on U.S. soil. Didn't he get that? What was wrong with men like him?

"Black Toyota Camrys," Max said.

"Okay." That was something helpful. "Do you know the location or the date the trawlers are scheduled for?"

"Nah. I gave him the number for the guy I use. Left it at that. The less I know, the better."

"All right. Then write down the guy's name and number." Declan slid a pen and pad of paper to Max.

Max scrawled down a first name and phone number.

"First name only?" Declan asked.

"That's how we do things."

"I'll bet it is."

A half hour of questions and answers later, Max was returned to his cell, and Declan and Tanner headed out of the prison.

"Do you think he was telling the truth about

everything?" Tanner asked, feeling like Max knew far more than he was saying.

"Doubtful, but he gave us some good leads," Declan said as they stepped out into the fresh air and crisp blue sky.

"You think he knows the target?" she asked.

"I doubt it," he said as they strolled through the leaves blanketing the parking lot on the way to his new Suburban, which they'd picked up at the Bureau. "But it is clear he knew exactly what and who Ebeid was smuggling in."

Tanner exhaled as Declan opened the passenger side door for her. She turned to face him, shielding her eyes from the sun. "So how do we stop something when we have no idea when and where it's taking place?"

"We check on Stallings' trawler connection. See if he can give us any information, and we go back through Burke's notations. The answer is in there. I can feel it," he said, shutting her in and moving around to the driver's side.

Tanner had a bemused smile tickling her lips.

Declan narrowed his eyes. "What?"

"Just you, going with your feelings again. I never thought I'd see the day."

"Then, clearly, I haven't been doing this right." He cupped her face in his hands and kissed her with a level of passion that caused her to melt into his strong arms.

• • •

Declan and Tanner sat on the rug in front of his fireplace as they worked back through Steven Burke's notations while waiting for Marco, Stallings' trawler connection, to return his call. Declan had left a message saying that he was a friend of Stallings, and was looking to arrange for a trawler, leaving his number and a false name.

Burke's magazines and maps were spread out in an arc around them. Their backs rested on his steam-trunk coffee table, their shoes kicked off to the side, letting the heat radiating from the flames warm their toes. The temperature was in the low forties and threatening to drop below freezing, but the sky was ablaze with a deep orange harvest moon. It was nearly as breathtaking as Tanner.

"15–8–G–10–H–4," Declan read off the numbers and letters again. "I'd say part of it was a lock combo or even latitude and longitude, but not with the letters." He grunted. "The letters are what's keeping me stuck. Though I still think there is a date in there somewhere. August has passed, and April is still a long time away, so let's assume it starts with the 10—October, this month. The fourth and eighth have passed, so if it is a date, it would have to be October 15 . . ."

Tanner's eyes widened. "Which is *tomorrow*."

Declan took a deep breath. "If we are correct about the date, that leaves us with 8–G–4–H."

Tanner tilted her head and studied the open Maryland map.

"What?" He'd seen that look before. She was on to something.

She grabbed the map. "I can't believe I didn't think of it before. Read off the remaining letters and numbers again."

"8–G–4–H."

"Hmm." She lay on the floor, elbows bent in front of the map, her legs kicked up and crossed behind her. Her index finger traced along the boxes. "G–8." Her finger settled on the corresponding square where row G and row 8 intersected. "Annapolis," she said. "Now H–4." She ran her finger the other way. "Kent Island?" She frowned. "I can see Annapolis would make a viable target with the state house there and large population, but Kent Island?"

"Maybe it's not the two separate places but what's in between," Declan said.

"You think they plan to contaminate the water?" she asked.

"Not with the IEDs, line charges, and whatever other weapons Carlos saw being loaded into crates," Declan said.

"Do you think Annapolis is the target?"

"No," Declan said, it all finally connecting. "Carlos said Steven Burke was killed because he found tunnel and bridge brochures in Darmadi's berth. G–8 and H–4. Look what's smack in the middle of the two."

"The bay?"

"The Bay Bridge. They plan to blow up the Bay Bridge."

40

Shock blanketed Tanner's face. "I can't believe it. I mean . . . I *believe* you've got it. I just can't believe that's going to happen tomorrow if we don't stop it."

"That's what the trawlers and line charges are for."

She frowned. "What?"

"The trawlers carry the line charges," Declan said. "Blow the bridge from underneath."

"That's brilliant," she said, "in a totally frightening way. But how, exactly, would it work?"

"I'm just spitballing here, but it would make sense if they used the trawlers or divers off of them to wrap line charges around the bridge's central pylons."

"To crumble it from underneath," she said, following his logic. "But that would only be the center. The bridge is over four miles long. It would be awful, but not the damage you'd expect from a terrorist attack."

"Don't forget the IEDs and black Toyota Camrys. No doubt they plan to set off car bombs, probably at both ends of the bridge. Blowing the ends would prevent emergency personnel from getting to the main blast in the center and likely undermine the entire structure." Declan shook his head. "We've only got hours to stop this."

He turned to Tanner. "Hand me the phone, love."

"Who are you calling?" Tanner asked.

"Noah Rowley."

Special Agent Noah Rowley, or "Row" as he was sometimes called, was a supervising agent with the Coast Guard Investigative Service. If there was going to be an attack on water, the Coast Guard needed to be involved. And having worked with him on the *Hiram* case, he could easily say Noah was one of the most thorough investigators he'd had the pleasure of working with.

Declan lay in bed, unsurprisingly unable to sleep. Too much was hanging in the balance. Max's trawler contact had never called him back, but it was a moot point now. They knew the target.

They could close the Bay Bridge for a time, but that would incite panic, which would allow the terrorists to achieve at least part of their objective. And they couldn't keep the bridge closed forever. But most importantly, the terrorists would know how closely they were on to them, and they'd most likely switch the target, and then they would have to start again from scratch.

After running it by their bosses, Noah and Declan agreed to let Ebeid think his plan was working and intervene at the crucial moment. It was a sound plan, but made for a restless night's sleep—well, total lack of sleep—on his part.

He shifted, adjusting his UMD sweatshirt. It was one Tanner had borrowed earlier in the night. He'd picked it up from the living room chair where she'd left it before heading to the guest room, and he'd slipped it on. As he lay there, the scents of coconut and vanilla wafted around him. It smelled like *her*.

He longed for her to be in the bed beside him—to see her face last thing before sleep and first thing in the morning. He knew they had a ways to go to reach marriage-ready, but he was thrilled they'd finally taken a giant leap onto the path. He longed for the day when she would be fully his and he'd be hers.

Tanner was brilliant, witty, savvy, compassionate, strong, brave, and grounded in her faith—rather soaring in her walk with God. Her vibrancy was contagious, her laughter tickled his soul, and her heart for others inspired him in a way he never knew could be experienced on such a profound level. She was making him a better man, and she didn't even know it.

361

Thank you, Father, for bringing Tanner into my life. Please, Lord, let me make her my wife one day. More pressing, let us stop those who intend to hurt our country. Let us get Ebeid behind bars where he belongs, and let us prevent the attack that could hurt so many. Equip us, Lord, and be with us always. In Jesus' name I pray. Amen.

41

After what seemed like endless travel, Griffin, Jason, and the Markums made their way into the precinct. They had arrested and Mirandized the Markums in Jamaica, and then escorted them back to Maryland—being careful to keep the couple separated.

Once the Markums had been fed and allowed to change clothes, they put them in separate interrogation rooms. Jason took John Markum, and Griff took the woman behind it all—Elizabeth Markum.

How could this couple, who from all appearances seemed to be upstanding professionals, actually be killers at heart? After observing Elizabeth's dominion over her husband and his subservience throughout their transport back to the States, Griffin was certain she was the one who'd murdered Haywood.

Griffin took a deep breath and said a prayer for God's guidance and wisdom before he entered the interrogation room.

He set a legal pad and pen on the table and slid it to Elizabeth.

"You've got to be joking," she said, sliding it back to him. "I'm a lawyer. I know my rights, and I want my lawyer, Trent Howard, here. Now."

Her resolve remained firm, and she remained silent until Trent Howard arrived.

"Don't say a thing" were the first words out of his mouth as he entered the room.

"Don't worry. *I* haven't." Which indicated she might not be so sure about her husband.

Interesting. Griffin was curious, what, if anything, Jason had gotten out of John Markum.

"What's this nonsense all about?" Trent asked.

"I didn't realize you consider murder and fleeing the country to be nonsense," Griffin said.

"My clients didn't kill anyone."

"The evidence begs to differ," Griffin said.

Elizabeth Markum snidely huffed. "He's bluffing."

"If you aren't involved, how do you know what evidence I'm referring to?" Griffin asked.

"I wasn't involved so I know no evidence tracks back to me," she said, her tone and expression smug.

"Okay. Let's start with the blood in your room."

"What does blood in her room have to do with Mr. Grant's supposed murder, which was in reality most likely suicide?" Trent asked.

"It was definitely murder. Autopsy confirmed it," Griffin said.

Elizabeth frowned, hard lines forming at the edges of her tight, thin lips.

"Be that as it may," Trent said. "What does blood in my clients' room have to do with Mr. Grant's murder?"

"Because it was all part of the Markums' plan to hide their disappearance by framing Haywood for their 'murders' and staging Haywood's death as a suicide to keep him from denying he had murdered them."

"My husband had an accident," Elizabeth said. "You're wasting our time."

"So you maintain you and your husband did not murder Haywood Grant?"

"That is correct, Detective."

"Then why did Haywood 'confess' in his fake suicide note to killing you and your husband?"

"I have no idea."

"Unless you have something more substantial, Detective McCray," Trent said, "I really must insist you let my clients go."

"Oh, I'm just getting started," Griffin said.

Jason knocked and popped his head in.

"Yeah?"

"Can I talk to you for a sec, Griff?"

Griffin nodded. "Of course."

Concern filled Elizabeth's eyes.

Griffin stepped into the hall, closing the door behind them. "What's up?"

Jason pulled a yellow legal pad filled with writing from behind his back.

Hope filled Griffin. "Is that what I think it is?"

"Yep. Mr. Markum just confessed, said it was all his wife's idea and doing."

Thank you, Lord.

"How'd you get him to talk?" Griffin was greatly impressed.

"I told him one of them was eventually going to talk, and whoever did so first would receive leniency with the judge. Plus, I got the feeling he doesn't like his wife very much."

"I'd say not, considering he just gave her up for murder." Griffin smiled. "I can't wait to see the look on Elizabeth Markum's face when I tell her the news."

His smile remained on his face as he strolled back into the room and said, "Your husband just confessed."

42

Declan met Row at the Annapolis Coast Guard station, only a matter of minutes from the Bay Bridge. It was the day of reckoning.

Crews had been watching the bridge all night. Everything was set, and everyone in place. Now it was just a matter of waiting.

"As soon as the trawlers move in, we will too," Noah said. "We have men watching the pylons from a good distance away, just in case they approach from a different direction than we're anticipating."

"I've got men stationed as construction workers at both ends of the bridge for the first quarter mile in," Declan said. "Once their cars enter the bridge, we'll seize them, and immediately stop traffic from entering the bridge while making sure all civilian traffic is cleared off. The bomb squad is ready and waiting." Thanks to Max Stallings, of all people, they knew exactly what make and model of car to look for.

Declan looked at his watch. "We probably have several more hours if they are planning on hitting the highest traffic time, but far better for us to be way early than even a second late."

Everyone was in place, tensions high, time moving slow as molasses, until finally two trawlers approached the bridge from the south.

"Here we go, people," Declan said over the comm system.

"Hold until they stop near the bridge before moving in," Noah said. "If it's not them, we'll have tipped the terrorists off to our presence."

Sure enough the two red trawlers slowed down twenty feet from the bridge. A diver from each ship with a black dive pack stood ready to enter the water when Noah and his team quickly approached, advancing from both sides.

The divers jumped into the water despite their arrival, but Noah had his own divers deployed. Declan prayed the terrorists' divers didn't disappear into the bay, that they didn't lose a single man. Led by Noah, the Coast Guard Investigative Service boarded the trawlers, taking the men into custody.

Meanwhile on top, the report came through that two black Toyota Camrys entered the bridge from either side at the same time. *This is it.* Declan ordered them seized immediately. On the north end he stepped from the faux construction site and approached the now-blocked vehicle, aiming his gun at the driver's head. "Exit the vehicle. Slow and steady. Keep your hands where I can see them," he ordered.

The southeast Asian man, no more than twenty, did as instructed.

"Up against the car. Do you have any weapons on your person?"

The man shook his head.

Declan patted him down, finding none.

His men searched the interior of the car, finding nothing.

"Trunk," Declan said.

They popped it open to find an IED counting down from three minutes.

Getting the same report from Barrows, he called for dual bomb-squad teams to begin.

The bomb squads moved in and began working on defusing the bombs.

"We have diver number one," Noah said over the comm. "Still searching for the second one, but we're keeping an eye on the pylons."

Great. They had two bombs counting down the mere minutes they had to stop them, along with an armed diver on the loose in the bay. At least he'd miraculously talked Tanner into waiting at the Coast Guard station where they'd started out this morning.

"Did Ebeid order the attack?" he asked the man he'd cuffed and had sitting in the back of a guarded FBI vehicle.

The man remained silent.

"You're either going to spend a long portion of your life in prison or we're all going to die—either way you might as well answer the question. You've already let Ebeid down."

"Not until you stop that bomb, I haven't," he said, defiantly.

"So it was Ebeid." He'd admitted as much without even realizing it.

The man's face scrunched in anger.

"Thank you." Declan stepped from the vehicle and to the bomb squad coordinator. "How are they doing?" Time was getting tight. They had less than two minutes. "Cutting this one a little close, aren't we?"

"I've never seen an IED rigged like this."

Declan exhaled. "All nonessential personnel clear the bridge," he ordered.

People began moving off the bridge en masse, but only one entered on. Was that . . . ? He squinted.

"Tanner? What on earth are you doing?" Was she crazy?

"I couldn't just sit in the office and listen over the radio. I needed to be here with you."

"I need you to go, honey, please." He glanced at his watch in a panic. "The bomb has less than a minute." His heart rate increased three-fold. "Do we need to evacuate?" he asked Justin, the bomb squad coordinator.

"No," he said. "One more . . ."

Don't say minute. *We don't have a minute.*

"Second," Justin said, then stood back and

wiped the sweat beading across his brow with the back of his hand. "All done."

Declan's lungs filled with an immense breath of relief. "Barrows?"

"Frank says almost there. Wait. Yes? Okay, Declan, it's disarmed."

Praise God.

Forty-five minutes later, Declan stepped to the rear of the police van where all the terrorists were now held. He smiled and then shut the door, banging on it to let the driver know they were good to head toward the federal building, where the interrogations would commence. Thankfully the second diver had been caught coming ashore a half mile south of the bridge and was being transferred to the Bureau office now.

He, Barrows, and Tanner would spend the rest of the day debriefing the terrorists. Tanner might very well be able to reach them on a level he and Barrows could not. That's precisely why she was on staff.

A crew was left in place to handle cleanup and containment, keeping the bridge closed until they deemed it safe to reopen.

Noah and his men were working their way through the trawlers, searching for any clues, and the cars were towed back to the Bureau's garage.

Now they just needed to gather enough

concrete information from the terrorists to bring in Dr. Ebeid. It might take hours or days of interrogation, but he'd get the evidence he needed to arrest Ebeid and put him behind bars, where he belonged.

Meanwhile, Luke waited for the transfer convoy to pass by him. His agency had coordinated with NSA and the CIA to ensure Dr. Susa Kemel wasn't heisted in transit. Luke's task had become even more important when hours earlier he learned that Dr. Bedan had entered the U.S. via Canada, but his whereabouts were unknown. Were the terrorists planning to have these two horrific scientists, who had no regard for human life, work together? And if so, what on earth was the scope of the project and the magnitude of destruction it would employ?

They needed to locate Dr. Bedan, and fast, but first he needed to make sure Dr. Kemel made it safely to Jessup Correctional Institution. He could rest easy knowing Declan had the diversion attack under control, but *this* is why he was in the U.S. He needed to remember that and not to let thoughts of Kate or the men who had once been his friends flood his mind.

Malcolm was right after all—attachments brought distraction that could not be permitted in his line of work. But attachments were what he wanted, what he longed for. He would do his job, prevent this attack, see Ebeid dead or behind bars, and then he was out. His soul couldn't take any more questionable decisions. He was no longer the agent Malcolm had worked so hard to create. The old Luke, the part he thought had died long ago, was reemerging.

Twenty minutes later, with his mind thankfully back in focus, the transit convoy carrying Dr. Kemel drove by. Luke followed at a distance, passing the agents positioned strategically along the various route options.

As they neared Jessup, unease settled in Luke's gut. The men who intel had indicated were going to attempt to break Kemel out during transit were quickly running out of time. Something was wrong.

Had he received bad intel?

The convoy slowed as they approached the prison.

Adrenaline burned through Luke's limbs.

An explosion rocked the ground, shaking his vehicle. Fire, smoke, and flying debris blew toward him in a blazing whirl. He dropped to the floorboard as his windshield shattered, heat blowing over, scorching his skin.

He prayed for the firestorm to pass, and after a few moments of feeling as if he were in hell's fires, it settled, his vehicle rocking to a stop.

He extricated himself from the vehicle to find shattered convoy debris littering the ground around him.

They'd blown up the convoy. It didn't make any sense.

He covered his face with his shirt as smoke engulfed the air, sirens wailing dimly over the ringing in his ears.

The ringing grew louder.

His phone. It was ringing.

Coughing, he pulled it from his jeans pocket and answered. "Yes?"

"I'm assuming you survived what I just heard was a convoy explosion."

"Yes, but I don't understand. Why would Ebeid blow up his own scientist?" He realized the reason before Malcolm answered.

"It appears they found a replacement with Bedan."

"Any idea where he is?"

"No, but that's not the worst of it."

"What happened?" What had they missed?

"Fort Detrick was transporting a supply of anthrax to the CDC, and it was just hijacked. The guards are dead, and the truck carrying somewhere in the neighborhood of six ounces of anthrax is gone."

"Why didn't we know about that transfer?"

"We did, but we didn't consider it would be a target."

That would have been helpful information. He was so sick of this game. Sick of only being given bits of intel when there was a far bigger game at play. His frustration with Malcolm soared. "And you can't find the truck?" Surely helicopters were in the air searching, but why hadn't he been on that detail? If he'd only known . . . Of course Ebeid would go for the anthrax. Dr. Kemel's transport was just another diversion. Ebeid had been feeding them false intel. Righteous anger flared hotter than the flames dancing a hundred yards from him as fire trucks converged on what remained of the convoy.

He covered his free ear, trying to hear as Malcolm continued, "We believe they must have switched vehicles somewhere undercover, but we're still looking."

His chest compressed. Both the bridge and Kemel's transfer were diversions. Ebeid and his team had just outmaneuvered them. But how did he know to play them? Did he have a man on the inside or had Ebeid discovered *their* man on the inside and fed him false intel?

Either way, Ebeid and his crew now had six ounces of anthrax along with Dr. Bedan. Luke fought the urge to stagger back. Instead he leaned against his car, which was still warm from the blaze that had engulfed it only moments ago. It was mind-numbing to think the convoy explosion and the diversion attempt on the Bay Bridge were nothing compared to what a few grams of anthrax could do. A few grams were deadly, and Ebeid now had *ounces* in his control.

Luke swallowed. He couldn't even begin to fathom the level of destruction Ebeid could cause or what deployment method he was planning. This case had just shifted gears— and the ramifications were terrifying. "We need to bring in the FBI. I'm sure they've already been alerted to the hijacked anthrax."

"Yes. I'll make sure the case is directed to Declan Grey, as he's already somewhat looped in. Looks like you'll be reunited with your old friends after all. Guess we're going to see how well trained you actually are in not letting attachments come into play."

Declan, Tanner, and Barrows spent hours interrogating the terrorists from the attempted bridge attack, but they remained steadfastly silent, so they'd given them a night in lockup and would start a fresh round of interrogations in the morning. In the meantime, Declan and Tanner headed for CCI, where they entered to the applause of their friends.

"Please, there's no need," Declan said, never one for accolades, though he had to admit he felt pretty darn good at the work they'd all accomplished in stopping a terrorist attack. Hopefully, they'd set Ebeid and his sleeper cells back years in their plans.

It bothered him that they still had nothing evidence-wise to concretely tie the attack to Ebeid, but tomorrow was a fresh day. They'd get something more concrete, no matter how much digging or how long the digging took, Declan would see Ebeid behind bars.

Entering the lounge area, he and Tanner both grabbed a slice of pizza and a Coke, and moved toward the couch.

He couldn't wait to head back to his house with Tanner tonight, though as this case wrapped up she'd eventually be going back to stay with Kate. He'd miss having her so near. He just yearned to spend time alone with her. Sitting and holding hands with the woman he loved was more than enough—for now. But a future awaited them. One he couldn't wait to get to.

"To Griffin, Jason, Parker, and Avery for catching Coach's killers, and clearing his name," Declan said, lifting his soda can.

"And to you and Tanner for stopping Ebeid," Griff said, lifting his own soda can as the rest of the gang joined in.

"Thanks, guys," Declan said, appreciating their kindness but never enjoying being in the spotlight. "But it wasn't just us. It was a lot of folks working together."

"But you did a great job." Everybody's attention swung to Luke standing in the doorway, a grim expression on his hardened face. "Unfortunately, we've got a far more lethal threat on our doorstep."

Acknowledgments

To Jesus—for everything. James 1:17.

To Mike—for being my best friend, soul mate, and for making me laugh like no one else.

To Kay—for putting up with "Deadline Mom," for your quick wit and sweet soul. You're precious.

To Ty—for keeping me on my toes and bringing adventure to my life . . . *daily*.

To Little Man and Chubbykins—your Nannie loves you silly!

To Dave—for your support, insight, patience, and friendship.

To Karen—for your thoughtfulness, thoroughness, and friendship. I treasure working with you.

To everyone at BHP and Baker—I'm blessed.

To my readers—I'm so blessed by your encouragement and support. A special shout out to my Armchair Adventurers—Tab, Misty, Rissi, and Eli—for always cheering me on. You guys are the best!

To my friends Lisa, Joe, Donna, and Katie—you make my life all the richer.

To Dad—for all the research help and vastly interesting discussions.

To Officer Barry Jordan—for all your guidance and feedback. Any mistakes are mine.

Praised by *New York Times* bestselling author Dee Henderson as "a name to look for in romantic suspense," Dani Pettrey combines the page-turning adrenaline of a thriller with the chemistry and happily-ever-after of a sigh-worthy romance novel. Her novels stand out for their "wicked pace, snappy dialogue, and likable characters" (*Publishers Weekly*), "gripping storyline[s]," (*RT Book Reviews*), and "sizzling undercurrent" of romance (*USA Today*).

Dani's adventure-focused ALASKAN COURAGE series climbed the CBA bestseller lists, with *Submerged* staying in the top twenty for five consecutive months. The five-book series also won multiple awards, including the Daphne du Maurier Award, two HOLT Medallions, and Christian Retailing's Best Award, among others. She turns her attention to crime and law enforcement in her home state of Maryland in her new CHESAPEAKE COURAGE series, starting with *Cold Shot*, which *Library Journal* called, "a harrowing and thrilling ride." For more information about her novels, visit www.danipettrey.com.

Books are produced
in the United States
using U.S.-based
materials

Books are printed
using a revolutionary
new process called
THINKtech™ that
lowers energy usage
by 70% and increases
overall quality

Books are durable
and flexible because
of smythe-sewing

Paper is sourced
using environmentally
responsible foresting
methods and the
paper is acid-free

Center Point Large Print
600 Brooks Road / PO Box 1
Thorndike, ME 04986-0001 USA

(207) 568-3717

US & Canada:
1 800 929-9108
www.centerpointlargeprint.com